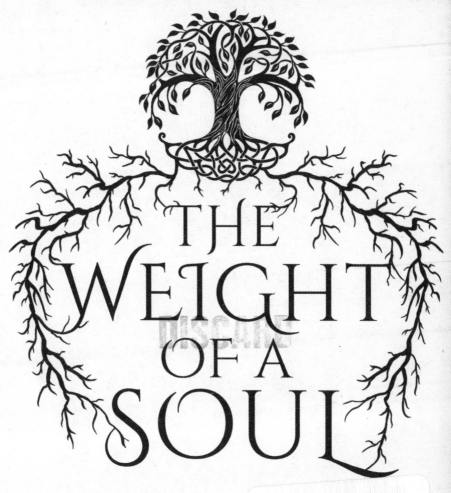

THE WEIGHT OF A SOUL

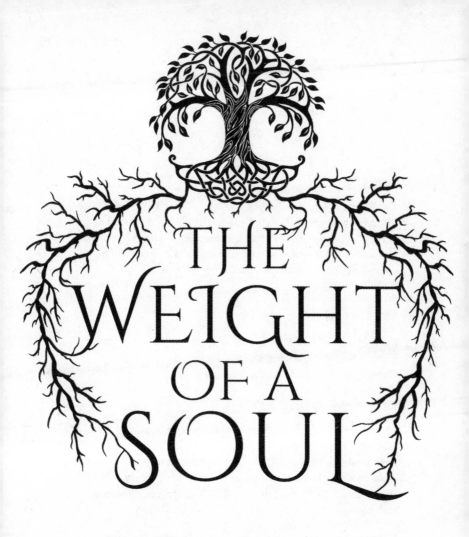

THE WEIGHT OF A SOUL

ELIZABETH TAMMI

Mendota Heights, Minnesota

First Edition
First Printing, 2019

Book design by Jake Nordby
Cover design by Jake Nordby
Cover images by artdock/Shutterstock

Flux, an imprint of North Star Editions, Inc.

Library of Congress Cataloging-in-Publication Data (pending)
978-1-63583-044-6 (paperback)
978-1-63583-058-3 (hardcover)

Flux
North Star Editions, Inc.
2297 Waters Drive
Mendota Heights, MN 55120
www.fluxnow.com

Printed in the United States of America

For my sister.

CHAPTER
ONE

Amal thrust his axe just shy of Fressa's right shoulder. Lena could see a thin sheen of sweat gathering above his brow from where she stood watching her sister expertly twist away from him. As Fressa plummeted into a crouch, Amal's momentum kept him tumbling forward and she reached up—almost daintily—to snatch his axe from his hands.

He stumbled to a halt, loose grass flying up in his wake, and glanced wearily behind him. "Why do I bother?"

Fressa shrugged, leaping back to her feet. "Again?"

Amal shook his head, though his easy smile returned; he did, despite it all, intend to marry Fressa. Above them, the sky was full of mounting thunderheads—grays and whites piled atop each other, a sure sign of storms to come. Still, it did little to dim the warmth in Amal's eyes;

they were starting to crinkle at the edges as he closed the distance between himself and Fressa. Lena rolled her eyes. She'd seen this scene unfold too many times.

"I'm begging you not to go any further," she said.

Fressa shot her a quick glare over her shoulder.

"*Begging*," Lena cried.

Mercifully, Amal held up his hands in surrender and took two generous steps away from Fressa. Lena laughed. The truth—which she could never tell them, or she would face eternal embarrassment—was that she thought they were probably the most perfect example of love anywhere in the nine worlds. Fressa and Lena had never known a time without Amal. He'd been an orphaned newborn when their father had brought him home from a trading trip to Baghdad just a year after Lena was born, and Amal had been eagerly adopted by Nana, their clan's apothecary. He was close to both Lena and her sister, but recently, Fressa's affections for him had evolved into something decidedly romantic, and he wasn't far behind.

Lena found the whole development to be an inevitable surprise—strange only in that she had not seen it coming. She'd never viewed Amal as anything but a brother, which was lucky for her, because after his and Fressa's wedding that's exactly what he would become.

"Why don't you try?" Fressa asked, holding out her axe.

Lena blinked while Fressa and Amal dissolved into laughter. Lena was on track to be the village's next healer—she could barely hold a small blade, let alone Fressa's weighty, frightening axe. She rolled her eyes, but couldn't quite tear her gaze from the axe in her sister's hands. Lena marveled at the relaxed curl of Fressa's fingers around the hilt; it was as if she'd been born with weapons in hand.

"You'd have died a thousand times without my skills," Lena shot back.

"And for that, I am grateful," Amal interceded. Fressa heaved a dramatic, amorous sigh.

Before Lena could think of an equally disgusting reply, a low horn echoed across the valley, down from the riverfront and sweeping past them into the village, taking their easy smiles with it.

"Is he back?" Lena whispered, even though the three of them stood between the river and their village, far away enough from both not to be heard. Amal walked a few steps closer to the river, squinting hard along the small strip of dark water that traced its way through their valley.

The serpent-head prow of their father's boat pressed its way into their vision with icy slowness. Lena struggled to remember how long he'd been gone this time. Well over a year. She couldn't even recall where he'd gone. Was it Francia? The Baltic? There used to be a time when her father and clansmen did trading missions, to Constantinople and Dublin and Paris—or, Lena's mother claimed they had.

Now they raided.

Lena's father insisted resources were thinning. That rival clans were pressing in from all around. She'd never seen evidence for either claim. A couple times a year, their ship would return to their valley bearing the weight of gold and jewels and fabrics they'd stolen from whatever poor monastery was brave enough to exist.

They mock our gods, her father would say. As if that was justification. As if their people did not ridicule the Christians. As if her very name—*Magdalena*—was not derived from their language. Her father had always been a hypocrite. Fierce and strong, she supposed. Attentive and doting enough when he was actually home.

But a hypocrite.

"I'd better get Mother," Fressa muttered. She burst into a sprint toward the tight, winding mass of their village, her auburn braid whipping behind her. The sound of the horn had reached the village—people were already emerging, their faces turned to the water. But Lena knew her sister well enough to know she would push off this reunion as long as possible.

Amal fidgeted as Fressa fled. His feet tapped the earth with a pattern so aggravating that Lena finally snapped. "*What?*"

"It's just . . ." Amal's black curls shifted across his forehead. "He doesn't know—"

Lena understood. "Your engagement." A stab of pity hit her. Of course, a father was supposed to give his permission before a marriage was arranged. But he'd been gone for over a year, and Fressa had promised Amal that they would ask upon his arrival—which meant that neither of her parents knew what their younger daughter had already planned. But Nana, Amal's mother, was aware of the engagement and had offered her support. That would be enough. They hoped. "Your mother will defend you both. Don't worry, Amal."

He nodded too many times. The ship was far enough away that they couldn't discern any figures, but it was no longer moving. They had reached the shore.

Lena glanced back, surprised to find a throng of villagers closing in. Some wore earnest hope across their faces, eager to see their husbands or brothers or fathers. Others wore the tired, sullen masks of a people who swayed between victory and desolation too often to have kept a steady footing in either.

One face, brighter than the rest, broke off from the crowd walking to the shore, and ran instead to where Amal and Lena stood. A brief burst of relief spread through Lena's chest as their friend approached. Bejla's hair glowed gold, even in the pale light. Here was one spot of calm in what Lena feared would be, at best, a tumultuous day.

"What is this ship?" she asked, her blue eyes wide. Lena and Amal exchanged the briefest of glances, trying to rein in their disbelief. Bejla was a sweet girl— eighteen, just as Lena was—but her perpetual supply of questions amazed Lena. Still, Bejla had only been in the village for less than a year, since that strange night she had stumbled into the village at winter's end, all alone and with little more than a pelt on her. That was one of this settlement's redeeming qualities, Lena supposed— like with Amal, Bejla had also been quickly accepted and brought into the village. It felt as if she had always lived just minutes away, on the fringes of their settlement, but with a start, Lena realized that Bejla would have no way of knowing that the ship returning was her father's.

"It is Chief Fredrik's," Lena explained, staring out at the water's edge in the distance. She could hear the elated cries of reunion as they caught on the wind, mixing with bird cries and bitter wind. "My father, I mean."

When Bejla did not respond, Lena glanced back to her. Her eyes were narrow now, sky blue reflected on a frozen lake. Wisps of blonde hair blew across her lips, some sticking to her mouth. Absently, she brushed them away and seemed to feel Lena's eyes on her.

"Of course," she breathed, letting out a shaky laugh. Lena frowned, tilting her head. Perhaps her friend was nervous at the chief's arrival, and what he might make of the orphaned girl who had wandered into the village in his absence. And stayed. "I should go be with Gunnar and Olaf."

Lena nodded as Bejla turned on her heels and jogged to the water, to the men who had taken her in all those months ago.

She heard Amal exhale beside her. "Your father will hear all sorts of news this afternoon," he muttered. She cut her gaze to him, and watched his shoulders slump with the weight of an unexpected burden. "Let us pray he is in the spirits to receive it."

Fredrik was the head of Clan Freding and chief of their village, but he never assumed the title of *king,* even though he could. Lena thought that was one of her father's less frustrating qualities. Still, as he strode closer to her and Amal, the villagers fanning out behind him, she felt that everything about him was . . . excessive.

She marveled that he could walk so steadily, even buried under draping robes of velvet and silk. He wore no crown, but his reddish-brown hair was cut short and close to his head—a jarring difference from the long-hanging strands the rest of the clansmen grew. A heavy circle of gold-encrusted sapphires hung around his neck. It must've weighed a great deal, but he kept his back straight as iron.

"Magdalena," he drawled, casually, as if he were just coming in from farming the fields for the day—not a yearlong raid half a world away. His voice sounded different every time he returned. She could never remember the sound of it, and even when he returned, she heard no recognition or familiarity in it. Lena inclined her head at him, but made no move closer. Amal did the same. Fredrik glanced at the boy, and braced his hands on Amal's shoulders. "How is your mother, Amal?"

"Fine, sir." Amal did not meet his eyes.

"Good," Fredrik replied, but his eyes were already focused on the village ahead. He started walking, a little too quickly, and beckoned for Lena and Amal to follow. Behind them, loud reunions and rushed conversation poured over the riverbank.

Lena glanced behind her, trying to remember all the faces of the long-absent men. The distance between them and the tents shrank quickly. At the fringe of their village, Lena's mother, Val, stood with her arms crossed. Fressa stood just behind her, wearing the same glare across her pointed features. Lena sighed through her nose. This was not the type of reunion she imagined most families shared.

"Fressa. Val," Fredrik proclaimed, in the same grandiose tone he'd used to greet Lena. Neither her sister nor mother made a move forward. They didn't acknowledge his greeting whatsoever. Fredrik cleared his throat, glancing behind him to the clansmen beginning to make their way into the village around him. He waited until they had some semblance of privacy before pressing forward with his winning smile.

"Where?" Val's words flung from her lips like a throwing axe. Even Lena straightened.

"England." Lena's father's voice betrayed no fear or worry. "Such a beautiful isle. Much greener and tamer than this place."

"And what glory and riches have you brought back with you this time?" Val's frozen tone ached with implication. Her mother's face held the blank stoicism that had earned Val such a formidable reputation, but her hazel eyes betrayed a deep-rooted anger and nervousness.

Suddenly anxious, Lena looked to Amal at the same time he turned to her. Lena's heart sank. He wore hope so plainly, like a luster exuding from within him, and the illuminating presence of it weighted her with pity. Fressa stood in the shadows beneath their home's massive thatched roof, swallowed up by her parents' loud rebuttals, her bright fury visible but dim between their rage. Lena ran a hand through her dark hair, subtly scanning their surroundings. Most of the villagers were still—seemingly—preoccupied with their own families.

But they were still outside, and her family had never been known for its silence.

She jerked her head slightly to the right, signaling Amal to leave them. He glanced at Fressa for a long moment, indecision piercing his dark gaze. Lena watched her sister give him a half smile, with the slightest shrug of her shoulders—and Amal relaxed, mumbling a farewell and walking over to the house next to theirs, where he lived with Nana.

"Inside," Lena murmured, keeping her tone casual enough so as not to attract any attention from their neighbors, but narrowing her eyes. Rage flashed in her mother's eyes, and Lena braced for her outburst. Val did not appreciate her eldest daughter instructing them, but Fressa was already throwing open the door, sauntering inside without a backward glance. Val sighed, and gave Lena a final warning glare before following Fressa inside.

Lena shrugged it off, waiting for her father to move in front of her. She had certain responsibilities as the eldest daughter of the chief, and she would act on them— her family always thanked her later. She'd certainly corralled her sister's tumultuous temper many times, and despite her mother's impressive self-awareness, Lena still found herself reminding them to keep their voices low and measured. And private. They did not understand people as Lena did; they did not understand how fast power could seep through fingers that weren't clenched.

She walked toward the door, following her father's footsteps in the trampled grass. Lena cast a glance behind her shoulder, down the roads snaking out in both directions from their threshold. Amal was with his mother, right nearby. Lena hovered in the doorway, looking in his direction, even though there was no way to see into his and Nana's home from where she stood. She tried to take a calming breath, gazing at the familiar traces of her village's twisting roads and thatched roofs with trails of smoke curling into the gray sky.

"Magdalena?" Her father's voice came from inside—commanding, but not cruel. Still, it raked across Lena's skin, and resentment crawled over her. It was bold of him to speak so confidently to a daughter he only saw once a year.

Still, she followed him—if anything, her sister would need her. But as the door shut behind Lena, she still resisted the urge to throw another last look at the village, as if casting a fishing line and hoping that something would bite, and soon.

Lena inhaled through her nose, the smoky dimness of their home slowly gaining definition as her eyes adjusted to the absence of light. Her shoulders relaxed a fraction of an inch. They were out of the village's sight, for now, but there was still much to negotiate. Lena made a mental tally—she would have to smooth out the anger morphing her mother's features, so no one doubted the solidity of her parents' marriage. She would have to urge her father, again, not to disappear so frequently, and remind him of the precarious edge his *voyages* had placed their family's position upon. She sighed as she stared at Fressa, her arms crossed and eyes cutting from the corner of the home she shared with Lena. Now that both of their parents were present, Fressa and Amal would have to breach the subject and make the official request for their marriage to commence.

Lena's mother glared at Fredrik and dragged a chair away from the table, sitting down and tossing her flaxen hair across her shoulders. Lena's father sat opposite Val, maintaining an infuriatingly neutral expression. Fressa sighed loudly and threw herself into the low bed of pelts and furs that she shared with Lena.

"Father," Lena began, since she knew all their family's troubles stemmed from his poisoned roots. She leaned against the doorframe, letting it brace some of her weight. "Your trips are getting longer."

Thankfully, Val seemed to wake at her eldest daughter's words. She straightened, placing her hands on the table between herself and her husband, and erupted into her grievances. "Surely you know how that makes us look. I cannot be everywhere at once. We have traders coming, and they want to know where our chief is, and they do not look at me—"

Fredrik tilted his chair back and slung his satchel to the floorboards. "I brought gifts."

Lena actually laughed. It was the same voice he'd used on her and Fressa when they were far younger and didn't want to sit through another meeting or run down to wash their clothes in the cold river. He would goad them to complete their tasks with the sing-songed promise of an extra drizzle of honey across their shortcakes or a story before bedtime.

Did he believe it would work on them now?

Nobody spoke as he reached inside the satchel. Wordlessly, he slid a golden necklace with inlaid rubies across the table to Val. She took it without thanks, but adjusted it around her neck.

"For Lena," he murmured, turning around to hand Lena an ivory comb. Lena took a step forward, snatched it from him, and made a grand show of tossing it over to her side of the room without even looking.

"And for Fressa."

Something in her father's voice had changed. Lena's neck tingled as her father reached out his hand, holding a plain, forearm-length blade toward his youngest daughter. Fressa rose slowly, her face stony and unafraid. She took the few steps that separated their corner of the room from the central table. Lena's heart stuttered, and she opened her mouth to interrupt, but could think of nothing substantial to say.

Fressa reached over, casually, and took the blade from her father.

Lena stared at her sister's hand, wrapped around the solid, unadorned hilt. Frankly, it was an ugly thing—compared to her mother's jewelry and Lena's comb, the weapon stood out in a boring, incongruous way.

She switched her gaze to her sister's face. Fressa's stoniness had melted away, and her hazel eyes were open wide in terror. For an instant, a green-tinted light seemed to spill across the freckled plains of her face, but then Fressa dropped the knife. It fell almost silently upon the packed-dirt floor.

Fressa's breath came in heavy, uneven bursts. She cleared her throat, her eyes darting to the dark corners of their home before locking on Lena's.

"What is it?" Lena asked, quickly closing the distance between them. Fressa shook her head once, her eyes begging Lena to drop it.

"Oh, Fressa," Fredrik laughed. "They say you're our village's most promising warrior! I never knew you to be so clumsy."

You barely know us at all, Lena thought.

Val said nothing, staring between her husband and Fressa with annoyance knitting her pale brows. Lena wished Fressa would say something. Do something. Instead, she just gave a short, polite laugh.

"Not to worry," Fressa muttered. "I still fight better than most."

Lena knew that was an understatement—she was the best—but she could not flaunt that title with too much pride. Their village appreciated her skill, but more as a novelty for her gender rather than the talent that it was. It helped that she was a chief's daughter, but it was another thing entirely to witness the way she could make weapons her own, like a wicked extension of her arm.

She was admired by teachers and elders alike, but some of the others her age were apprehensive at best and exclusive at worst. Lena felt ashamed of herself for ever envying the wonder that widened her village's eyes when Fressa gripped a blade. Astonishment was all well and good, but it would never replace acceptance.

Fressa stayed perfectly still, and the fear in her sister's eyes remained, pulsating with a barely reined restraint that Lena alone seemed to notice. The energy between the four Freding family members grew further strained. Lena paused, considering her next move. She needed to cast her sister a line, and soon—before she melted into one of the tantrums or tirades her younger years had been full of. If this family befell another ounce of scrutiny, the scales of their fortune and position would surely tilt out of favor.

"Fressa," she said. "Remember we promised Amal we would help him with the nets before sundown."

Her eyes lightened with fake recognition and very real relief. "Oh, yes!"

"And Father," Lena said, trying to keep her tone light enough not to anger him. "I heard some of the villagers had questions about the raid—shall you hold an audience this evening? Before they get too impatient?"

Fredrik's eyes settled on Lena. They were nearly the same hazel shade that all the Freding women shared, but in certain light, they could look venomously green. Lena kept her face placid, her breathing steady, fearing she had overstepped too far this time. But he only nodded, offering a hand to help Val up.

"Indeed," Fredrik said. "I had planned to do just that. Your mother and I will make our way to the ceremony house now."

Val adjusted her necklace and braids quickly before grabbing Fredrik's arm. Lena watched her parents step into the sunlight—the clouds that had reigned just minutes before were shifting slowly away, showing the sun still burning high through the sky. Midsummer could not be far off.

As soon as the door shut behind them, Lena whirled on her sister. "What's wrong?"

Fressa's chin trembled, and Lena's stomach churned. The defiance that ruled her sister's features into haughty, self-assured lines had vanished. Fressa braced her hands on the table, shaking her head. "I don't know."

"Fressa—"

"Did you see it? The light?"

Lena hesitated. "I am not sure."

Fressa sighed through her nose and crouched down to the ground—her hand hovered above the knife below, but did not reach down. "Father and Mother said nothing. Maybe it was nothing. I don't—"

"Just pick up the knife, Fressa."

Her pale fingers grabbed it in a swift movement. Fressa seized the blade, and stood back up. For a moment, both sisters stared at the knife, uncertain of what they waited for.

Lena's hands flew to her mouth as the green light she thought she'd imagined burned across the blade in arcing lines and strange runic symbols she had never been taught to read. Fressa's hands trembled wildly, the illuminated patterns wavering and glowing as the weapon shook.

"What is this?" Fressa whispered. Though she had dropped the blade the first time, now Lena saw that Fressa held the blade so tight that her knuckles whitened. "Some invention from abroad? Then why did Father say nothing? Why is it *our* runes—"

Lena reached over and grabbed the blade from her sister's hands. Perhaps that was not the wisest move to make unexpectedly, but Lena knew enough of how to hold a weapon—it was just the fighting in which she did not excel. As she suspected, the blade returned to its ordinary behavior in Lena's grasp.

Fressa raked her hands through her auburn hair. "What—"

"I don't know," Lena murmured. She set the blade down on the table, and it looked perfectly normal, placed between the knives Val used to cook and the tools they used to maintain their small farm.

Lena's body felt cold, but her skin burned. Her mind ached for an explanation, and she wished more than ever before that her mother had allowed her to learn the runes. She filed through any information or point of action, before realizing—

"Amal!" Lena exclaimed. Fressa tilted her head, confused, though Lena did not miss the slight relaxing of her sister's shoulders at the sound of her betrothed's name. "He can read runes. He'll know what this means."

Fressa nodded, already moving for the door. Lena hesitated, grabbing the knife before following Fressa. She did not like the feel of it in her hands—not after seeing what it did in her sister's. Still, she would hold it as long as Fressa needed her to.

CHAPTER
TWO

The walk to Amal's was not long, and Lena and Fressa had walked the path between their house and his so many times that grass had not dared to grow after their footsteps. Amal and his mother, Nana's, house was built much the same as Lena's family's, just on a smaller scale—a wide thatched roof spread over dark, tightly nailed planks of wood.

But a smaller hut stood behind their home, where Lena spent most of her time as an apprentice for Nana, the village's apothecary. The hut was made entirely of wood, with a swinging barn-style door serving as the entrance. Smoke trailed its way into the clouds, a sure sign that someone was inside.

Wordlessly, Lena and Fressa rushed to the hut and opened the door to find both Amal and Nana sitting beside the fire, smoking meat. Lena normally would feel no disappointment to see her mentor, but now a wave of irritation slammed into her. They needed to talk to Amal—now, and in private.

"Oh, Lena," Nana trilled, standing up. With her age, it was no longer a swift or easy movement. Lena tensed until she was sure Nana had her balance. "I didn't think we had a session today."

Lena smiled, folding her hands—one holding the blade—behind her back. "We don't," she said. "But we did promise your son that we'd assist him with the nets by the river."

Amal looked up to them, wiping away ash from his cheeks. His sleeves were rolled up, and sweat shone on his forehead, brought out by the heat from the fire and the summer sun. He frowned, and opened his mouth, but Fressa cut him off with a look. Quickly, he cleared his throat and nodded. "Right," he said. "I should go do that, Mother."

If they had been ten years younger, Nana might have expressed doubt or scrutiny, but now she only gave a soft, vacant smile as Amal placed a rushed kiss on her cheek before leading the Freding sisters outside.

The three of them walked side by side to the river, with Lena sometimes falling in step behind Fressa and Amal in the busier straits of the village to make way for passersby. Despite the sun, clouds still scattered across the sky and the wind held an undercurrent of chill. Lena heard Amal and Fressa whisper to each other as they walked, and guessed that her sister was filling Amal in on the strange gift Fredrik had given her.

Once the houses thinned out, the river stretched before them. It yawned and widened in the distance, and Lena knew that once it passed out of sight between the mountains that held their valley, a whole body of water waited. Sometimes, she thought she might understand what made her father want to stray.

The water that licked the shores was crystalline and cold, though in the distance the dark-blue hue of the river seemed solid and impenetrable. The three of them came to a halt and sat down on the rocky shore. Lena stared over her shoulder for a long moment, making sure nobody was observing them. The ceremony house where her parents should be holding an audience was close, but hopefully they would be too preoccupied to notice a group of teenagers by the water.

"Let me see it," Amal said, his voice troubled. Fressa held out her hand to Lena, and took the blade. Her expression did not alter as the green light reflected in her eyes, even as Amal leaned over her and stared at it for several minutes. He made no exclamations, no outbursts—he was calm, always the water to Fressa's fire.

"And it only does this with you?" he asked. Fressa nodded. Lena was unsure of how much the two of them had discussed on their walk over, but Amal clearly had grasped the situation. He studied the green lines intently, taking Fressa's hands in his own so he could get a closer look. Lena averted her gaze, looking back over the waters ahead. She had not seen the ocean her father spoke of so fondly; she could not imagine a body of water bigger than this.

"What do these runes mean?" Fressa asked, breaking the silence.

Amal shook his head, his dark brows knotted in uncertainty. "I really am not sure," he muttered. "Runes can vary so differently between villages and lands—"

"Amal," Fressa begged. "Please."

He sighed, his eyes darting to the sky as if he might find the answer there. "If I had to guess, the closest translation might mean . . . *master of the wolf.*"

Lena and Fressa exchanged a dubious glance. Wolves were always a threat, Lena supposed, though they typically never dared enter such a densely populated village.

"Well, what does that have to do with anything?" Fressa snapped. She let the knife fall onto the stones with an ugly clatter.

Lena bit her lip, disappointment closing in on her. She had not realized how much hope she'd pinned on Amal's answer—without it, they were faced with an unsettling truth.

Amal put his hands up. "Why don't you just ask your father?"

Fressa's face burned red. She stared down at her hands, wringing them together. "What would he know about this? It—whatever this is—only seems to happen when *I* hold it. I don't need another reason for the village to think me strange," she added, voice low.

Lena's chest hurt. She couldn't imagine the frustration her sister felt—her greatest, defining talent for weaponry and fighting was also the thing that isolated her. As far as Lena could tell, none of the other girls in the village—and definitely not herself—had even a fraction of the same gift for it, or maybe just not the motivation or status to pursue it.

"Still," Amal urged. "This is too strange to ignore."

Fressa closed her eyes. Lena hesitated—as she often did in their presence. Sometimes, she got the sensation that Fressa and Amal were aware only of each other. Still, she made herself speak.

"Amal is right," Lena said. "We should ask Father."

He shot her a quick, private glance of gratitude. She nodded subtly. The two of them knew an awful lot about how to take care of Fressa. It was strange, sometimes— how often had it been just Amal and Lena together, best friends for longer than they could even recall? Lena was constantly at Nana's home growing up—it was only natural that she would strike up a friendship with her son. Fressa had always been there, in a sense, but only over the past couple years had she really become a constant companion.

Lena knew both of them better than anyone, but even she had no way of knowing who had fallen first, or if it had been entirely mutual.

Amal helped Fressa to her feet as Lena rose, taking hold of the blade without being asked. The three of them began the trek back home, and this time, no one spoke.

It was late, Lena knew, by the time her parents returned from the ceremonial house. Midsummer approached, and the sun still clung to its place in the sky, dragging very slowly to the mountaintops; it might not even dip beneath the horizon tonight. Summer in these lands split the world open with light. The sun glowed and burned until they began to forget the aching cold of winter that laid crouching and waiting for its turn to reign.

Amal, Fressa, and Lena sat outside the apothecary hut, scaling a bucket of fish at Nana's request. When they got back, Nana had either forgotten or pretended to ignore the fact that they had left earlier to go "help with the nets by the river" only to return empty-handed. Nana sat inside the hut, framed by shelves full of jars of herbs and pastes, with lines of dried flowers and branches hanging from the ceilings. She hummed a jaunty tune to herself as she worked, the strains of the melody reaching them outside.

Once Lena saw the outlines of her parents walk closer, she rose to her feet and motioned for her sister to do the same. Amal asked a silent question with his eyes—should he stay?—but Lena did not answer. This was Fressa's decision.

"My daughters." Fredrik smiled. Val moved around him, going inside to greet Nana. "You look distressed. Is all well?"

"We are fine," Fressa whispered. She stared at the ground. "Father, I—I need to ask you something."

Lena started to hold the blade out to her sister, but her father cut her off. Amal stood with his back to the hut, watching the scene unfold with a calm but vigilant gaze.

"Ah," Fredrik said. He smiled, but Lena thought it looked terribly sad. Lena glanced over to the hut, wishing her mother or Nana would intervene. She heard straggling pieces of their conversation through the open door. "I believe I know what you want to ask of me."

"Y—you do?"

Fredrik nodded, releasing a loud sigh. "Yes, darling, and I am sorry. Truly." He pointed at Amal, who went rigid under his gaze. "Come closer."

Fressa laughed nervously. "What does he have to do with the knife you gave me?"

Fredrik pressed on, as if he had not heard. "I understand that the two of you desire to be wed."

Now he had everybody's attention. Val and Nana's conversation cut off abruptly, and they walked outside. Amal and Fressa turned to Lena, outrage and confusion burning their cheeks red.

"I said nothing!" Lena insisted.

The two of them would believe her, she knew, but it still prickled her to see the judgment that had flashed in their eyes—the assumption that she would sabotage them. Fressa switched her gaze quickly to her father, her fists already clenching in preparation for a fight. But Amal's eyes lingered on Lena's. He was asking her a question, but Lena could not tell what it was. It was a relief when his gaze returned to Fredrik.

"You want to *what*?" Val snapped, her voice lashing through the air like a whip. "Fressa, you cannot be serious."

Dimly, Lena wondered if she should bring up the knife just to distract from the disaster erupting. She had helped Fressa and Amal meticulously plan how they would go about their request—they needed to wait until both of Fressa's parents were present. They had Nana's blessing secured already. How could her father know?

He'd been gone when the engagement had occurred and Nana would not have had time to tell him.

Fressa and Amal stayed several feet away from each other, both of them burning red.

"Chief Fredrik," Amal tried, his fingers shaking slightly. "I love your daughter—"

"I'm sure," Fredrik said. Val moved to stand beside him, and her features were indignant and unrelenting. The resemblance to Fressa was uncanny. "But, my son, you are not truly so naïve as to misunderstand how and why marriages work in this settlement." Amal clenched his jaw as Fredrik took a step closer to him. "And surely you are not so stupid as to forget what was sworn upon a decade ago."

Fressa and Lena exchanged a puzzled, desperate glance. How had her father known to ask this of them now?

"It had not been spoken of in years," Amal said finally. Quietly. "I assumed it was not binding."

Val barked a harsh laugh, turning to Nana with disbelief. Lena's heart beat an unfamiliar pattern—never before had she doubted or questioned Amal. But here he was, chin downturned and fists clenched. What had he done?

Nana cleared her throat. Her voice shook with age and trepidation. "I must admit that I thought so too. We discussed it so long ago . . . perhaps my memory—"

"And would you not want it for your son?" Val demanded. She reached out her hand, as if to grab Nana's shoulders, but stopped herself halfway. "For him to be chief?"

Lena's blood chilled. The diminishing rationale within her whispered to turn around and see if any villagers were observing this exchange. The desperate part of her wanted to take her sister and run, to go to Bejla or Estrid's homes, where they had always been welcome, or maybe even board a ship. For there was only one way Amal would ever be *chief.*

"He was always meant for Magdalena," Fredrik said. His voice was gentle, but reproachful. "You all knew this."

"*I* didn't," Lena said, soft at first. She saw the stricken look on her sister's face, and the shame on Amal's. "I was never told of this!" Lena whirled on Amal, grabbing his shoulder hard. "You knew of this?"

His hesitation was answer enough. Lena's vision tunneled. She moved to stand next to Fressa, clutching her wrist.

"Fressa, please," Amal said, his voice shattered. "I only overheard our parents discussing it—I was so young, I did not realize they were serious."

Val shook her head. "Lena. Your younger sister cannot and will not marry before you. Amal is perfect to reign beside you: trained and proficient in trading relations and the economics that keep us afloat, not to mention his knowledge of the apothecary and runes—"

"I don't care!" Lena shouted, reputation damned. "I am not the one engaged to Amal. He is my friend, yes, and soon to be my *brother*, but he can never—"

"You cannot rule this village without a husband." Val said the words evenly. "You *know* the law."

Lena opened her mouth—but shut it.

She would never forget these seconds of silence, when the rift roared open.

Because for an instant, Lena felt a dark fear at the idea of *not* being chieftess, the title she had trained for and desired her whole life. The role she had always been meant to play. She could not do that without a husband—without a chief to rule beside.

As soon as the fear crossed her mind, rage chased it away. This was Amal. Though Lena had always known she would likely never marry for love but for power, the thought of marrying her best friend—and her sister's lover—was repulsive. The thought vanished as suddenly as it had appeared, but she knew her hesitation was an instant too long.

Fressa tore her arm from Lena's grasp, backing away from her parents, her fiancé, and her sister. She stared at each of them in turn, her cheeks redder than her hair, frantic tears pooling at the corners of her dark gaze.

"Fressa—" Lena and Amal both rushed.

But she only shook her head. She wiped at her eyes and turned from them before breaking into a run. Lena surged after her, but Amal's arm lashed out and held her fast. He stopped her with a subtle shake of his head, and she sagged against him—he was right. Though no one knew Fressa better than Lena, Amal knew her in ways Lena never would.

She needs to burn it away, Amal often said. When Fressa felt something strongly, it came out in bright conflagrations. She returned to normal quickly, but only after releasing whatever tears or laughter or rage or love that built up. Lena would give her a few minutes alone.

Dimly, Lena registered her parents speaking to Nana in hushed, angry voices. Amal and Lena watched Fressa sprint down the main thoroughfare of the village, nearly tumbling straight into Bejla and Estrid as they walked with baskets of laundry balanced precariously against their hips. Lena watched Bejla's gaze follow Fressa as she tore through the village, headed for the tree line.

Lena felt a dark, unforgivable shame within her. Fressa had needed her more than ever—to stick up for her and stand by her in this—and she had . . . what? Hesitated? She cut a sidelong glance at Amal, who stood only a couple inches taller than her. For him, she had hesitated? Lena loved him, but not as Fressa did. He would be her brother and friend; anything else would be a betrayal of the worst kind, a rejection of the fundamental trust and unity that she shared with her sister.

No—she had hesitated for power. For her rightful place as the leader of this village and its clans. Her mother was right in that these people would not accept a single woman as their sole ruler, but surely Amal could not be the only candidate. There was her friend Estrid's older brother, Sven, or all those young men who followed her father across seas unknown—Lena found she did not care who else it was. But it could never be Amal.

Amal coughed slightly. "Lena—"

"What?" she snarled, glaring at him. He looked stricken and ashamed. Good. Lena didn't understand what to do with this growing anger and confusion inside of her. Had he known all along that he had only ever been meant for her? Had he misunderstood, or hoped he could will it away with his love for Fressa?

"I'm sorry," he whispered. He spoke to her alone, but his dark eyes stayed on their parents, who were still conversing. Lena found that she did not care to hear whatever excuses or insults or explanations they had. How had her mother never explained that Lena had been engaged her whole life? Was it truly so obvious, or had she hoped to put the confrontation off as long as possible?

"It wasn't supposed to be this way," Lena groaned. Amal nodded, but said nothing. She wanted to get away from him before she said or did another thing she'd regret. "I hope you know what you have done, Amal. Now it's at the forefront of their minds. Who knows what—"

"Your father brought it up," Amal hissed. "Not me. None of this was my idea."

They locked gazes for a moment, sensing a divide growing between them. Nothing had broken their bond—Lena had feared it might be awkward when he started his relationship with Fressa, but it had not changed their friendship. Nothing, she believed, ever could. But if he really had known, or even suspected, all this time, that her parents wanted him to marry the older Freding sister? The rage simmered to life again.

"If they ask, I went back to the fishnets," Lena growled.

She pushed past Amal, not particularly gently. Now that she'd given Fressa a few minutes alone, she needed to find her sister and fix this. Amal made no attempt to stop her, and she jogged down into the village the way Fressa had run. Lena's speed built as she tore past the thatched roofs and billows of kitchen smoke that grew thicker toward the village center.

"Everything all right, Lena?"

Lena stumbled to a halt as gracefully as she could manage, and imagined the furrow in her brow melting away—she fixed a practiced, cordial smile upon her face as she swiveled toward the girl who had spoken.

Estrid stood outside the blacksmith shop where her father worked some days of the week, hanging wet clothes upon lines in the sunlight. She watched Lena as she worked, and the tilt in Estrid's face made Lena stand straighter. Estrid was one of the only other girls Lena's age, and had thin, brown hair that curled slightly across her shoulders.

"Where are you off to, then?" Estrid prompted. Her voice was perfectly pleasant and casual, but Lena did not relax. On any other day, Lena would have been happy to stay and talk with her friend, but the forsaken look on Fressa's face resurfaced in her mind, spilling urgency into her veins. Her chest tightened, though she tried very hard to keep her spine erect and chin up. She trusted Estrid, of course, but could not afford to bare her family's vulnerabilities. Not so soon after her father's return.

"Just—I'm catching up with my sister," Lena said. A half-truth told with a steady voice. Estrid nodded, and wiped her hands on her apron.

"I saw her go that way," Estrid said, nodding her head in the direction Lena had already been heading. Lena resisted the urge to tap her feet. "Is she off to see Amal, I assume?"

Lena crossed her arms, barely registering Estrid's voice. Her stomach wrung itself out over and under and again. "I have a question for you, Estrid."

Her friend's eyebrow raised. Lena swallowed—she

prided herself on staying aware of how she and her family were perceived, but what if she was wrong? Helplessly naïve? She and Estrid had been friends their whole lives—though she was not as dear as Amal, she was still a solid, dependable companion. Bejla was nice, too, but it was easier to be friends with a girl who had spent her whole life in the same place as Lena. "If I were to marry someone, say, tomorrow, who would you think it would be?"

Estrid barely looked over her shoulder as she hung an apron on the line. "Amal, right?"

"Are you serious?" Lena ran a hand across her face. She was supposed to know these things—how she and her family were looked at and spoken of, what was expected of them. How had she been so blind? What else had she missed? "But . . . he loves Fressa."

"Well, sure," Estrid admitted, but her tone held its same steady cadence. Her gray eyes flicked over to Lena as she worked. Lena's fears were confirmed, and now the terror of what else she had incorrectly assumed wrapped like a heavy, tight scarf around her neck. Her gaze gravitated back toward the path her sister had fled down. Who else had seen Fressa run? Had she been crying?

Lena blinked as she realized Estrid was still speaking.

"Lena—why are you bringing this up? You're of marriageable age. You're always with him. Marriage is an arrangement, nothing more. I assumed your parents had arranged it, what with you apprenticing with his mother all your life."

Lena clenched her fists. "I see."

"Lena—" Estrid sighed. "I don't mean to upset you, I'm just confused."

"So am I," she muttered. "I have to go, Estrid. I'll be right back."

Lena's mind swelled with information it refused to fully absorb. Her stride broke into a measured sprint, in case anyone was watching her. She didn't break into a full run until the houses thinned out and the trees hurtled closer. Lena plunged into the shadow of the canopied leaves, and shrugged off the gaze of her village.

These woods were refuge for the Freding sisters, and Lena knew exactly where to go.

CHAPTER
THREE

S he slowed for an instant as she entered the forest. The sky was still light, but the closeness of the trees was hard to peer through. She realized she had never ventured in here by herself before. Lena cursed her sister, then stepped inside. The branches rustled with thick leaves, setting off an eerie cacophony of whispers.

There was a thicket just a few minutes past the tree line that she and Fressa liked to visit in the summer months. They didn't visit as often as they had when they were children, since Fressa liked to be with Amal more these days, or to practice her axe throwing and arrow shooting and whatever gods-forsaken weapon she'd chosen to become an extension of her ferocity.

Regardless, Lena set her feet on that familiar path— if Fressa had run for the tree line, this was where she would go. A few harsh bird cries ripped across the valley, and her own feet crunching through the dirt and leaves seemed deafening. Lena quickened her pace, her eyes scanning the distance. Relief slammed into her as she saw her sister's figure on the ground of the thicket.

Lena heaved a relieved sigh, only now realizing just how nervous she had become. She jogged over, calling Fressa's name. She already dreaded trying to convince her sister to return to the village and face their father. Lena slowed to a walk as she approached. Had her sister fallen asleep? She supposed the day had been going on for a while, though it was hard to tell in summer.

Lena knelt down, shaking her sister to wake her. Fressa was on her back, her hair still tied away from her face. Any trace of tension and anger was gone from her sleeping features, and Lena marveled at how different Fressa looked asleep and awake. Lena sighed, shaking harder.

"Come on, Fressa." Lena shook her again, and Fressa's body remained limp and motionless.

During one Yuletide when they were children, Fressa had jokingly shoved an icicle down Lena's dress. She'd howled from the icy pain while her sister had howled with laughter. Still, as soon as she'd managed to remove the icicle, Lena found herself in hysterics too.

Now, that same biting, solid cold began to drip down Lena's back. She began to claw at Fressa, grabbing her by the shoulders and opening her eyelids, nauseating panic spreading through her veins. Lena tried to say Fressa's name, but her jaw couldn't unclench. She fumbled for Fressa's wrists, clutching them both just as she'd been taught. Nothing beat beneath her sister's skin. Wordless, heaving syllables tumbled from her lips.

Lena let Fressa's hands fall. Choking silence held for just one instant, and then Lena had to breathe—one gasping, frantic inhale.

And she screamed.

CHAPTER
FOUR

Amal took years to arrive, it seemed.

Lena alternated between bouts of hoarse wailing and numb stillness, and didn't hear the crash of Amal's legs until he was beside her. She tried to speak as he ran through all the motions she had just completed: the desperate shaking, the stuttered words, and waiting for a pulse that would not come. She tried to tell him to stop, that it was no use, but then the other villagers began to tear through the forest, their loud shouts echoing dimly around her. The sun glowed red, low on the horizon. The light still blinded her.

"Mother," Amal whispered suddenly—as if stricken by a bolt. "She can save her."

She knew she should try to stop him, but even his fruitless hope struck a flint within her. Lena found the strength to stand, while Amal scooped Fressa into his

arms—an impressive feat, given her tall frame and mus-
cled limbs, but he bounded effortlessly from the forest,
dirt flying behind his pumping legs.

She watched him go, her sister in his arms. Another
wave of confused grief collapsed her lungs, and she staggered back to her knees, gasping for air. A few of the
villagers had followed Amal, but others remained, reaching down to hold Lena up. She couldn't bring herself to
identify or process who they were.

The next thing Lena could comprehend was the familiar scent of her home. She blinked slowly, her ears
ringing with cries that must have come from her mother.
Some part of Lena knew, even then, that their family's
fragile foundation had just been ripped from beneath
them. Her mind worked through half-thoughts, but nothing made sense. The grief and the confusion held each
other at bay, barely, and Lena's heart beat either too fast
or too slow. She turned to her side, blankly registering
the empty pelts beside her. Fressa had been here. She
had been here just an hour ago—minutes? Days?

The sun cycled its way through the sky. At least, Lena
had to assume it had, because darkness had somehow
fallen. Here was another impossibility: midsummer had
not been far off, and now the sun had fallen below their
world, Midgard. The light should have kissed the edges
of the sky, bouncing across the horizon but never vanish-
ing. Lena's stomach ached with hysteria and hunger and

the knowledge that something big had just happened. Something she did not understand.

She hadn't moved or eaten all day. Through the doorway, she caught glimpses of Amal as he displayed a grief worthy of the two of them combined—pacing the length of the village, screaming inarticulate pleas and questions and cries, not stopping to sit or breathe until Nana had shaken her head and ushered him into their home. Lena swore she heard his sobs from within her own walls.

Other villagers had stepped into her parents' roles. They offered broth to her in too-soft tones and it was all she could do to muster a shake of her head.

It happened when exhaustion finally took Lena's mother—her father was off somewhere trying to figure out why his daughter had fallen victim to a silent kill. When the quiet overtook the room, Lena felt the absence of noise and it drew her raw devastation back out from beneath the dreadful, surreal dimness she'd hidden under all day.

A few choked sobs tore through her, and Lena's body slid from her pallet onto the dusty floor. She pitied her mother enough to not want to wake her from her sleep. To not want to come back to this terrible world. So she crawled her way to the door, her body aching from hunger and anguish. Lena pushed her way into the night, only standing when she recognized her father's figure by the central fire—his men standing around him, huddled together against the cold.

She stumbled her way to them, wondering if her father had found some explanation. Anything but this aimless black that had consumed her. When the men beside her father noticed her approach, they stared at the flames with panicked, pitying faces. Her insides lurched.

Her father turned to Lena. His face was tense, a bright inferno. With a stab of disappointment, Lena saw no evidence of tears in his eyes or across his face. Her own cheeks felt stiff with traces of salt.

He must have seen Lena's question on her face, because he offered her an answer before she opened her mouth.

"It must have been one of those southern clans," he said, his voice hard as flint and shaking with a barely restrained anger. "They push in closer every day. Like the one your friend came from."

He meant Bejla. Olaf pursed his lips—he had taken the girl in when she stumbled to their settlement all those months ago, freezing and distraught. He kept his voice measured and low, and countered, "But there were no wounds or injuries on her. It must have been some sudden sickness . . ." Olaf faltered, bracing a hand on Fredrik's shoulder. "Sometimes, these things just happen."

Fredrik jerked his shoulder hard, and Olaf darted

a glance at Lena. She stared at him, realizing he was right about one thing—there had been no cuts or blows to Fressa's body. But he was wrong, too; these things couldn't just *happen*. Not to Fressa. She'd been the village's model athlete. She hadn't even been gone for long—just the time it took for Lena to stop and talk with Estrid. The image of Fressa's face—deflated and shocked by Lena's hesitation—slammed into her again. Was that supposed to be the last time Fressa looked upon her?

No.

Lena's fingers trembled, and she could not control them. If she had only rejected her parents' insistence on her marriage to Amal right away. If only she had not stopped to speak with Estrid. If only she had sprinted after her sister, Amal's warnings be damned. Lena's blood was threaded with a pain that roared through her veins—a pain only held at bay by the strangeness surrounding it all. That glowing knife, the darkness, and the unsettling chill of the night that should not have existed so close to midsummer.

But her father was especially wrong in one thing. Lena was too tired to feel the anger she should've felt at his baseless accusation about other clans.

Fredrik had latched onto his theory, it seemed, because he stomped his feet into the earth with enough force to make the fire bend away from him for an instant.

"We need to assign more guards to our borders. I will not be scared off from my destiny."

He ground his heels into the earth, and stalked back toward home with one pointed look at Lena. She understood his command and followed. It took all her strength to put one foot after the other.

Lena guessed morning came because the sun rose. The black sky leaked into dark blue and then periwinkle as she sat outside her home, watching the spectrum unfold with unsettling confusion. She stared into the village and saw others doing the same—their faces upturned to a spectacle of nighttime. Lena pulled her arms over her knees. There was a coldness in the air too, subtle enough for now, but with the whispered promise of ice yet to come.

Lena twisted Fressa's knife in her hands. Grief pulled her body down like a millstone, but she focused on the metal in her hands and the sun rising before her. These two incongruities. It was easier to focus on the puzzle before her instead of the terrifying reality that her sister was—

She set the knife down hard and tried to exhale in a slow, controlled breath. Tears still pooled in her eyes, and she debated crossing the distance to Amal's home. But inside Nana's apothecary hut, her sister's body lay beneath a heavy cloth, pale blossoms scattered across her.

They were to burn her today.

Lena stared at the sky again, her body aching like a chasm had opened within her. Only one thread of thought allowed itself clarity within her, and it was the knowledge that Fressa's death had coincided with the alarming occurrences. The blade and the darkness were tied to her sister, somehow. Lena knew it.

A blade of light, a sky of black.

And her sister, between them—dead.

She swallowed back a howl, clawing at her hair and trying to think.

What happened, Fressa? Where did you go?

Her sister's story was not over. It did not *feel* over, and Lena would not allow it. She promised herself that she would find whoever or whatever had done this. Lena would fix this. That was what chiefs did. Even as her parents—red-eyed and silent, in a startling moment of genuine unity—walked outside and beckoned her toward the river's edge to see their daughter sent to the next world, she promised herself it was not the end.

It could not be the end.

Fressa was the fiery hearth that all their lives centered around. Fressa was two years younger than Lena, but Lena could not remember a day or moment where she had not had a sister.

It was not the end, because if her sister was gone—truly—then there was nothing left.

Amal carried Fressa, again. Lena looked at the whole ceremony without truly seeing it. She was elsewhere, even as she stood between her mother and father, her dark hair pulled back in a series of braids that Estrid had spent an hour arranging. Lena watched as Amal laid her sister's body down upon a pile of wood, not bothering to conceal his tears. Some part of her felt pity, but she fought the desire to run to him—to her.

She clawed the pity out of her. Pity would mean accepting this.

The sun was high again, as if the surprising interruption of night had never occurred. But Lena could tell, as she observed the congregated village, that stolen glances confirmed her suspicions. They were worried too, that it might sag and disappear again. There were harvests at stake, and trading missions planned around the cycle of their seasons.

Good, Lena thought. *Let them see that there is something different. That something is very wrong.*

It connected. She sensed it, feeling her certainty align with the steadying of her heart and breath. She watched as Amal lit the pyre, throwing a torch upon her sister. Lena did not flinch as the flames erupted into orange sheets of light. Bodies were not so important to their gods, or to the travel between their worlds. In fact, the absence of body made it easier to traverse realms, which was the purpose of cremation.

Their god Loki could change bodies and forms easily. Loki flowed between species and gender and age, assuming any guise he wished, even as his true essence was chained to a rock in a world far from this one. Lena could admit that Loki was not a kind god, but he was clever—and if he could change forms and bodies and exist in multiple realms at once, then that was proof enough that what seemed impossible lay beyond a terrifying border. One that Lena could cross, if she was brave and cunning enough.

She tore her eyes from the flames at the sound of her mother crying beside her. Lena hesitated, remembering that the village thought Fressa was dead. They were watching as her body burned. Lena bit her lip hard, fighting the tide of disorienting nausea that surged closer as Val braced her hands upon Lena's shoulders. She reached to rest her hand atop her mother's, hoping that would look like a semblance of the grieving sister they thought she was. It was not too difficult—a shadow of grief fell innately, like a destructive instinct, as Lena watched her sister disintegrate.

Lena looked away from the pyre. *No.* None of this

made sense, and she would not succumb to grief before she solved this problem. She tried to meet Amal's eyes, but tears cut down his cheeks until his whole face shone. Lena's heart raced, and she switched her gaze to the villagers holding flowers, gathered in haphazard rows behind the Freding family and the fire.

Bejla stared right at her. She stood by her guardians, Olaf and Gunnar. Her ice-blue eyes did not dart away when Lena met her gaze. Bejla offered the smallest, most tentative smile that Lena had ever seen, and her chest warmed slightly. It was a relief not to see tears or pity. Estrid and her older brother stood beside them, their eyes reflecting the dwindling flames. They either did not sense Lena's gaze, or wished to avoid it. She could not blame them.

As the fire faded, so did the crowd, until just Amal, Lena, and her parents remained. Even Nana had retired to her home, her old legs too tired to stand so long. Amal walked to Lena slowly, and she felt the world spin beneath her. It was plain to see that Amal believed his fiancée was gone entirely, and some part of his shattering sadness wore her down. She threw her arms around him, and let him sag against her as they all watched the fire burn into nothing.

The next day, Lena's father vanished in the early dawn. Since the funeral, Val had not risen from her pallet for more than a few sips of water and broth. Lena had not slept, and watched as her father threw stores of dried meat into his satchels and sheathed two swords through his belt. Her eyes felt bleary, but her mind felt clear and awake—though she struggled to sort through the labyrinth of thoughts winding through her. This house was torture, with Fressa's absence such a palpable, physical reminder. Lena said nothing as her father left with nothing more than an indecipherable nod in farewell.

She heard the rest from Estrid that afternoon. Apparently, what he'd said the night after Fressa died was the one thing keeping him strong. *I will not be scared off from my destiny.* He gathered some men again—those too worried or stupid to speak back to him in such a breakable state—and set off with vague, ragged notions of tracking down their alleged rival clans, despite the strange darkness pressing in harder around them.

The decision made little sense to Lena, but she couldn't bring herself to care. His absence, if anything, was the most normal thing she had felt in days.

Another couple days, by Lena's best estimate, passed in this strangling haze of pain and confusion. Lena had committed every wooden panel's pattern to memory by now. She had the jumbled pieces of a problem set before her, and she turned them over like stones in her mind again and again, still without an answer. She figured she'd lost weight. Even sitting up made her dizzy. With the help of many neighbors, Lena's mother had begun to stand and function again—barely. She could make herself go through the series of motions that allowed them to survive, but Lena could tell that half the life behind her mother's eyes had been killed. Her mother had learned how to look without seeing. To listen without hearing. She never commanded Lena to rise or contribute. Sometimes, Lena wished she would.

Lena felt shame when Amal came to visit in the days after Fressa's funeral. He should've been in the throes of grief at losing his would-be fiancée—he must be drowning in his own private ocean. But here he was, sitting with Lena and silently giving her broth while her body diminished to nothing and her mind struggled for a foothold or even a feeble grasp of the situation before her. She wanted to act—her limbs and heart begged for movement, or any sense of direction. But the enormity of it all felt too impossible to comprehend. The rigid assurance she'd felt at Fressa's funeral compelled her to investigate, but first she needed to figure out where.

Lena started by making herself finally sit up and look

at Amal. She felt a crushing need to shatter the silence that had buried this house for too long.

"My father said it must have been one of the southern clans."

Amal stared back at her for a few moments. His dark eyes were dull. Pronounced bags puffed beneath them. "I heard."

"Olaf said it must've been a sudden illness."

"My mother thinks the same."

"Do you believe her?" Lena's throat already hurt from using her voice again.

Amal braced his hands together, and his shoulders began to shake. He looked away, but the thickness in his voice was enough evidence of his tears. "I have to. What else could it have been?"

Lena's mouth opened, but she had no answer to give.

His voice shattered. "What does it even matter?"

Amal disintegrated for the thousandth time, and Lena managed to wrap her arms around him as he collapsed into her shoulders. The weight of him was hard to bear, but it was a relief to have proof that someone else in this world had loved Fressa so unconditionally and completely. It seemed for everyone else life was moving and steering back into a semblance of what it had been before.

They were all changed in small ways, she supposed, with the strange lengthening nights and the growing dissent toward her father's missions. But no one spoke loud enough or pushed hard enough to make any difference.

And Lena had felt no change in herself since she'd touched her sister's still veins. No release or relief from this mystifying loss. She clutched Amal to her, her perpetual supply of tears opening again.

"I'd give anything," Amal sobbed against Lena. "To even get to say goodbye."

She murmured words of comfort to him, but latched onto that thought—*to say goodbye.* Lena stared at the wall over Amal's heaving shoulders, a cautious beam of hope glowing within her. If Fressa's soul was no longer in Midgard, then there was another world she must be in. It was the one they all feared and despised, the one world in all of the universe that cared nothing for wealth or occupation or age.

Lena's heart began to race from dread and assurance at once. Fressa's soul was not in Midgard, the human world of the living—so Lena knew where she must be.

Their people had a dangerous language. It wasn't so lethal to be spoken or heard, but when written, their markings could have incomprehensible effects. The runes, therefore, were an art taught only to the most trusted and intelligent of their clan. Nana knew it, and in turn, had taught Amal the basics, once he'd grown old enough to show an appropriate amount of fear and respect. Val had strictly forbidden Fressa and Lena from learning runes.

It would be like climbing Yggdrasil, the World Tree, she'd always said. *Impressive, yes, but one misstep and you fall between everything and into nothing.*

Now, Lena stared at the runestones in Amal's hands and prayed she wasn't making a mistake.

"Lena," Amal warned. They stood at the riverbank. It wasn't quite cold enough to freeze the dark waters, but the night air still cut straight to her bones.

She turned to him in an angry flash. She'd built up a little more strength over the past week, but even that movement alone felt like being stabbed. "No, Amal. You promised me."

He knelt to the ground, spreading his mother's stones around him. Lena looked over her shoulder again, to make sure nobody had followed them here.

"I know," he murmured. He glanced up at her uneasily. "I just don't want you to get your hopes up."

"You said it yourself," Lena whispered, a fresh batch of nerves roiling within her. "Just to say goodbye."

He nodded, then examined the stones in the dirt. Amal inhaled, and began to arrange them. Lena avoided looking at him, so he wouldn't feel the pressure, and also because she still heard her mother's nervous warnings about these runes. She made herself stand straight and stared across the river. She had to rid herself of that fear, or this was never going to work.

Summoning their gods was usually a practice left half-complete. Fervent prayers for luck at sea from Rán, or success in battle from Odin. Rarely did they expect or attempt a true response. Lena clenched her fists, wondering if Amal understood the depth of her plan. He wanted closure. She wanted an explanation as well, but was only standing here because she wanted more.

And who better to ask than the goddess of death herself?

Hela is not a kind goddess, Amal had warned her, when she'd first brought up the idea. But his curiosity had won, and her growing, rebellious hope had propelled them both to this night. To what, Lena feared, was her only chance at moving forward.

Her only reason.

She heard the faint clicking of stones as Amal arranged them into letters, and heard his frustrated breathing as he attempted to concoct a summoning message. Each of the stones bore one of their runic symbols—her village believed that their intentional arrangement could summon blessings, like a strong, seafaring wind or a bountiful harvest in midsummer. Lena wondered how her and Amal's intentions would be interpreted through this message. She shut her eyes and prayed hard that Hela would respond. The runes, after all, were sometimes only half the importance in these matters. The other half was the power of will alone.

The faint clicking grew louder, slower, more erratic, until Lena realized it wasn't from the stones at all. Her stomach twisted, and she slowly pivoted around to find Amal staring into the shrouded darkness at the end of the river. The stones beneath him seemed to glow, their markings taking on the same green hue that the ones on Fressa's blade had. Another stab of pain entered Lena's heart, but it was quickly replaced by fear.

Lena had to remind herself that the water was not actually frozen, which only made the sight before them so much stranger. A pure-white horse strode erratically toward them across the water. It had no rider, but there were a saddle and stirrups strapped to it, almost like an invitation.

"Lena—"

"Shh!"

As the horse got closer, Lena understood why it had such an unusual gait—it had only one front leg, its left one. The horse examined them, and its black eyes held enough intelligence that Lena knew it was not of Midgard.

"A hel-horse," Amal choked. They shared one

shocked, terrified look. He'd been supposed to summon the goddess Hela, not her horse.

"But that's not what we asked for!" Lena exclaimed. Frustration tore through her. The hel-horse tilted its head, almost like it was nodding at its back. Lena exhaled. "Did you do this right?"

"I don't know." Amal's voice shook. He staggered his way to his feet, moving to stand beside Lena. They stared at the tri-legged hel-horse, and Lena clenched her fists tight to keep them from trembling. "But I think it wants a rider."

CHAPTER
FIVE

Lena stared at the white horse. It was unnerving to see the imposing animal without its left front leg, but her attention was pulled by the gaping darkness of its eyes. Even in the black of night, its eyes were darker still—the boundless, aching emptiness that affirmed Lena's hopes.

This horse was from Helheim, the land of the dishonorable dead.

"Lena."

Amal's voice came soft and urgent. She turned to look at him over her shoulder. His dark eyes caught the hazy reflection of the hel-horse's white hair. It was hard to be sure from where she stood, but she swore his eyes watered. He reached out a hand, but she didn't know if it was in warning or farewell.

"I'm going, Amal." Lena felt relief to hear her own voice like this again—strong, assured, driven by purpose.

"You saw that knife. You see this darkness, yes? We need answers or we will never move on."

Move on. A lie, of course, but the only words right now that might release the fear widening Amal's eyes.

"I thought we wanted a goodbye," Amal said hesitantly. "This is not what we asked for."

She turned her gaze back to the horse. Lena knew Amal would be tested by this—by leaving Midgard, by confronting forces beyond their comprehension and design. But she was not asking him to go with her. He had summoned Hela, and this hel-horse had arrived in her stead. Lena found the course of action obvious. She would ride it wherever it went. She would not fear her destination, for she had little left to lose.

"Are you sure?" Amal asked.

She didn't turn back to look at him. In that moment, she resented the anxiety that lifted his shoulders and clenched his fists. Couldn't he see that this was the only way to make things right?

"I'm certain."

Lena reached out a hand to the hel-horse. The creature was male, and roughly the size of the horses in Midgard. His mane was cold to the touch, but she steadied herself and stepped into the stirrup to haul herself over. The added weight did nothing to shake the horse, which was already starting to turn around to the direction he'd come from.

The gait beneath her felt unsteady—she felt herself lurching precariously to her left with every step—but she gripped the reins tight and kept her legs firmly wrapped around his flank. She did not look back as they rode across the unfrozen river and broke into the shrouded darkness the hel-horse had emerged from.

Never again, Lena promised, would she describe her home as *cold*. This world took the word and gave it new meaning. She had no doubt that she really was in Helheim—the air felt like invisible ice. Solid and brutal. Despite her unsteady steed, she risked riding with one hand so she could breathe warmth into the other before switching every few minutes.

At least the cold distracted from the fear. She couldn't fully focus on the terrifying new reality she was traversing. Lena wasn't just between the worlds—she had entered a new one. No human was supposed to leave Midgard . . . not *alive*, at least. Some part of her figured she should fear what that meant for herself, but Lena could not bring herself to worry much about that. The freezing air whittled her down, and the only thought strong enough to hold onto was of her sister.

Through squinted eyes, she could discern the jagged tops of black mountains surging upward all around her.

Beneath them, coils of mist and fog sat suspended—frozen into stillness—in the air. Lena pressed her lips together tight, willing her teeth to stop chattering. The light in Helheim was strained and weak, filtered through the deepest roots of Yggdrasil.

Lena's legs were so numb that it took her several seconds to register that they'd stopped moving. She frowned, trying to blink moisture back into her eyes, and scanned the space in front of her. As far as she could tell, more dimness and solidified fog awaited. But her horse was unmoving. Expectant. He tossed his head, agitated, his white mane shifting.

She sat shuddering on the horse for another minute. Now, Lena felt the fear. She was in the realm of the goddess of death. Hela had something that Lena wanted—*needed*—and Lena had no idea how or when she could return to Midgard. Frantically, she tried to summon the faces of Amal and Fressa. Lena shut her eyes tight, remembering the one thing that mattered now. She was terrified, yes, but the thought of returning back to Midgard without Fressa—back to that place scarred and mauled by her sister's absence—scared her far more.

Lena squeezed her toes, trying to keep the blood coursing through her veins. As steadily as she could manage, she dismounted and crouched into a landing on the solid, frozen ground. She nearly slipped, realizing that there was no soil beneath her. Just impenetrable, dark ice. Lena found her footing, keeping her knees bent.

There was nothing ahead of her. Lena whipped her head back to the horse, but he only nodded again, and she hoped he meant she should continue forward. She put one leg in front of herself, and half-walked, half-slid her way into the dimness. There was only a crevice between two colorless mountains, and it was the kind of black that she feared meant a true darkness—an infinite one. But the hel-horse began to tread his way behind her, so she felt a little better.

Her lungs burned with cold fire. She'd hoped she might manage to summon Hela with Amal's help, but she certainly hadn't planned for the other way around. If she had, Lena definitely would've worn her snowshoes and draped herself in every single pelt she owned.

She noticed the mist around her beginning to move— to flow and tremble, as it might in Midgard, not like the solidified clouds hovering behind her. But when she squinted closer, she thought she could make out faint shadows of eyes. A reaching hand. A mouth open, but silent. Lena swallowed, jerking her gaze forward. She shouldn't be surprised. This was Helheim, the realm that most of her people would someday reside in.

Valhalla was an option for those who died fighting, but there were strange necessities to gain admittance there. Lena had been taught that you had to be holding a weapon, and one of Odin's servants—the winged Valkyries—had to choose and deem you worthy enough to enter that hall of fighting and feasting where you waited for your true, final death during Ragnarok. The twilight of the gods.

This place—this world, Helheim—was for everybody else. Some called it the realm of the dishonorable dead, which Lena felt was highly unfair and circumstantial. Those who died of age or natural causes found themselves here. Nothing about Fressa's death felt *natural* to Lena, but the hel-horse would not have led her here without reason.

Lena shuddered as the spirit-mists drew closer to her, nearly converging. She tried to avert her gaze, terrified she might find Fressa buried somewhere among the dead. Lena knew rationally that must be where she was, but she couldn't allow herself to imagine it, let alone see it.

In the distance, she could see where the tendrils connected. They branched out on either side of a daunting throne of ice that soared upward, disappearing into darkness. Hela's domain was the vastest of the nine worlds, ironically serving as the most shared, communal space in all of Yggdrasil. The final resting place for nearly everybody. Lena clenched her fists to keep them from shaking.

"My father told me you might come."

Lena jumped. She hadn't realized there was a figure sitting upon the throne. The goddess was murky and translucent enough that Lena may never have noticed her if she hadn't spoken. Hela's voice lilted in low tones, but she spoke far more quickly than Lena had imagined. Not that she had truly imagined she would get this far. Lena froze, terror pinning her as she studied Hela's face. It was split in two, straight down from the temple of her brows to the tip of her chin. The right side was pleasant enough, the pale face of a woman with smooth, raven-black hair and an inquisitive gleam in her dark eye. But the other side was a shifting, terrible conglomeration of the spirit-mist, writhing and whirling death. Lena trained her eyes on the right side, and focused on Hela's words. Her voice was surprisingly feminine—youthful, almost.

"Y-your father?" Lena asked. She coughed, her throat throbbing from the cold. "Loki, right?" Lena felt suddenly grateful for her mother's lessons about the gods, like Loki, the trickster god of chaos who had birthed the death goddess with a giantess. Another fear struck Lena. "Why does Loki know about me?"

Hela tilted her head. "Hmm. He does keep an eye on these sorts of things. Bargains."

"You know what I want, then?" Lena dared a step closer. Her mind still spun with the information that one of the most powerful gods *knew* who she was—for better or worse.

"I could sense it as soon as that boy drew the runes." Hela paused, lacing her hands together. One elegant, one marred. "I haven't felt a rage like that since—"

"Balder?" Lena interrupted, jumping at the opportunity. This was one of her primary arguments. "I remember the story. The god of light and goodness. He was killed, wasn't he?"

"Yes," Hela said slowly. The mist around her seemed to churn faster. "And Odin—the All-Father himself—dared to enter my realm and beg for Balder's life back."

Lena swallowed. She feared Hela's pointed words were a challenge. A threat. But she made herself finish the story. "You said you would. If every single living creature in the nine worlds wept for his soul."

"And they all did." Hela smiled, but it only reached the right side of her face. "But for one."

"So you kept Balder," Lena finished. She realized then that the dead god of light and love was somewhere in the mist thronging Hela. Somewhere in this realm. "Because a bargain must be met."

"I felt guilty," Hela admitted. Lena's eyebrows shot up—she hadn't expected Hela to care much about her souls. "I would have returned his soul to Asgard had my conditions been met. But if death has no rules, no limits? Nothing does." Lena's stomach dropped, but Hela continued. "Now, I believe you have a question for me."

Lena faltered. Her nerves felt shattered. Hela spoke

so strongly of rules—nothing like the goddess's father, Loki. How could Hela say yes, then, to Lena's impossible request? She struggled to think through the pain and fear and horror threading its way through her mind. Rules, limits, balance. She needed to convince Hela not just that returning Fressa wouldn't disturb the worlds, but that it would *help* the worlds.

Fressa, Lena thought. She shut her eyes, letting the memories she'd tried so hard to suppress over the past weeks slam into her. Fressa was there, through them all, every single day—braiding Lena's hair by the fire, arguing with their mother, throwing her arms around Amal, out in the fields with weapons in her hands and perfection on her mind. Lena's eyes flew open.

"She had a weapon."

Hela only blinked, and Lena's voice made her sound braver than she really felt, but she forged onward.

"Fressa had a weapon," Lena rambled. "A knife given to her by my father just days ago—it glowed when she touched it. It didn't do that for anybody else. She was a good fighter. Our best. Maybe that weapon meant something, or maybe it could do things—to help . . ."

Lena couldn't finish the argument. Nobody had known what that knife was capable of, least of all Fressa. She dared to look at Hela. Lena couldn't tell if the goddess was unsurprised, or simply bored. Desperation flooded her.

"Hela, please." Lena raked her hands through her greasy hair. Should she have better prepared herself for this encounter? She would have to say something incredible and pray it worked out later. "That weapon is powerful. Fressa would be much more help to you—to us all—in Midgard than stuck down here. Strange things are happening. Night has fallen in the middle of summer, and—"

"She is your sister," Hela countered. The eyebrow on her human half raised delicately, pointedly. "You want her back."

Lena tried to hold her chin steady, but she couldn't. It trembled, and her body sagged. "I *need* her back."

Hela sighed. "There is a balance to these worlds, Magdalena. You have to understand that."

"Then let's keep the balance!"

"Do you understand what you're saying, girl?"

Lena's mouth hung open. She turned the words over in her mind, considering. "Yes. What if—what if you took another soul in exchange for my sister's? You have her—you can give her back."

Hela rose from her throne, staring down at Lena. "I never said I had her soul."

"Wh-what do you mean?"

"Fressa is dead." Hela's words were casual, but they stung Lena like a slap. "But she is not in Helheim—your sister is in Valhalla."

Lena bit her chapped lips, frowning. "But she didn't die fighting. She wasn't *holding* a weapon, and I thought that was one of Valhalla's requirements."

"I'm aware," Hela finished. She walked closer to Lena, and Lena resisted the urge to bolt. "So it seems we have a strange situation on our hands."

Lena wasn't sure how she felt about the goddess of death using the word *our*. But she had ventured too far to turn back now, so she made herself stare into Hela's face. "Fressa belongs in Midgard. She can wield this blade."

Hela said nothing, and Lena bolstered herself. "Please, Hela. I will honor you forever."

"That would certainly be a first," Hela laughed. It was a strange, cacophonous noise—death laughing. "I am not concerned with how humans view me. But I can sense your sister is not where she belongs, and that is what concerns me. I am still Hela. Even if Odin has her soul, I can feel her. Perhaps I can control her, though I make no promises. I am very true to my word. If I am to interfere, it is to help the balance of our worlds. You promise your sister has something to offer, but you will have to do the worst of the work. You have to be the maintainer."

"Of what?" Lena whispered, half-knowing the answer.

Hela studied her, leaning close enough that Lena held her breath. "You're a healer, aren't you?" Lena risked a nod. "This will be difficult for you, then. But you say you *need* your sister back—that we all *need* Fressa returned. My father sensed this imbalance as soon as it occurred, and I am a good daughter, just as you believe you are a good sister. I will help you to the extent that I can, but I am not of your world—and Loki can only sense so much from where he is trapped. Yet even the All-Father Odin has limits in my domain. Death is mine."

She paused, and Lena's mouth felt frozen shut. This all boiled down to one question, of course, but one that required several heavy moments of silence to linger between them before Lena found her voice.

"You want me to kill?"

Hela relaxed back into her throne, giving Lena another inspection. "How else is this to work? Now, your best bet is this—maintain the balance. Bring me a soul equal to hers so the weight will not be uneven when I remove her from Valhalla. Do you understand?"

Lena took a step back. She wished she could slow Hela's words, or retrace her way back through the conversation, to find out how in the worlds *this* had become the solution. But she could not afford to lose the goddess's interest now. "There is a weight to the soul?"

"Like you would not believe."

Lena swallowed, her knees almost buckling. It was hard enough to register the goddess's words, but even stranger to hear herself speak back. "As in—I need to find someone my sister's weight?"

Hela's human eye rolled dismissively. "Well, not *literally,* of course. Think of who your sister is. How would you define her, or how would your parents? Consider this."

"Fressa is—" Lena cut herself off. It was a relief to speak of her sister in present tense, but her answer stopped in her throat. Hela wanted Lena to define Fressa in what—a few words? Sentences? She blinked, her jaw quivering. Her heart raced. Hela waited for her answer. "Many things. My sister can braid hair better than anyone I know. She can ride horses bareback. She's a real warrior, like the type most of the men in the village wish they were, and—"

Hela sat up slightly. "A warrior! Excellent—perhaps another soul as physically able as hers could replace her in Valhalla without notice. Yes. Start there."

"*Start* there?" Lena moistened her lips, but the goddess gave no reply beyond a raised brow. "How—how would I bring it to you?" Lena murmured, half in disbelief at the words coming from her lips. Half knowing she would do it anyway.

Hela pointed her hand at the hel-horse still standing silently behind Lena. "The souls come straight to me. As for you, my steed has the power to venture between worlds. It is the only way you can travel. Do not lose him, or you will be lost forever in Ginnungagap, the nothingness between our worlds."

Lena nodded, barely fazed by Hela's warning. "And if I meet your conditions?"

"Then I will follow through as best I can. I will try to retrieve your sister's soul without Odin noticing."

Lena didn't like the words *as best* and *try,* but she was struck with a hope so strong that the clouds smothering her soul began to lift. She didn't realize she was nodding until Hela nodded in return. The bargain had been made.

Hela strode back to her throne, sitting down to face Lena. "Best of luck to you. If what you say is true of Fressa's weapon, then perhaps my father was right."

Lena's mind spun again, and she stared at the goddess. Dread trickled down her spine. "You keep talking of Loki. I don't understand—"

Hela waved her fingers dismissively. "It doesn't concern you. Truly. He just senses imbalances in the worlds as I do, and it is in all of our best interests to ensure our worlds are not tilted. That is all."

Lena frowned. She wasn't convinced, but she couldn't risk pushing Hela any more than she already had.

"I'll see you soon, I presume?" Hela asked. There was a subtle hunger beneath the goddess's syllables that made Lena uneasy. She wasn't asking a question, but voicing a prediction. Lena considered the task ahead—she felt a trapping fear, a smothering weight, and the lingering sensation that she had just walked into a world far wider than she anticipated. But it was all buried under the one thing that was left.

Fressa.

She gave Hela a nod, and walked with careful steps back to the hel-horse. It was hard to mount with the icy ground and Hela's eyes on her, but she managed to swing her legs across the horse. Lena looked up one last time at Hela, who offered her hand in farewell. The hel-horse began to move away, and Lena's breaths came hard and fast as soon as the death goddess was out of sight.

Lena felt like sobbing, but whether out of fear or relief, she couldn't tell. She held tight to the hel-horse, remembering Hela's warning to never leave him. The mist turned from liquid to solid again, and the light slowly grew brighter. A fraction warmer. Something pulled Lena's eye, and she saw a familiar female silhouette vanish into shadows. For an instant, Lena wondered if it might be Fressa, but the figure was too short and slim. Lena flicked the reins, urging the horse faster. Now that she knew Fressa was in Valhalla, there was nothing in Helheim she wanted.

Now that she knew how Fressa could come back, there was nothing else.

There could be nothing else.

CHAPTER
SIX

The riverbank emerged from the fog. It was still dark, but was it the same night? The hel-horse stopped abruptly, and Lena patted his neck once—he had allowed her to travel between worlds, after all. She swung her legs over, her feet splashing into the cold, shallow water that the horse seemed to easily stand on top of. Lena walked to his front, staring into his eyes. "Come back for me, okay? Don't forget."

The horse didn't nod, but Lena prayed he understood—and that the horse's master, Hela, would be able to understand once Lena's half of the bargain was met. She blinked back a wave of nauseated panic as he trotted his way back the way he came, disappearing into the darkness. Lena shivered, though it was positively boiling here compared to Helheim.

"Lena!" Amal's voice came from the trees. It was

such a relief to hear the warmth of his tone that Lena's knees swayed. She made herself jog up the riverbank, until she nearly collided with him.

"What just happened?" Amal rushed. He looked haggard, his eyes wild.

"How long was I gone?" Lena asked, grabbing his shoulders.

He shrugged. "Maybe ten minutes?"

"*Ten minutes?*" Lena barked a laugh. "That's not possible, I . . ." She faltered, realizing hardly anything that had occurred should be *possible.* Perhaps the thwarted passage of time was the least baffling aspect of what had just happened.

Amal stared at her, waiting for her to finish. His brows drew close to each other, and his skin looked far paler than usual in the moonlight. She half-hoped, half-feared he might ask her what she'd done. Where she'd gone. He looked like he wanted to—his hands were restless, tugging at the tips of his dark hair.

She'd nearly forgotten what he thought this was all about, until his voice dropped to a whimper. "Did you see her?"

"Oh—" Lena's lungs collapsed. That fast, his grief threatened to crush her. She tried to remember the deal she'd made, the weight of it. This suffocating bargain was the only thing that kept her breathing. "I didn't, Amal. I'm sorry."

The problem was that there was a very good reason why Amal had been chosen to learn the runes: he feared them. He feared it all—the other worlds, the gods and the giants—and he called it respect. He respected them enough to fear them.

When they were children, Fressa went through a stage where she'd convinced herself that all sorts of spirits lurked in corners of her house—serpents, ghosts, or wolves. She'd never seen them, of course, but Lena remembered the youthful fear that dragged Fressa's face downward as night fell. Amal had told her, in a voice far too serious for a ten-year-old boy, *don't go looking into the dark if you don't want to find what's there.*

And Lena had done a lot more than look.

Amal had impressed her, admittedly, by even agreeing to attempt to summon Fressa's spirit. She wondered how the grief weighed upon him. He had loved her sister differently, of course, but she wasn't sure exactly how to ask how he was dealing with the death of his fiancée. Maybe he could help, maybe—

"It's okay," Amal whispered, staring across the dark waters. Lena blinked, remembering her apology. "She's gone—I can feel it."

His voice broke off with a jagged, carving sob. Lena stared at their feet, not sure how to offer the comfort she desperately wanted herself. *No*, she thought. *I can fix this.* Amal cleared his throat again, and Lena glanced up.

"Fressa—she would want us to be happy," Amal said slowly, as if he were trying to convince himself. This was a practiced speech—one that Lena had heard at other funerals many times, but a burst of rage flamed up now. "She would want us to live our lives the best we can. To move on—"

"*Move on*?" Lena yelled. Amal flashed a surprised look between her and the village behind them, reminding her to be quiet. He raised his hands defensively. They were shaking.

"I'm sorry—I'm sorry, Lena." He sighed, tears welling up in his eyes. "I shouldn't have said that."

Lena shook her head. "It's okay." The rage in her was quickly washed away by a hollow disappointment. She'd figured this would be the case, but now she knew for sure—she would have to do this alone. All of this. Amal didn't understand. To him, Fressa was *gone*. Fressa wanted them to be happy.

But Lena knew Fressa wanted to live. She wanted to marry the boy standing in front of Lena. Fressa needed to master her archery—she'd been so close to shooting perfect rounds with a whole quiver.

Fressa wanted to live.

Amal nodded his head back to the village, a weary look of defeat easily claiming his features. Lena glanced back at the river one more time. She would have to come back soon. She prayed the hel-horse would remember.

He slung an arm around Lena's shoulders, holding her close as they walked side by side back to their tents. It was meant to comfort her, she knew, but she only felt sicker as they left the river—her gateway to Helheim and getting Fressa back. The impossible night was clear but starless at the same time, with only a thin strip of clouds burning white in front of the moon.

Lena tried to build up the courage to ask him what he thought about the darkness shrouding the sky, but suddenly Amal peeled away from her, hugging his arms across his chest. Lena slowed her pace, blinking at him.

The pale light made him look as if he were glowing, and with a cutting ache, Lena remembered the night a few years ago when she began to realize how things were going to change for Amal and her sister.

"Amal?" Lena had shrieked, dissolving into disgusted laughter. She fell back onto her bed pelts, while Fressa sat upright in hers, holding her head in her hands. "Fressa, what are you even saying?"

Fressa's face burned as bright as her hair, but she giggled too. "I don't know. I just mean, maybe he's kind of handsome." She laughed harder. "I don't know!

"You're crazy." Lena shook her head. "Utterly senseless."

Amal cleared his throat, and Lena blinked. Her sister wasn't here, and the familiar pain settled over her again—though this time, at least there was hope. She tried to focus on Amal's voice.

"My mother told me something the other day," he murmured, cutting his gaze down as they walked. Lena fought to keep her expression neutral, but her heart lifted—had Nana noticed something that could help? A clue?

She watched Amal moisten his lips, but his voice only grew self-conscious and rehearsed. "She said, 'There is a way back to the light.'" Amal paused. He winced, as if the words had left a sour taste upon his tongue, and Lena's spirits plummeted. "'Crawl to it, if you have to.'" Amal faltered, and they came to a pause outside Lena's home. She had not realized they had walked so far. He gave a meager attempt at a shrug, barely meeting her eyes. "I don't know if she understands."

Lena nodded once in response. "I'm not sure I do, either."

Amal and Lena stared at each other, but no words came. The best she could manage was a slight lifting of her hand in farewell, and she slipped silently through her door after a moment, relieved to be free of his gaze. The soft, even breathing of her sleeping mother filled the room, and Lena felt her way through the dark to her bed. Lena couldn't see Fressa's empty bed space through the blackness, but she knew exactly where it was—a glaring opposition beside her own.

Waiting.

CHAPTER
SEVEN

"Now that you're well enough to roam around in the middle of the night, I'm sure you'll find no problem in helping to prepare the riverbank for the incoming traders." Val's voice filled up the empty spaces of their one-room home as Lena shoved her way into a sitting position the next morning. Her mother stared at the light seeping in through the boards of their home. "Maybe the last traders of summer, with the winter coming in so fast."

Lena winced. Perhaps her entrance last night hadn't been as stealthy as she'd thought. The morning light was overwhelming, with the exhaustion of a sleepless half-night already setting in. As the dawn filtered through the cracks in their walls, Lena stared at the rays until her eyes burned. Her heart felt fragile in her chest, but it still pounded like a drum. *There is a way back to the light*, Amal had said.

"Fine," Lena whispered, distracted.

Her mother inhaled—it was the usual sharpness that always preceded the scolding and lectures about *respect* and *authority*. On instinct, Lena hunched her shoulders in preparation for a verbal onslaught. But her mother only let out a haggard sigh that seemed to deflate her. Lena's stomach lurched in discomfort. She'd rather endure a lecture than see her mother so broken.

She kept her eyes fixed on the sunlight, and had to remind herself to blink. Lena heard her mother's trudging steps leave their home. Silence settled in, and Lena leaned back on her hands, resisting the urge to collapse back into her pelts.

Her eyes fell again upon Fressa's bed space. Her blankets and pelts were still strewn across it. Fressa had never liked to tidy them, and in death, it seemed neither Lena nor her parents could manage to do it for her.

Lena knew she should feel incapacitated with fatigue. And she was, in a sense—her body felt as brittle and breakable as a charred crust of bread. Exactly as if she'd traversed between the worlds, which to her knowledge, no human ever had.

Until now.

But there was no room for fear or pride or amazement—she had work to do. Lena hurled herself onto her feet and swayed on unsteady legs for a moment before balancing. She squared her shoulders as she pushed her way to the threshold and walked into the light.

Lena tried not to wince at the onslaught of it all. The day was bright, as if the darkness of just a couple hours ago had been a bad dream. She faltered outside her home, taking in the slow-moving morning. There were only a few people around—some farmers on the fringes of their settlement, pulling at straggling weeds—but she felt their eyes on her and wanted to scrape them off. This world without Fressa was unsteady and incapable of being righted. She'd gotten enough attention being one of Fredrik's daughters. But to be the only one? Lena tried to swallow, but her throat was too dry.

That, at least, was an easy fix. Lena set her gaze on the distant river, the one she'd ridden across just last night. She would drink first, and then consider how to balance the worlds. Lena kept her gaze on her feet. Her leather shoes were crusted with dirt from the riverbank. She stared at them as she walked, marveling that they, too, had been to Helheim and back. Her stomach throbbed with anxiety and hunger. Lena didn't make it far before Nana's lilting voice ricocheted out of her tent.

"*Le*-na!" she crowed.

Lena stopped and tilted her head up. She mustered a smile, which wasn't terribly hard to do—she loved Amal's mother, with her face webbed in laughter lines and a mind wide enough to cure almost any ailment that befell their people.

Everything would've been so much easier if she'd been able to cure Fressa from whatever invisible killer had taken her. Lena tried to suppress the shock of icy rage that surged through her veins and walked over to Nana.

Nana was half-shadowed as she stood at the threshold of her apothecary tent. Bouquets of dried herbs, flowers, and roots hung suspended along the walls by ropes. Small containers of melted elm bark and mead sat haphazardly on short oak tables.

"How's my Lena?" Nana asked. Her voice had the subtle warmth of a thin blanket. It wasn't stifling or obvious. Just enough to know it was there. Nana betrayed no pity in her clouding blue eyes, though Lena knew it likely lurked beneath the surface.

Lena's throat grew thick again, but she managed a shrug, and Nana nodded with squinted eyes. She pressed no further, but nodded her head back toward her tent. "Come back whenever you're ready."

The familiar scent from within—subtle smoke intertwined with fading flowers—reminded Lena of *before*. That glorious realm she'd spent every moment longing to return to. She was hit with a brutal pang of longing to reclaim at least a fragment of the familiarity and comfort that her training could bring.

"How about now?" Lena dared to ask.

Nana cracked a smile. "There's no better time."

Lena followed her inside, her mission to the river forgotten. Her deal with Hela was not so easily brushed aside; it simmered at the forefront of her mind, but first she needed to figure out which warrior was worthy and equal to her sister's soul. For the moment, she allowed herself to breathe in the hut's scent, letting her lungs fill completely before exhaling. Her eyes adjusted to the dimness, and Nana knelt down to light a small fire in the center hearth. Nana's fingers shook wildly as she scraped the flint down a slab of oak. After a few moments, Lena gently leaned down and finished the task for her.

Nana laughed, rolling her eyes at her age, but Lena sensed a frustrated sadness lurking behind her eyes—which were not as clear or bright as they'd once been. Amal had never seemed to find it strange calling Nana his mother, despite the fact that she was at least twenty years older than Lena and Fressa's mother. But then again, he had never known anyone else. Nana was so obviously Amal's mother—he'd grown up into her best qualities.

Amal's self-deprecating laugh was a younger, male version of what Lena had just heard Nana dissolve into. Amal had loved to spend his days wandering the forests with his mother when she was younger, finding new uses for the roots and flora that grew around them. Whenever a merchant or visitor from another clan came by, Amal would sit eagerly behind his mother, his head on his hands, listening as Nana interrogated the foreigner on all the methods and medicines they used to see what she could learn. Lena missed that expression on Amal—his dark eyes almost glowing with excitement, and a smile that drew out so many laughter lines. He wore that smile most with Fressa—

Twin snakes of regret and fear uncoiled in her core. Hela's words, again, hammered themselves into her mind—right behind her forehead, in agonizing repetition. But Lena made herself offer Nana a hand up, and they brushed themselves off as the fire grew. An awkwardness she had never known with Nana suddenly settled between them as they faced one another. Partially caused by Nana needing help to stand up, perhaps. But a flash of indecision crossed the apothecary's face—a slight open-then-close of the mouth. The whisper of a frown drawing her brows together.

Ducking her gaze, Lena hoped Nana would not speak of Fressa. To hear her spoken of as *gone* or *beyond* or simply *not with us* would be too incapacitating. Fressa was within reach, Lena reminded herself.

Thankfully, Nana cleared her throat and instead asked, "So, where did we leave off?" She hobbled to the table, Lena trailing behind. "Elm bark?"

Lena's brow quirked. She was unsure whether or not

Nana was joking; the functions of elm bark—to soothe the throat and bolster the voice—were fairly rudimentary. It must have been one of the first things that Nana had taught her.

"Elm bark?" Lena repeated cautiously. Nana turned over her shoulder to frown at Lena, but it dissolved fast—a quick flash of confusion banished with a smile.

"Oh," Nana laughed. "Of course, not elm bark. I meant to say, ah—" Lena watched her examine the roots spread across the table. "Rotabagge."

Careful relief relaxed Lena's shoulders. "Oh. No, we haven't done that yet."

Nana straightened her back as best as she could manage, seemingly bolstered by the normalcy of the task ahead. This, at least, was charted territory—Nana with the answers, Lena the attentive pupil. Without further ado, Nana launched into demonstrations and explanations of the vegetable's functions and qualities, her previous confusion forgotten.

Lena half-listened. She was glad to be in the company of Nana, but at the same time, felt guilty and wasteful for doing so when she could be helping her sister. It had been less than a day since she had visited a whole other world. Lena thought the sense of direction and purpose would make things easier for her. Now, with the sun back in the sky, it was difficult to wrap her head around what she would have to do. In the back of her mind, lingering in the space below Nana's words, Lena thought she heard other voices—Hela's, with those gracious but damning instructions. Amal's, his tone neutral and dull, as it'd been since the day Fressa died. And Fressa's, the quietest of all. She was saying something, Lena swore, but she couldn't decipher it.

Don't worry, Fres, Lena thought. *You'll be back before you know it, I promise. I'm coming for you.*

CHAPTER
EIGHT

After a day full of apothecary training, Lena deflated when she remembered her promise to her mother. Exhaustion pooled within her, but an incessant desire to fix more pressing matters also raged at her. It was not a conducive mindset for adjusting their village's banners along the shoreline, or for helping set up tents and tables for trading.

She heard mutterings among the village about the setting sun as she worked in silence. Everything swam through a murky, golden light, dense and dewy in its sinking. Lena's heart pounded as she dug another flag-pole into the stony side of the river so the boats would know where to port. The soft rush of ripples kissing the shore roared in her ears.

Lena did not want to be here.

Last month, she imagined she would've sprinted

across the village in a frenzy, making sure all the vendors were ready and that enough guards were posted along their fringes in case any traders turned out to be less than friendly—but they could not be conspicuous, of course.

Now, Lena barely reacted at the first shout announcing a boat on the horizon. She wanted to be elsewhere, by herself, ciphering out Hela's words and to complete this generous, devastating task—a soul for a soul. She should not have wasted the day training with Nana; part of her knew she was stalling the inevitable, afraid of what she had promised despite her willingness to see it through for Fressa, whatever the cost. Lena sighed through her nose and wiped her hands on her skirt, staring at the approaching boats. There weren't many, and they were the usual clans from just north up the river. In her pe-riphery, she saw Estrid and her older brother, Sven, look across the waters.

Lena nodded at them in greeting, but could think of nothing that mattered to say.

But Estrid spoke, which was hardly surprising, though her words made Lena sicker. "This darkness is strange," she said. Lena turned to look at her. Estrid's gray eyes stayed locked on the horizon, her jaw taut with worry. "Did your father say anything before he . . . left?"

Lena sensed a barely concealed rage born of fear. Sven glanced over at Lena, then down. He had not ac-companied her father on his most recent mission—not many had, fearing the unexpected darkness. Lena did not blame them. Even now, when she could tell her own friend harbored obvious resentment for her father, she could not muster the fear she should have been consumed by the notion that her father's position as chief might be in question. She could not break through the anxiety of her promise that numbed her to everything else.

"He did not," she said, trying to erase any inflection from her voice. Lena hated the way it sounded—unassuming, brittle. "But my mother says this is nothing to worry about. Storms pass."

"This is not a *storm*," Sven said. Lena blinked—he was a man who rarely spoke. Even his sister jolted slightly. Sven sighed as the ships neared. "I apologize—I mean no offense. But this is why I could not accompany your father this time to Francia. Something might be wrong, and I must tend to the harvests more carefully."

Lena tilted her head. "He went to the southern clans."

Sven stared blankly back at her. Estrid glanced between them, crossing her arms. Behind them, voices ricocheted between the houses and stables—the traders were near. The scent of smoked meat wafted toward them on the wind. Lena's spine felt cold, though she was unsure of why.

"And my father's never been to Francia—he's only

raided England," she said slowly, not sure why Sven was confused.

"England?" Sven raised his eyebrows. "That place is a myth. Some of these men"—he motioned at the traders disembarking their boats—"claim they've been, but I doubt it. If it was real, it would be simply too far for any of the missions your father leads. We always went to Francia."

Lena opened her mouth, but held her tongue. She would not press this further for fear of seeming ignorant, but why would her father lie? Or was Sven merely confused?

Before anyone could speak, a small girl burst between Estrid and Sven—it was Kiali, their youngest sister. She had the iciest eyes Lena had ever seen, a crystalline blue so piercing that they could have been made of glaciers. Her ash-blonde hair hung loose across her thin shoulders. Estrid leaned down to pick her up.

"Are you ready to help at the market?"

"Yes! Mother sent me to tell you that we need your and Sven's help."

Estrid glanced at Lena across her shoulder. "Will you and your mother need any help?"

Lena shook her head quickly. Estrid meant well, but there was an undercurrent of doubt beneath her words—the doubt that Lena and Val could effectively lead this village without Fredrik.

Or Fressa.

As they walked, Sven raised a hand in an awkward farewell. It was too bad that young children did not know to lower their voices, because Lena heard Kiali's high voice ask, "Is that the girl whose sister died?"

Lena clenched her fists, walking fast toward the water. Her passiveness toward the trading session melted quickly—darkness was falling, and she would not let anyone think that Clan Freding could not lead this village. She caught up with her mother, who stood by the boats, directing the visitors toward the main thoroughfares. Val was flanked by some of the village's bulkier men in case anyone gave a sign of trouble, though it seemed to be going smoothly.

She smiled as Lena walked closer to her. The next crew unloaded, dragging a few chests of summer fruits and gold-inlaid cloth. They nodded to the men surrounding Val, and bowed for her. Lena thought she recognized them from years past, but couldn't be sure. When her mother turned to face Lena, she saw a tightness in Val's jaw that hadn't been there before. But then her face broke into a proud, rehearsed smile as she motioned toward Lena.

"My daughter," she introduced. "Magdalena."

Lena's neck prickled at the sound of her full name in her mother's magnanimous *chieftess* tone. But she tried to arch her back, and look as serene and stoic as possible. The leader stepped forward—he was about as old as her father, with a full, dark beard shot through with white. He eyed Lena, giving her a private smile. Lena offered a polite nod in return.

"She can lead you to the market center," Val explained. "Lena, would you?"

"Of course," Lena said, willing her jaw not to clench. "Follow me."

The village was not far, but Lena felt conscious of her every step. She kept her shoulders perfectly squared and tried to exchange pleasantries with the leader, who introduced himself as Jannik, and the three men who had come with him.

"Where is your father this year, eh?" Jannik asked. Lena winced—she had hoped he wouldn't ask that. The tension within their village was quelled only through the wealth they brought back. But it was bad news that other clans had started to hear of her father's trips.

"England, I believe," Lena lied, not wanting him to know of her father's alleged insistence on investigating other clans. Fredrik's whereabouts were not up for speculation among any outsiders. The din of voices around them grew louder. Lena exhaled slowly as they walked. Just another few houses to go.

"It's strange," Jannik said. Something in his voice had changed. Lena glanced over at him, and noticed the rest of his band had fallen several steps behind them.

He grazed her arm in what she might have believed to be an accident, if not for the look in his dark eyes. She gritted her teeth, fixing her gaze forward, hoping to find Amal or Bejla or Estrid. "Him leaving all you women by yourselves in this valley. All alone."

Lena stuttered a small laugh. She was not afraid of this man, though frustration surged strong. "We manage."

"It's still a shame," Jannik lilted. "Are you married?"

She flushed, and shook her head. Lena knew she was older than most married women, and she disdained the instinctual shame she felt. Who was this man? Lena thought she recognized him from previous years, but she had always been so busy during trades—examining ribbons with Estrid, or begging Fressa to help her set up. Lena realized they had stopped moving. The market was all around them now. Those who had arrived already shouted their wares, or adjusted the display. Torchlight rippled across the crowd, though the sky still burned in twilight-blue.

Despite the crowd, Jannik reached for her arm again. Lena lurched away, but at the enraged flash in his eyes, something clicked. She had seen that rage in the worst kind of men before. She had heard the stories, and knew of the unspeakable evil men who felt wronged or led on could commit.

"Are you a warrior, Jannik?"

His eyebrows raised, and he burst into laughter—Lena knew it was a peculiar question to ask, but she kept her chin firm nonetheless. Jannik's lips curled into a haughty smile. "The best of my village, they say."

Lena smiled back, her stomach flipping. This was almost too perfect. Maybe even divinely ordained. She had spent all day agonizing over the brutal simplicity of her task. A soul for Fressa's. Lena realized she was still grinning, and Jannik reached for her arm again. This time, she let him. She stared into his eyes, surveyed the insatiable and selfish hunger in them, and let the affirmation she desperately sought rush through her. There was no good in this man.

Lena leaned in, slightly, and dropped her voice into a whisper. "It is difficult," she breathed. "With no men around. You understand my meaning, I'm sure?"

His grin was a wolf's.

CHAPTER
NINE

The sky turned almost black as Fressa's blade bounced where it was tied against Lena's hip as she walked quickly over to Nana's apothecary hut. Smoke curled into the darkening sky, and Lena's heart felt too slow. Could she go through with this? She had promised to meet Jannik in his tent within the hour.

She paused for a moment before the hut, bracing herself against the sturdy wood. This was not a matter of *could*—she would do this, no matter what it required. Lena exhaled, keeping her sister's face clear in her mind. She would not let it fade before it was back in this world where she belonged.

Lena swung open the door and froze. She had counted on everyone being down by the river, but she was not alone.

"Amal?"

He turned to face her. His eyes looked red, and his dark hair plastered itself to his forehead. Amal crouched on a low stool, stirring a pot hanging above the flames. His shoulders shook slightly.

He didn't move once he saw her. Instead, he tried to laugh, but it rang out more like a cry. "Why has night fallen in the middle of summer, huh? Is it winter so soon?"

Lena approached him carefully, crouching by the fire opposite from him. She wanted to ask him if he really meant the darkness surrounding their settlement, or something else. That different type of night that had crept into every corner of their lives.

"Where is your mother? I did not see her by the river."

Amal wiped at his eyes. "She—she isn't feeling well."

"Oh?" Lena asked. She leaned back on the heels of her hands. "Well, it's convenient that she's an apothecary, then."

He hardly smiled at that, his shoulders offering a faint shrug. Lena felt like she had somehow failed him.

"Medicine cannot stop age," Amal said. He clenched his jaw, avoiding Lena's gaze. "Medicine can't stop a lot of things."

Lena's stomach pitted. Another tide of grief started to pull at her, growing with the quaver of Amal's voice, but she blinked hard to hold it back. She had a plan.

Lena stood up fast, her head rushing from the sudden motion. She turned her back on Amal, and pretended to examine all the roots and flowers strewn across the tables lining the perimeter of the room.

She glanced once over her shoulder, back to him. He stared into the flame, and so Lena made her move. The hemlock lay beside the other pale flowers, inconspicuous and unmarked. It was just another reason why only those trained by Nana could enter this room. She grabbed a handful of the small, white flowers and transferred them to her satchel, praying that Amal wouldn't look up.

Once she felt them drop into her bag, she exhaled and turned around. "Give your mother my love. I'm sure she'll feel better soon."

Amal opened his mouth, but hesitated long enough that she felt uneasy. Lena half-hoped and half-feared he might mention their time by the river—the runestones, the hel-horse . . . there was so much more that he didn't know. Couldn't know. He seemed ready to put it all behind them, and to focus on this world—Midgard—alone.

Lena loved him, certainly, and she could not blame him for fearing the cosmic unknown. Still, the lone burden of her bargain rested uncomfortably upon her shoulders. She raised a hand in farewell, and left him alone, staring into the open flame.

Jannik's tent was situated by the edge of the village, along with most of the other traders' tents—and Olaf and Gunnar's home. Lena walked quickly past their home, which looked downright inviting next to the dismal white tents lined up next to them. The two men had a few rows of cabbage and barley planted outside, with a small stable filled with a few beautiful horses. Smoke billowed into the sky from within. She imagined the couple with their pseudo-adopted daughter, Bejla. Then she wondered if they might see her from inside, and part of her wanted Bejla to run out and stop her from what she was about to do—but that was only the fear.

Fear could be crushed and suppressed. Fear was nothing compared to the gaping hole in her heart; fear was a flea, and Fressa's absence was a thousand knives impaling her at once. Lena reminded herself that she was not unarmed, in many senses. Poison or a blade—one way or another, she would fix things tonight. Lena cast one glance behind her. If anyone saw her here, it would raise too many questions.

A flickering above her tore her gaze upward. Billowing sheets of green light emanated between the stars, rippling like an open sail. Lena's breath caught, and a momentary wash of calm doused her. The northern lights rarely showed themselves in summer. The beauty was as fearsome as it was entrancing, and Lena knew only the gods would send such a sign.

Satisfied, Lena squared her shoulders. She did not hesitate now—the gods watched and waited, and Lena knew at least one was on her side. Lena remembered Jannik's directions and flung open the flap of his tent once she found it.

"Magdalena," he drawled. His speech was sloppy, and Lena took notice of a half-drained bottle of wine. *Even better.* It was as if Hela wanted Lena to succeed in this. The thought bolstered her.

"Am I allowed inside?" she asked, demurely.

"Of course," he slurred. "Come here."

Lena smiled, ducking inside. The tent was only a tent, of course, but Lena felt suffocated almost instantly. A bedroll lay unfurled on the grass, and a few small bags of his belongings were strewn opposite it.

"I—I thought you might be hungry," Lena said, as she'd rehearsed on her way here. "I brought some of my mother's leftover oatmeal."

Jannik blinked. "Oatmeal?"

Lena had expected as much—she smirked, lifting one shoulder in a shrug as she unslung her satchel from her shoulders. "It is very good, I swear," she assured. Lena took out the canteen-like container and held it out for him. "Besides, I have a feeling you will need the strength . . . for what is to come."

Lena fought the urge to cringe. The words left a bitter taste in her mouth, but they had the desired effect. He raised his eyebrows, his lips curling into a smile. Already, he reached forward to receive it. Lena had ground so many poisonous flowers into the meal, but she prayed it was dark enough and that he was drunk enough that he would not notice. He must have been pretty far gone, since he did not even ask why she had none for herself.

Lena seized slightly as he brought the container to his lips. She felt little pity—not with this man's character and her sister's life in the balance—but she had still crossed some invisible threshold. Lena knew, even now, that something in her soul had shifted irreparably. Though she took no joy in this, there was a grim sense of satisfaction at the power she now knew she could exert.

He wiped his mouth, and Lena smiled at him. Waiting. It was hard to tell if it had begun to affect him—he was already loose and clumsy enough from the alcohol. But then he stood up and walked toward her. Lena kept her face hard, but her heart ticked out a faster pace—had she calculated the hemlock incorrectly?

No, she promised herself. She would not ruin this. Subtly, she reached behind her to ensure that her sister's blade was still on her. While her hand was still behind her, Jannik lurched forward suddenly, grasping Lena's waist.

She bit her lip, clutching at his arms. "Not so fast," she trilled.

"I'll admit," he said, laughing. "It is nice to be fed

first. So rarely do I get that luxury with the women I take in other villages."

Lena winced, her heart pounding now. She reminded herself that there were people nearby. Bejla was just next door, but the thought made her feel worse, somehow. Jannik moved his hands lower, from her waist to her hips, and Lena tensed.

She should have calculated the poison's acting speed more carefully. Lena had been so ready to jump at this chance—her chance to save Fressa—that she had let it make her rash. She bit the inside of her cheek hard, knowing that she had, at the very least, prepared a lethal dosage—it would take effect. But when?

He leaned in to kiss her, but she could not risk any residual poison—let alone stomach the thought of his lips on hers. She turned her face, offering her neck instead. Lena exhaled shakily, clinging to the reminder of her bargain with Hela and steeling herself not to bolt.

Lena stared hard at the fabric of the tent as he kissed her neck with a terrifying hunger—she blinked rapidly, trying to focus in on the tiny spots of the weathered cowhide, and not the way his arms wrapped around her entirely, pulling her too close to him.

One good thing came from his proximity—she saw the faintest look of confusion pass through his feverous gaze, and felt the first trembling in his arms. But with her body pressed along his, she also felt him hard against her. A bolt of panic swept through her, and a strength she had never known in her spindly limbs propelled him away from her.

Lena had never even been *kissed*—she could not participate in this charade any longer, not if she saw the poison finally acting. Lena had felt plenty of moments of confused heat in the past years—mostly when she was alone, and mostly without a specific face or body to name. Some puzzling dreams came to her on longer winter nights. The figures were mostly anonymous, but sometimes took on the features of Sven or Bejla or once, disturbingly, Amal—and Lena always awoke frustrated, in many senses. But she did not know what to *do* with the heat, and she certainly felt no hint of it now with Jannik.

Cold dread spooled from her stomach as he pulled her back to him. *Please, Hela,* Lena prayed. She felt his limbs begin to weaken and tremble, but he still wasn't hesitating or slowing down. Her breaths came in crashing, panicked succession—her vision tunneled and twisted as she felt his hands begin to gather her skirts, pulling them up.

"No," she said.

Quickly, she slammed her knee up into his groin. He grunted, tripping backward. Lena gasped, adjusting her skirts. Jannik *still* hadn't collapsed from the hemlock, though his eyes grew unfocused. He was too big, too strong for poison alone to act so fast. Lena cursed herself under her breath.

Fear and anger combined within her, and before she could stop herself, Lena reached over to the table and grabbed hold of his wine bottle.

"Stop," she warned. But he only rolled his eyes, and tried to stumble to her again.

Lena gritted her teeth, raised the bottle over her head, and brought it down as hard as she could. She did this not just for Fressa, but for herself, and for the other girls she was now doubly certain this man had hurt. The bottle didn't even break over Jannik's skull, but it was enough to bring him to his knees.

"Wh—" he choked. He touched his head, then examined the blood on his shaking fingers. Jannik fell forward onto his wrists, and his breathing became labored—of course, *now*, the poison laid its claim. Lena's chest heaved, but she couldn't look away now. Her breaths were audible—loud, ricocheting through the small tent, so she clapped her hands across her mouth and swallowed down the rising nausea. She made herself watch to the end. Lena had not come this far for nothing.

Finally, the panic in Jannik's eyes leaked away. His limbs fell limp. Lena did not move for several minutes, though she knew she needed to be far from this scene. She could not guess at how the other traders who had arrived with him would react, so Lena set down the bottle, and forced one foot behind her, then the other, until the crisp outside air filled her lungs.

She had done it.

Lena let her hands fall back down to her sides. She swiveled around, part of her half-hoping to find Fressa safely returned. But though the task was done, she would have to retrieve her reward. Her heart thrilled with a hope she tried to rein in, but it grew too strong to contain.

And despite what she had just done—despite the poison in her satchel, the shadow of his touch across her waist, and the empty silence within the tent—she grinned.

She turned toward the river, ready to complete her bargain. But her eyes caught on a figure standing outside Olaf and Gunnar's home—Lena froze. The distance and darkness might hide her, but she feared it did not. Bejla stood just outside, emptying a pail. Lena wondered if Bejla had seen her emerge from Jannik's tent.

Lena's first fear was not that she could now be tied to Jannik's death if Bejla told anyone. It was that Bejla had seen her, and believed that Lena had lain with him. She swallowed hard, clutching her satchel against her. Once Bejla finally returned inside, Lena ran with as much speed and silence as she could muster. There was a far more pressing matter to see to.

The hel-horse was waiting at the river.

Lena's heart raced, but this time from cautious excitement. This meant Hela knew Lena had acted, that she was completing her end of the bargain. Lena felt none of the trepidation and unease she'd felt the first time she saw the horse without its front left leg. She leapt onto its back easily—something she could rarely do with any horse, let alone with a primordial, three-legged one. Part of Lena feared she should have dragged Jannik's body with her to Hela, but she knew they were dealing with the weight of souls alone. Fressa's body had burned down to ash, and Lena had watched her sister turn into smoke that faded into air. This transaction did not require a corpse, which was lucky—there was no way Lena could have carried the man's body this far, especially without getting caught.

The journey Lena had taken last week—had it only been last week?—whipped by fast and fluid this time. The river rushed beneath her, but they rode on with ease into the thickening shroud of darkness at the end.

Hope surged within her, even as the dark grew blacker and tangible, almost as if she could grab at it with her fists, feel it curl and writhe between her fingers. She was certainly not in Midgard anymore—jagged, black mountaintops clawed their way upward into thick, hovering mist until they disappeared.

Her nerves only returned as the mists coiling through the realm assumed shapes, or hints of them, at least. She swore she saw flashes of gaunt eyes and screaming mouths, but the mist shifted constantly, too fast for her to discern anything. She kept her gaze trained ahead as best she could as the mist surrounding her on either side converged on Hela's throne. The throne that had haunted Lena's thoughts and dreams. The throne that was her only hope.

Lena could not read the goddess's expression. It was rather impossible, especially with her divided face. The left side, with its sagging skin and empty eye socket, made her focus intensely on the right face: smooth, pure white, almost like the porcelain Fredrik sometimes brought from the far east. Her eye was a rich, earthy brown that glistened when she smiled. Or half-smiled. It was equally impossible to guess her age from looks alone, though Lena understood that Hela must be thousands of years old, if Loki had fathered her so long ago.

"I saw his soul tainted by you," Hela said. There was no greeting, which Lena supposed was fair. What could possibly have been said to precede this situation?

"Tainted?" Lena asked. The word cracked open some crevice within her, undammed doubt pouring forth.

Hela's half-smile didn't waiver. She flipped her right hand in a dismissive gesture, as if it was nothing to worry over. "I must admit, you took the *warrior* instructions to heart. He was certainly strong."

Lena's heart stuttered as a few seconds of strained, unsettled silence poured between them. "Our deal," she prompted.

"Yes," Hela said, steepling her hands—one of flesh, the other of bone. "Our deal. To find me a soul equal to that of your sister's, so we can switch her from Valhalla as best as we can manage."

Her use of *we* was a slight comfort, but Lena wasn't sure why the goddess felt the need to recite their plans. She squinted her eyes. "I killed that man. Like you said."

It wasn't as jarring as she had feared it might be to say aloud, but the temperature still seemed to plummet, impossibly, further—the cold sliced straight into her bones, but she tried to keep her body from shaking.

Hela squinted back at Lena. "I need a soul equal to your sister's."

Lena faltered. "Y—yes, a soul for a soul." She cleared her throat. Tucked her hair behind both ears. "An eye for an eye. All that."

Before she even finished, Hela shook her head. "Lena. This is more complicated than even I anticipated.

It seems this is not a matter of mere *quantity*." Her voice cut Lena deeper than the cold, and she felt ashamed before she felt angry. "After all, do you believe Odin, the All-Father, is concerned with *quantity*?"

"Quality," Lena realized. Her cheeks burned, even in the depths of Helheim. Legs swaying again, she had to steady herself against the hel-horse's flank. "Quality."

Hela nodded, and Lena noticed that the goddess's fingers twitched. Was Hela nervous too? "Yes." She sighed once, raking her humanoid hand through the swathes of raven-black hair that fell across her right shoulder. "A mere warrior to replace another warrior will not appease Odin. This man has a very dismal, terribly unbalanced weight—a strong build with a weak mind. And your sister is not weak, is she?"

Lena's mouth fell open. A furious flurry of questions raged within Lena, and the hope she'd cautiously opened herself up to morphed into a dangerous, charged creature with fangs. Her vision blackened as she realized she would not be seeing her sister tonight. The path she'd been following this whole time, dark and cold and lonely, hadn't come to an end—it was merely the first bend in the road. Her fingers trembled with rage and fear as she searched for the right words to say—to make Hela understand, to make *herself* understand what was happening. Lena hesitated, but voiced her concern out loud.

"What does Loki have to do with any of this?"

Her voice quavered, and it was not the first question she thought she might ask, even though it had lingered in the back of her mind ever since the first time she made the trek to Helheim. But as soon as she spoke the words, she knew she needed that answer. Her sister's fate was wrapped up in some strange, confusing chaos that spanned the worlds. Lena did not care much for the Aesir or Vanir gods, the two tribes of gods that held a very fragile peace between them, but if it brought her even a step closer to Fressa, she would unspool this thread as far as it allowed.

She watched Hela tense, her fingers curling into her armrests. Loki was this goddess's father, Lena remembered. Perhaps this had less to do with Fressa and more to do with Hela's own obligations. Lena cursed herself for blurting out her question.

She was angry still, at Hela's vagueness and flippancy. But the goddess was her only well of hope now, and she would sooner drain it then let it dry.

"All I mean," Lena backtracked, "is that if Loki wants me to succeed in this, as you mentioned, then why will you not simply take this man's soul?"

Hela inspected the fingertips of her human hand, but they trembled just enough that Lena knew she was entering dangerous territory. "I just said, girl—the man could probably fight as well as your sister, sure, but he is not *worthy* of her."

"But we agreed—"

"Keep trying." Hela's voice snapped through the air like a whip. "We can do this, but not with this man's soul. We cannot risk it."

"We?" Lena asked. Her anger was giving way fast to teary frustration, but she tried to hold her voice steady. She asked the question she was afraid to. "Why are you helping me?"

The darkness shrouded all around them seemed to converge around the goddess, and Lena instinctively took a step back. "You said your sister was special, didn't you?"

Lena nodded. "I only mean—"

"Like you said, your sister is *useful*," Hela said, her voice grating across the distance between them. "And right now, I cannot say the same of you."

Lena took another step back, the goddess's words driving her away. Maybe they literally were. Her father, Loki, was supposed to be able to do that sometimes: say something so clever and crafted that it could wring out very tangible consequences. Whatever the case, Lena would not let Hela see her cry.

She ducked her head. "I will try again."

Hela nodded once, deep and swift. She glanced over at the hel-horse, snapping her human hand. The horse kneeled slightly, as Lena pulled herself atop it. The erratic but familiar gait began to take her away from Hela's throne room, but not before Hela's voice rang out behind her.

"This is bigger than you, girl." Lena shut her eyes tight, not daring to turn around, the hel-horse still striding away. "You want your sister back, but we *need* your sister back."

Lena yanked on the reins, her back stiffening at the goddess's words. But the horse would not stop. She turned around, her back cracking from the motion.

"What do you mean?" she screamed. Hela was small now, shrinking away until the darkness crowded her from Lena's vision. She pulled at the reins helplessly, but the horse did not react. Helheim returned to its foggy darkness, and Lena only felt the tears streaked across her face when the air froze them to her skin—icy rivulets carved into her, a mask of perpetual despair.

Her body convulsed from the cold, and she slumped forward onto the hel-horse's neck for the rest of the ride, trying to steal any warmth from the death goddess's creature. Lena wanted to scream at the hel-horse for not stopping or turning around or ever obeying her. Questions piled up, and even though this was supposed to be *Lena's* quest and *Lena's* mission, control had been torn from her. She felt like dissolving into sobs, but her body was too tired and numb, so only silent tears came, slowly melting away the icy ones.

Gradually, the air warmed. Even as she started to recognize the Midgardian stars emerging above her, she could not muster the strength to sit back up.

Hela was right, had always been right.

Your sister is useful.

Lena was barely comforted by the goddess's use of the present tense about Fressa.

I cannot say the same of yourself.

If Lena could not save Fressa, what was she doing? What *was* she? Who had she ever been, since she was two years old, if not Fressa's sister?

It took her several breaths to realize that the hel-horse had stopped moving. Lena slid off, glad to be away from the creature. But as she watched him walk back into the darkness, her eyes still blurry with tears, she remembered the goddess's final words to her. Something much larger than Lena, or even Fressa, was at play. She traced the flat edge of Fressa's blade, still secure at her hip, wondering for the thousandth time since her father's return last month why the runes had never danced or lit up for her.

A coldness worked its way down her throat, and Lena staggered to the riverbank. Had it been so recently that she had dragged Amal here, begged him to cast that terrible spell? If the goddess was so invested, it couldn't possibly have been mere runestones that set this all in motion.

She stared up into the sky, so bright and pierced with the stars and constellations she knew well, like the giant Thialfi's pair of eyes boring down upon the worlds, blazing eternal light. She liked that story, especially the way her mother had told her: as a vengeance for her father's death at the hands of the gods, Thialfi's daughter Skaldi had made the gods swear that he would be remembered for all the days and nights that would ever be.

And they had cast his eyes into the sky, where all could see them.

Lena would do the same for Fressa, she knew, if only she knew who had killed her. And *why*. Lena stood up, her knees cracking—perhaps she had been chasing the wrong questions, or rather, not allowing herself to get wrapped up in the details and nature of her sister's death. She was so concerned with getting Fressa back that she had never truly allowed herself to consider who had taken her, and why. To do so would be to accept that she was actually gone. Her knees went weak at the other prevailing realization—Lena would need to find someone equal to Fressa's character and worth, beyond her fighting skills. Lena blinked hard.

Valhalla. Odin. There were names and places, but with no connection Lena could fathom. She'd feared considering the specifics, had hoped for a simple—even if dangerous—way out. But now she had to figure out what the gods knew of her sister.

And what could they know that Lena did not?

CHAPTER
TEN

In the darkness of Midgard, Lena could not tell precisely how long she had been absent this time. She rolled her shoulders as she walked back to her home, keeping to the darkest shadows. She had not dared walk past Jannik's tent after returning from Helheim—Lena couldn't look at a corpse she had created. The thought was too unnerving, too outrageous for her to wrap her head around without going faint.

And it still had not been enough to save Fressa.

Lena bit her lip hard, and hoped her mother was asleep as she creaked the door open as quietly as she could. The sound of her mother's snoring resounded through their room, so Lena sagged with relief and tiptoed to her pallet. She had been prepared to tell her mother that she'd spent the night at Bejla's after staying up too late at the markets, but that would've made matters worse if word got back to Bejla. She had already—maybe—seen Lena with Jannik.

Her heart seized again, and she laid flat on her back. Her body ached with relief, but she was far too wired and frantic and muddled to sleep. Time leaked away as Lena stared at the wooden panels, waiting for the light to seep in.

When persistent knocking sounded across the door, Lena sat straight up. It took Val only a few seconds to wake and fling the door open. Lena listened—it was Olaf's voice. She had never heard his deep voice verge on hysteria, but it took on a wobbling tone that pierced through the room. Lena kept her face perfectly neutral as she stood to hear them.

"—the other men in his party did not see him at the tables this morning," he heaved. One of her mother's hands was braced upon the oak door. Lena moved to stand behind her. "They went into his tent—he's dead."

Lena watched her mother's hand fall. Lena knew Val was already sorting through all the repercussions that could befall their village.

"Dead?"

"We couldn't find a pulse, and we—we think there might be some blood and bruising on his head, though there's not much—"

Olaf fell silent, and Lena realized he had spotted her behind Val. The sky was a dark blue cloaking his silhouette. Lena made her lips quiver an appropriate amount, which wasn't terribly difficult—adrenaline pumped through her, swift and electrifying.

"One of the traders?" she asked, eyes wide. "He's not waking up? Do you know why?"

Her mother exchanged a troubled look with Olaf, and neither of them answered. Lena froze—were they onto her? Had she not been convincing enough? Lena switched her gaze from her mother to Olaf, trying to understand why their lips pursed.

"Oh, Lena." Her mother put a hand upon Lena's shoulder, and her grip was soft and soothing. "These things just happen sometimes."

Lena gasped an inhale, ice shoving down her throat, because how could she not have seen what she had walked into? The man's death. There had not been much blood on him—it was the poison that had ravaged him, and she had not been strong enough to do much damage with the bottle. In their eyes it would be quiet, inexplicable, almost peaceful.

Just like her sister's had been.

Now she understood their pity, and wanted to scrape it off of her. She shook her head, her voice coming out in stutters.

"It's all right," Val whispered, nodding to Olaf to leave them alone. He stepped away as Val turned to Lena. Val tucked a dark, unwashed strand of Lena's hair behind her ear, and Lena almost relished the attention from her, but felt sick to her stomach with the knowledge that it was entirely undeserved.

"I—I'm fine," Lena finally managed. "You should go see."

Val started to object, but hesitated as she stared through the doorway at the throngs of people already making their way back to the markets for another day of trade. Lena knew her mother would go to them—her visitors, her people. It was her responsibility now to decide what to do with the man she had no idea her daughter had killed. Lena sent a silent prayer to Hela that the body would show no signs of the poison she had fed him.

"He and his men have long caused trouble during trading seasons," Val murmured, mostly to herself. "If they try to dispute this, our village has more than enough leverage."

Lena nodded, though Val didn't look at her. That much was a relief, at least—another assurance that she had not killed an innocent man and that the village would not suffer. She watched her mother stride outside, joining Olaf and leaving for the tents. Lena realized Amal was there too, outside his house. The thought of him seeing what she had done to the man made her skin flush, despite the cold pressing into her skin.

Lena dug her nails into her skin, trying to ground

herself. She made herself remember the takeaway from last night—the new implications of her task, and the reminder that something or someone had stolen her sister's soul and placed it in a world far from here. Lena closed her eyes and forced herself to imagine it. Only it was not mere imagination; the certainty that Fressa was alone, in Valhalla, of all the strange worlds and places Lena had sometimes only half-believed . . . it was enough to make her spine rigid. Desperate tears prickled at her eyes. Her mother was gone, off to tend to the unfortunate situation of a dead trader-guest. Lena stared from her vantage point in the doorway until Amal walked back inside, and then she walked from her house, full of purpose. She realized, at last, where she needed to go.

The sun was high again, and the air around Lena felt temperate enough that she could wear her dress without any shawls or pelts. She could almost pretend that the summer hadn't leaked away so suddenly—that maybe she was simply on her way to meet her sister in their favorite spot of the woods, avoiding their chores in favor of picking their own stash of blackberries.

Almost.

But nothing could loosen the grip of the heavy steel wrapped around her heart. Nothing could undo what she had done last night, and as she tread the tainted familiar path to where she had found her sister's body, her fingers twitched, no matter how hard she tried to clench her fists tight. She grasped at her satchel, and focused on the rhythm of her sister's knife hitting her thigh as she walked faster and faster. She needed answers, and would seek the root of it all—the place it began. The worlds were all of Yggdrasil, the World Tree. Everything, all realms, came from the same roots.

Lena exhaled as she turned the final bend, pushing aside a leafy throng of branches. She fixed her gaze ahead, and froze when she realized she was not alone. Bejla stood in Lena's clearing, her blonde hair tucked behind her ears, head ducked as she talked in quiet tones with a young woman Lena dimly recognized as one of the visiting traders.

It was entirely disorienting to see anyone else in this clearing. In her shock, Lena's hand released the branches, and they sprung back into place with a rush of noise. The two figures whirled around, and Lena did not miss the way the tall woman with Bejla reached for her scabbard without a second thought.

Bejla squinted into the trees. Lena hesitated, before stepping forward with an embarrassed smile. This would be only slightly less awkward than trying to retreat.

"Lena?" Bejla asked.

Lena waved, and walked over to them—she tried

to swallow the sting of Bejla's nervous tone and caged expression. Did she not want to see Lena?

"I was just leaving."

Lena glanced up, surprised to hear the other woman speak. She stared down at Lena, even though Lena was fairly tall herself. Her hair fell in sleek, raven-black plaits, and based on Lena's understanding of her village's trading systems, she guessed the woman was from the eastern lands.

Bejla and Lena exchanged a look, until Bejla finally broke into a smile, "Oh! Okay—well, it was nice to speak with you . . ."

". . . Zhao," the woman supplied, with a tight smile.

"Zhao," Bejla finished. "Will I see you at the market before the trading season ends?"

"Perhaps," she said, her tone dry but placid. Lena watched the way Zhao and Bejla looked at each other, unease trickling down her spine. The words, Lena sensed, were staged. But why?

Lena watched Zhao stride out of the clearing and back toward the village. Something about the way she walked seemed too fluid, but she was out of sight before Lena could pin it down. Beside her, Bejla exhaled a breathy laugh.

"I just met her earlier today," Bejla said, though Lena had asked no question. "She came to sell the most beautiful porcelains and silk, you should see her wares—"

"Why are you here?" Lena snapped.

Bejla blinked, because she understood very well what Lena meant. She had to. Everyone in the village knew that this was the spot where Fressa had been found. Lena held Bejla's gaze. A new tension threaded between them; for all their closeness, it was hard to remember it had barely been a year since Bejla had joined their settlement, fleeing a disastrous famine that had ruined her clan.

"I—this was random, Lena, I promise. We went for a walk together and—"

Lena sighed, stepping around Bejla. Her mission would have to be postponed again, she knew, but she couldn't help but start looking for any clues or markings that might have been left from Fressa's absence. Lena certainly hadn't been in the headspace to observe her surroundings when she first found her sister here.

At first glance, nothing seemed amiss. The same circle of trees shot up around them, creating a fan of leaves poised beneath the sky that let only dappled light onto the moss-choked ground. A constellation of memories lived here, and Lena was surprised at how many good ones could coexist alongside the one devastating, final tableaux.

But it was hard to focus while feeling Bejla's eyes on her. Lena tensed. Her instincts told her that Bejla had, indeed, seen Lena enter Jannik's tent last night.

Bejla's gaze felt weighted. Different. She knew something about the night the trader died, Lena guessed, but Lena would not be the one to bring it up. A distant raven's cry tore through the valley, shattering the fragile silence between them.

As if heralded, more footsteps sounded. Lena sagged slightly from relief—here was something to break up the mounting tension between them. She actually smiled when she saw Amal make his way toward them, though his face looked gaunt.

"Lena!" Amal said. Bejla strung a lock of hair around her finger, looking between him and Lena, and she stepped backward as he ran up to Lena.

But something in his voice felt very off, and the flash of joy Lena had first felt at his presence swiftly dissipated. He'd spoken her name a thousand times, but it had never sounded so jagged and mournful, like he was reciting her name off of an execution order.

"What is it?" she whispered. He avoided her gaze relentlessly, his cheeks blotched red and white. Amal ran his fingers through his thick hair, exhaling slowly.

"You—my mother," he stammered. "And your mother. They . . . they said we need to—"

"What, Amal?" Lena begged. A raven's cry ripped across the valley again.

"She's gotten so much sicker." Tears slipped down his cheeks. "It was never supposed to be like this."

"Like what, Amal?" Lena pressed, her fear rapidly morphing with frustration.

"They say we have to marry."

Her chest seized for a moment. "But that was before—"

Amal stopped her with a shake of his head. "No, Lena. Our families say we have to marry each other—and soon."

CHAPTER
ELEVEN

Lena and Amal stood staring at each other for far too long, Amal's words sitting between them like a boundless chasm. She did not cry. She did not scream. She did not laugh. Lena stayed very still, until the cold made her fingers numb from lack of circulation.

Marry each other.

But they did not register, not fully, refusing to pass the threshold of her comprehension. At least, not until Amal whispered, "I am so sorry. I put her off as long as I could."

The words edged and shoved their way into Lena's mind, a syllable at a time, and she still stood frozen. Hazily, she recognized Bejla's taut outline hovering beside them—unsure of what to say or where to go. The painful silence she had just shared with Bejla suddenly seemed far more preferable, far more casual, than the

mere idea that Lena would . . . that Lena and Amal would
. . .

It was as if her mind could not even think of their names together. Not like that. For so many years now, it had been either *Fressa and Amal,* or sometimes, *Fressa, Lena, and Amal*—it had rarely been just *Lena and Amal.* And certainly not in this context.

He raised his hand so slowly that Lena did not realize he was trying to comfort her, and the moment she felt his hand brush her shoulder, she slapped him away. Amal blinked fast, panicked tears spilling over. Now, the words processed and registered, and Lena shoved her way past Amal, breaking into a sprint toward her mother, toward their home.

Not even two months ago, Lena had been helping Fressa make wedding arrangements—or, at least, wedding dreams, since their father was still gone and away. Fressa had asked Lena to weave her a circlet of flowers. They were going to ask their mother to make those sweetbread pastries the clan loved so much.

Lena staggered at the threshold of her home, hearing Amal crash to a stop behind her. She gritted her teeth, bracing herself; she had never been a fighter before, but she would have to be now. *I will not do this, Fressa. They will not replace you.* Frustration surged up along with disbelief—what sort of twisted timing was this? Impatience slammed into her, and she had to catch her breath. Lena should be out solving Hela's bargain, not negotiating her way out of a marriage that everyone besides herself had planned for so long.

She let out a haggard breath, and saw her mother and Nana both sitting in the dim hearth-light, not looking at each other, and not looking at Lena as she burst inside with Amal right behind her.

"Mother?"

Lena had meant for the word to come out fast and damning, urgent and furious enough to startle her. Instead, her voice tumbled out weak and shaking, her accusation diminished into a quiet, desperate plea.

"Sit down, Magdalena," Val murmured. She blinked slowly, as if she knew this would be difficult. As if she knew even a sliver of the anxious rage Lena was drenched in.

Lena heaved two more breaths, staring at her mother. When she said nothing, Lena's stomach lurched, and she sank into the empty chair opposite her mother and Nana. There was no seat left for Amal, who paced the floor so fast that Lena got dizzy watching him. A small fire fought to stay lit in the hearth. Lena clenched her jaw hard to keep the sob of panic from wracking through her. Her face was strained, her fists shut tight.

Val leaned forward, as if to reach out and comfort her daughter, but apparently thought better of it. She sank back into her seat just as fast, a sigh stuttering out of her. Nana's eyes were vacant, staring ahead into nothing in particular. She was such a gentle person; her eyes always crinkled at the edges, and she was quick to offer an embrace or encouraging word. Her mind, even if it wasn't as sharp as it had once been, still sought the good first.

So Lena was a little scared of the anger that simmered inside her chest, directed at Nana. Why was she doing this to Amal? To Lena? Why?

"Why?" Lena finally managed to ask aloud.

"I'm sure you feel upset, Lena," her mother tried. "But we discussed this earlier—this is no surprise. Try to remember that these things are rarely ever intertwined with actual love." Val's voice quieted as she reached the end of her sentence. Perhaps, Lena thought, she was thinking about her own marriage with Fredrik. Before any pity could worm its way into her, her mother continued with a shake of her head.

"This is just keeping order. This is moving forward. You more than anyone should understand how property laws work in this clan, do you not?"

Lena set her jaw. The implication beneath her mother's words wore Lena thin. It was something she had heard, however unspoken, her whole life, but was now amplified with Fressa gone. *You should understand, Lena. You are daughter of the chief. Are you not?*

You more than anyone.

But Lena knew what her mother meant. It was a fundamental law that protected the properties and belongings of the clan, that left no room for trivial disputes. Eldest children inherited property—eldest children *married* to ensure that the line of succession was rigid and unchangeable.

Lena realized two facts at the same time. Firstly, if Nana was suddenly so concerned about her property's succession to Amal, her health must be worse than Lena thought. Secondly, the true implication of *marriage* in the clan's laws was really *children*.

It was simply a contract to ensure that a family's lineage would extend and live on, with future generations ready to inherit property and bolster their name.

Oh, Freya, save me.

"You cannot be serious," Lena whispered. "After Fres—"

"It was supposed to be you." Her mother spat the words. Through her peripheral vision, Lena could see Amal wince. "All along. You are the eldest. That is how these things go—you cannot seriously believe that *emotion* goes into these things. If that were the case, our whole clan would have fallen apart years ago."

Lena tilted her head. Was her mother so dissatisfied by her father? Lena stared back at Amal, whose gaze dragged across the sodden floorboards.

"But even after everything that's happened? You still

would ask this of me?" Lena kept her gaze on Amal, even though it was his mother's haggard voice that answered.

"Before you could even utter a word," Nana said. She coughed, once. "When Amal was first brought back here by your father, we knew—due to your similar ages, my standing as the apothecary in this settlement and my lack of an heir for my property, and above all, the fact that you are the eldest daughter of the ruling clan's leader—this would be the most advantageous match for you both. Your parents and I agreed to it. We even swore an oath to Freya."

Lena made herself look at Nana—her teacher, her second mother. And yet Lena could not keep her fists from clenching as Nana continued to speak. She remembered the vague, almost dismissive acceptance she had given Amal the one time he'd been brave enough to ask his mother about wedding Fressa. He, Lena, and Fressa had really believed that she would support them if and when their relationship was called into question. Had it always been a misunderstanding? Had Nana merely forgotten, or was she intentionally backtracking to appease Lena's parents?

Lena's heart raced, but only one image forced itself into her mind—her sister's shocked face as Lena hesitated, just for an instant, to consider the idea of chiefdom through marrying Amal. After Fressa—Lena had not dared to consider they would bring this up again ever, and not so soon. She choked on her rage, her limbs trembling.

"*You* said he could marry Fressa—"

"Lena!" Her mother's voice leapt like dried leaves on a fire. "We are not discussing that again. Nana was just confused."

"When your younger sister came along," Nana continued, as if she had not heard, with a ghost of a smile flickering across her lips. "We never considered an alternative, not even when Amal took an interest in her. It hardly mattered if he favored Fressa. It's unheard of, you know. For sisters to marry out of succession."

Lena hated the small stab of insecurity that punched through her. She swallowed roughly, staring down at her white-knuckled hands. Her throat ached as slivers of uncertainty and loneliness raked through her. She kept her gaze locked on her hands, afraid to breathe or speak or move without breaking. *It is no matter,* she told herself. Lena had never once loved Amal as anything but a brother or friend. She felt no anger or envy that he'd fallen for her sister, and not her.

But remembering what the initial intention had been for Lena and Amal, and knowing how hard Amal had recoiled and raged against it, all without Lena ever knowing . . . it hurt. Deep, penetrating, and almost tender in its unexpectedness. She had never wanted Amal. She certainly did not want him now. But she had never truly seen herself as the anomaly she was—old to be unmarried, especially with the prospect of assuming control of the village so close.

"I had not realized," Lena whispered, heat rising in her—equal parts shame and fury. "That I was such an oddity."

Her mother sighed. "No, Lena—"

"I'm sorry."

It was Amal who cut her off. He was in front of her, suddenly, his eyes dark and afraid and drenched in guilt. Lena wrenched her gaze back to the floor, too scared and angry to look at him. She wanted to seep into the ground. She wanted to tear through the door and run far from here.

She wanted many things, but she needed her sister, and for that, she needed time.

"My father," she managed. "Would he not need to be here? Do you expect them to respect a marriage without my father present?"

Her mother rose from her chair, stalked over to her. She tilted Lena's chin up with one finger. Val's eyes were dark hazel, like Lena's, but bright with offense. But when she spoke, her voice was threaded with a timidity that made Lena hesitate. "Since when have you respected your father's presence in matters like this?" The implication was clear—Lena was directly challenging her mother's individual right to the village and its authority.

Lena held Val's gaze, and watched as her eyes narrowed. "You do not get to pick and choose when to follow these formalities."

Val only held onto Lena with one finger, but Lena felt trapped enough by the confusion in her mother's eyes. She looked old, all of a sudden. Her cheeks dragged just slightly downward and the lines beside her lips and eyes seemed carved into her skin, more pronounced and permanent than Lena had ever seen.

"But if it is truly so *important* to you," Val muttered, finally, "we can wait for your father to arrive before the wedding ceremony occurs." Instantaneous relief slammed into Lena, and she sagged backward. "But make no mistake, Magdalena. Preparations will still commence in the meantime. You and Amal are betrothed."

Lena gripped the sides of her chair hard. "But I cannot see why preparations must begin so soon. I need time—" She cut herself off. If they asked questions of her, they would not like her answers. Once she had Fressa, they would understand.

Another glance between her mother and Nana was exchanged. Or, rather, Val looked at Amal's mother. Lena imagined Nana withering slowly under her gaze, a long-faded rose shrinking into itself before disintegrating. She blinked as her mother continued speaking.

"If I do not uphold what rules we have left," Val said, turning her gaze back to Lena. "I will not keep this settlement in line. I have to manage the repercussions of that trader's death, and figure out how the barley will manage in this interrupted summer. It is hard without your father. I am not looked at the same—you know."

Lena did. The villagers looked at her mother with pity, and pity did not inspire reverence. But still, she'd hoped her mother would not expect *this* of her, to wed her sister's fiancé in the same year she died.

At least she had postponed anything from happening until her father returned, giving her time to finish Hela's task. She had done *something* to save herself. Pride swelled from her core, victory and shame blooming intertwined within her. She rose to her feet, making eye contact with no one.

"Lena—" her mother called.

But she was already outside. Lena stared at the too-dark sky, trying to remember what the stories said about unexpected winters. Would this be a winter?

"Is the sky so enchanting?"

Lena jumped at Amal's voice; he must have followed her outside. It wasn't even that he had startled her, it was that she feared his voice would never be just the voice of her friend or brother again. She did not want to look at him, or listen to him, or—

She breathed once, steadying herself. This was not his fault. Lena turned around to face him. In silent agreement, they walked away from their homes. Lena kept her gaze focused straight ahead, and her skin burned with shame and grief and anger.

"That was a good move," Amal said, after minutes of silence. They still walked, though Lena had a feeling neither of them knew where or cared, so long as it was away. "About your father."

Of course he knew it was a ploy. Amal always knew, and Amal especially knew how she and her sister had long felt about their father's strange obsessions with faraway isles and near-permanent absence.

"Yes, well. Hopefully it will hold." Lena's voice was brittle, breakable, and hollow. It hurt to even breathe, and she crossed her arms tight across her chest. "I had not realized Nana was so . . ."

Amal faltered. They stood at the fringe of the settlement, rows of barley stretching before them. "I suppose I never realized I knew until she admitted it herself. That takes a lot for her."

Lena had to smile at that. Her teacher was many things—stubborn, gentle, sharp—but certainly never one to admit a weakness or fault of her own. But the darkness settled again, and quickly. She felt bruised by Nana's decision to force her son into marriage with his rightful fiancée's sister—even when she'd claimed, before her father's return, that she was okay with him marrying Fressa. Everything felt tainted with betrayal by the fact that this had been the initial arrangement all along.

And Amal had known it too. Even if he only overheard it—he had never asked for clarification, he had never once tried to speak out.

She finally bolstered herself to look up at him. He was only an inch or two taller than her, but he felt impossibly far away.

Make no mistake, Magdalena. Her mother's voice pierced through her. *You and Amal are betrothed.*

Lena wrenched her gaze away again. Had everyone she'd ever known been keeping secrets from her? Her whole life? Even Fressa, maybe, if what Hela had said was true. *Your sister is useful.*

"Amal," Lena started, her voice rushing to catch up with her realization. She grabbed Fressa's blade. "You remember the runes on this, yes?"

"I thought that was established knowledge," he muttered. "What does that have to do with any of—of *this*?"

"Don't you wonder why there were runes on it when she, when she—"

"When she held it," he finished, his gaze growing guarded. "And no one else."

Lena nodded, and moistened her lips. "Remind me again what they read?"

Amal paused, his boots shuffling through the layers of dirt beneath them. He exhaled, and when Lena looked up to him, she could see him squint his eyes, scouring his memory. She was half-surprised he hadn't teared up at the mention of her sister, like he usually did.

"That knife scared her," Amal murmured. His voice softened into the gentle tone reserved for speaking of Fressa—like liquid gold spilling from his lips. "It still—I don't know."

Lena nodded, urging him on. Her chest thrilled at the reminder that Fressa's capability with this blade marked her as different—she was either blessed or cursed by their gods, and she had not lived long enough to find out which one it would be.

"Amal?"

He sighed again, his shoulders shrugging slightly. "Was it not something like . . . master of the wolf, maybe? Or it could be translated as *beast*. I might have missed some markings, or misread . . . she only showed me that one time . . ."

"I know," Lena said. "I know."

"Why?"

Lena studied him. She wondered what he might say to her, if she told him the truth. If she told him exactly what had happened after he'd summoned Hela for her— he'd wanted a goodbye, or maybe an explanation. Did Amal love Fressa enough to understand why Lena had ventured so far into Helheim? Would he understand how Lena felt? What she'd already done?

He couldn't.

"I just—" She paused as the cry of ravens ripped across the valley again. Amal did not seem to notice. "There are many things about her that I want to know, now that she's . . . not here."

She had to catch herself before she said *gone*, because that was not the truth. Amal nodded. He reached out, maybe to touch her shoulder, but stopped himself short. He knew as well as she did that things between them were never going to be the same. Their once-easy friendship would now be another death to mourn. But she had put off marriage as long as possible—long enough, at least, for her to make things right.

Amal deserved to marry Fressa. Lena had to fight for him—for both of them.

"I understand what you mean," Amal said. Lena offered a tight smile. He probably did understand a little of what she meant, in his own way. He glanced behind him, at the fires in the village glittering to life. The sky was the darkest gray now, close to total blackness. Not even the stars poked through the constant veil of clouds that never seemed to move. "But that isn't why you asked, is it?"

She raised her eyebrows, begging her eyes to betray nothing. Maybe he knew her better than she gave him credit for. "What is that supposed to mean?"

He leaned close enough that she could feel his misted breath. "What happened that night, Lena? At the river? Because now you're asking more questions about runes, about Fressa—" His voice caught, and he stared upward, taking a steadying breath. Lena's heart raced.

"Amal, believe me." She made herself meet his gaze, even though he was standing far too close for comfort. "We all have questions about what happened, is all, and I just . . . want to know my sister."

"Know her?" Amal barked a laugh, but it didn't sound happy at all. "Even I never came close to knowing her like you did."

Like I do, she corrected silently.

He stared at her hip, until she realized Fressa's knife was still visible. Of course it was—Lena had kept it strapped to her since the day Fressa left, even though she was wretched with blades in comparison to her sister. She shifted her skirts so they covered the weapon.

Finally, he looked away. "I should go back. I'll need to prepare supper. But Lena—you know, you can tell me . . . whatever it is. All right?"

She nodded once, wanting him gone, suddenly. He stared at her—his face tight with questions he clearly wanted to ask—but he stayed silent, and trotted back to his home. Lena watched him turn into a silhouette.

Already, she turned over his translation in her mind: *master of the wolf?*

The wolf? As far as Lena knew, Fressa had no special affinity or remote interest in wolves. Amal's translation must have been off. Or maybe the runes meant nothing at all. She shook off the numbness seeping from her limbs to her core, and tried to focus in on the village. It was getting dark—she should return to the warmth.

But the early arrival of the too-dark darkness kept her where she stood.

Lena realized that just as she had always expected the summer to stay, she had always expected her sister to be at her side. Because for her whole life, the summer meant sunlight—always—with no unexpected night cutting through it. Her sister had fallen asleep each night across from her, and Lena assumed she would wake with her each morning.

Now, neither was true, and she saw how blinded with assumptions all the humans of Midgard were beneath it all. Despite whatever dangers they knew lurked, humans took for granted that life would continue as it always had—that the world would cycle through its seasons. That they could build their lives around their husbands or wives or sisters or brothers or chiefs and that when they woke each morning, everything would be just as they had left it.

Lena had been oblivious while Fressa was—what? Killed? Taken?

Lena could not ignore Amal's translation, or the fact that darkness had not merely arrived, but persisted. She could feign disbelief, and choose to assume the events were unconnected.

But the nine worlds, separate and distinct as they are, all branch from Yggdrasil. Actions in Midgard, or Helheim, or Asgard all strung together and knotted from one single root. Lena knew now that what had begun as a selfish, contained act was spilled across the worlds. Or maybe it had always been that way, and Lena had merely walked in on this cosmic disarray.

Either way, Lena was willing to admit to herself that Fressa's fate was wrapped and interwoven with more than Lena could ever guess. Maybe Fressa was a bystander, or some pawn, or the key to solving this sudden darkness. She realized she was only staring at an iceberg's tip—an inconceivable mass of solid ice plunged into the black depths below, and she saw none of it from where she stood.

She *knew* this.

And though she stood at the silent outskirts of the village for nearly an hour, weighing the strange facts that she knew against the murkiness of all this mounting and unattainable knowledge, Lena still could not bring herself to feel afraid. Her focus had to be honed on her sister—the iceberg's visible point—or she would never succeed in her task.

Beneath it all, the rest of the iceberg loomed below the surface, solid and impenetrable. And if Lena stared at it for too long, it would freeze her.

CHAPTER
TWELVE

The next morning felt as strained and tense as those seconds before an arrow was released, or an axe hurled toward its target. Unspoken words stacked high into the air between Lena and her mother as they both rose with the sun. Lena had to commend her mother for her valiant efforts at pretending her daughter was not also in the only room they shared. Weak light fought its way through the slits of dark wood built around them, and did nothing to chase away a growing cold that no one could deny had begun to make its permanent home in their valley.

The fire in their hearth kept burning all day and night now, filling the air with so much smoke that Lena's first breath outside was almost pleasantly crisp. She shivered against the air—had it grown so cold in only one night? Her mother had tried to explain away the growing darkness, assuring the villagers that it was merely a storm or a miscalculation on their part. But the traders had almost all left, cutting their usual stay nearly in half, out of fear that the cold would grow too dangerous to travel in.

No one had brought up Jannik to Lena. She knew they assumed she was too fragile, with two inexplicably dead bodies in the span of weeks. Whatever the case, Jannik's companions left without any obvious contempt that Lena could detect—it was not too surprising, Lena supposed. If he had been a good man, someone worth missing or whose death warranted further investigation, then her sister would be standing beside Lena right now.

But she stood alone, staring across the swathe of lanes weaving through the village that seemed disturbingly quiet and empty with the traders gone. But the strain of the weather and the forced marriage discussed last night had placed a crushing weight upon Lena's house, and it was a relief to be out of her mother's gaze—even if she was only trading one disappointed woman for another. She walked over to Nana's, because her training was to be completed as usual, now that the market season had swiftly arrived and left. Or maybe Lena wanted desperately to keep at least one thing in her life normal while she considered her next move.

Her boots crunched into frosted grass—the ice must have settled overnight. Lena gritted her teeth against another tide of worry that she suspected the rest of the village dealt with as well—*this is not normal.*

"Lena," Nana called from inside the apothecary hut. The grass crunching beneath her must have announced her arrival. Lena tried very hard to keep her face blank as she ducked inside, suppressing as much of her frustration at Nana as she could. She was here to learn how to heal, which she had always wanted to do. And now, it was something Lena figured she needed to do more than ever. She did not feel guilty for what she had done so far—but Hela's quest and its qualifications had grown darker, and Lena could not deny the mounting panic at what was yet to come.

She exhaled through her nose and gave a quick look around the small room, relieved to find Amal not present. He sat in on some sessions, since he was moderately interested in his mother's work. Lena realized he hadn't really done that since Fressa went away. Amal spent most of his time overseeing the market by the river and affirming the trading relationships between them and their neighboring clans. He could count money faster than anyone in the village, and maintained a fair and balanced judgment in trading disputes that earned him respect both at home and abroad.

She wondered what the traders made of this darkness, and how far it had spread. How badly would it affect their trade? Their village relied on the work of their blacksmiths and textile workers, yes, but above all, they were an agricultural settlement. It was the barley, wheat, and fish that sustained them.

Lena swallowed back another wave of anxiety, and blinked until she focused back on Nana, who stood hunched over the fire, leaning too much on a stick that Lena had only seen her use a few times before. She squinted up at Lena through the smoke, and Lena made herself take a few steps closer.

"I did not know if I would see you here today," Nana managed, each word careful and deliberate in inflection.

"Neither did I."

The words hung suspended between them. Only the veil of smoke separated Lena from her would-be mother-in-law, and she wondered if she should have bothered to show up.

"But I am here," Lena said, her voice leaping from her throat without the grit and steadiness she wanted it to have. "So let's get to work."

Nana stared up and blinked at Lena as if she were dumb. Lena splayed her hands, considering if she should ask if Nana needed help standing up. But she stood up all by herself, just a little shaky, and that was what made Lena say it.

"Why now?"

Nana sighed, shuffling over to her table of dried, dead flowers. When she did not respond, Lena walked behind her and raised her voice. She would make herself heard.

"Nana. Why now? Are you even sick—really?" Lena hadn't meant to make her voice quite so loud, but she could find nothing within her to feel sorry for it. She stood right behind Nana, and she still said nothing. "What is it then? You want your son to marry the chief's daughter for some kind of power?"

Nana spun around with more speed than Lena had anticipated. She grabbed Lena's wrist tight, and stared straight at her. Nana's eyes were cloudy, but they still burned. Lena braced herself for the words that would come. She watched Nana's mouth fly open, and—

She coughed.

Hard.

Lena froze as small droplets splattered across her face. Blood. Nana doubled over, her coughs achieving a terrifying crescendo until she fell to her already-frail knees. Lena still stood with her arm outstretched, where Nana had latched onto her only seconds ago. Panic rose up, and Lena swiveled around the room full of tables of herbs and flowers and spices, with branches and barks hanging from every wall, all supposed to heal. It wasn't that Lena could not recall the function of the plants, but that she knew none of them could erase the pain in Nana's joints, or stop the heaving breaths that crashed through Lena's ears as Nana tried desperately to catch her breath from the ground.

"Amal," Lena murmured as way of explanation, motioning to Nana as best she could. Lena sprinted out of the smoky room and into a shock of icy cold. Her boots kicked up dirt and frost as she ran over to Amal and Nana's house, stabbing drops of freezing water working their way in through the weathered soles.

Her fists flew upon the oak door.

"Amal!" She screamed his name again and again, until the door disappeared from beneath her fingertips, opening to reveal Amal already pulling on his boots and pushing past Lena for his mother. They had needed no other words for him to know.

He and Nana lived right next to the apothecary hut, but the distance stretched and writhed. Lena was tall, but Amal was taller and stronger—he shot out like a perfectly primed arrow, already inside the room as Lena ran as hard as she could behind him. Her legs felt leaden. Lena's chest felt cracked and frozen, like a pick slammed into a winter lake's surface.

What if she were dead? Would Lena have to watch her die?

She was relieved that those were her first thoughts, because the ones that followed were not as nice. For if Nana died that day, Amal's future within the settlement would become incredibly uncertain. If he was unmarried,

Lena's family would have to make the decision between bending their strict property rules for him, or punishing the man who would have—should have—been Fressa's husband.

And if Nana lived, was this how desperate her health had become? Then perhaps Lena could understand the urgent panic for Amal's marriage. Understanding, however, was still a far cry from acceptance.

Lena skidded to a stop at the threshold, her heart seizing. Amal had already lifted up his mother and brought her to a chair, where she had a swathe of fabric pressed against her mouth. Lena sagged against the wall, pushed down by relief and fear pressing in on either side.

When had this happened? Any of this? Had Lena been so focused on her sister that Nana had slipped so far without her noticing?

Lena ran her hands through her hair, which was becoming thinner than she cared to admit. Amal glanced up at her, his brown eyes cutting through the space between them, diminishing her.

They asked, simply, *What happened?*

"We were just"—Lena flicked her gaze downward, focusing on the glowing embers of the fire—"in training. I don't know."

She heard Amal's sigh fall through the room, and the subtle cracking of his knees as he rose to stand. He walked over to where she leaned against the wall, and grabbed Lena's arm.

"Has this happened before?"

Lena shook her head. He reached his hand beneath her chin, forcing her gaze up. She winced as he traced his thumb across her cheek, until she realized he was only wiping the blood away—his mother's blood was still sprayed all across her face. Still, she pushed his arm down, and stared behind him.

"Nana—" she tried to say, regret threaded through her voice. Amal cut her off with a pointed stare.

"We will speak later, Lena," he whispered. "Let me handle this."

She held his gaze, trying to decipher the guarded darkness in Amal's eyes. He used to be easy enough to read, or at least Fressa had managed to detect how Amal felt or what he wanted. Now, Lena was unsure if she should feel insulted or reprieved or both. His face betrayed no anger or worry. It was like when she looked at rune markings—she knew they meant something, and she could make out the individual signs, but the fact that they held a meaning, which she had no way of comprehending, left her paralyzed with frustration.

Lena held up her hands, muttering as polite of a farewell as she could muster, and walked alone outside.

The few hours of daylight left grew and shrank away too fast to hold on to. Lena sat outside her home, staring into the waning light, wishing the sun would bounce and hover across the horizon like it should in summer. She made a passable effort at mending the soles of her boots, pushing her needle into the fading leather whenever anyone walked by so she appeared occupied.

It worked until her mother came back from another meeting about the weather with the clansmen.

Val stepped in front of Lena, blocking the already-dim light. Lena stared up with reluctance, holding her boots closer to her chest. As predicted, her mother wore a look of displeasure, the hard line of her mouth sloping downward on one end. Lena could not conjure up an image of her mother smiling at her. Not since Fressa.

"How thoughtful of you to work on a task that only helps yourself." Her mother's voice snapped through the distance between them like a whip.

Lena pulled her knees closer to her, letting her gaze fall. Her cheeks burned with the cold and the hurt. She fought hard to suppress the rising sob in her chest. If Fressa were here, none—

She shut her eyes tight, and heard her mother kneel to the ground so she was eye-level with Lena.

"I told you weeks ago that the home needs serious work, Lena," Val whispered. Her voice was soft, but in the way that a snowfall was—stinging cold, and more dangerous with every second it lasted. Lena could not recall her mother asking such a thing, but she could not recall much of the past weeks besides her two trips to Helheim.

If only Midgard could just stop for a week or two more, Lena could fix this. Fix her sister, which might fix this premature winter—she just needed the time.

"Well?" Val asked.

"What—what in the house am I supposed to do?" Lena asked.

"The notion that you even have to ask is astounding," Val said, with a disgusted shake of her head. Lena winced. The meeting must have gone poorly. She had never seen the lines bunched around her mother's lips and eyes so deeply engraved. "You can start with replacing the rotted panels and fixing the roof leaks. We'll need all the protection we can get, with the climate as it is. Then, you can move on to your sister's things."

Lena's head jerked up. "What?"

Her mother's face softened a fraction, the lines receding enough to make way for earnest guilt. Lena rose to her feet, her mother following suit.

"What do you mean?" Lena whispered.

Val opened then closed her mouth, her eyes watering. Lena shook her head, her throat aching with the effort to keep down her cries. They escaped anyway, and Lena shrank against the outside wall of the house, the wood damp and cold with melted snow.

"Please—"

"Magdalena," her mother said, tracing a tired hand through her grease-dulled hair. Whenever her mother said her full name, it was usually in a serious, scolding manner. Now, it rang out with all of the finality but none of the sting. It was a resignation. "We have put it off too long already. You know this."

"No!" Lena shouted. "No. We just need to wait—"

"Wait?" Her mother frowned at Lena. "What for, Lena? What is left?"

"But—"

Val did not interrupt her, but Lena had no way of finishing her sentence. Her mother would kill her if she explained how she'd convinced Amal to deal with the runes, how she had faced the goddess of death more than once, how she had poisoned that trader.

The memories felt foreign and detached in her mind, like they were not quite hers. And so the words left her mouth in a shaking sigh and not with a voice. Her mother sighed too, moving past Lena as she whispered, so quietly that Lena was unsure if she had heard her, "Tomorrow, then."

Lena blinked fast, her breaths coming hard. It felt like those first days after Fressa all over again—the crushing weight of her absence, acknowledged and discussed so openly by everyone around Lena. She'd tried then to complete the thought, to accept it: *your sister is dead.* Each time she tried, it felt like placing her hand on that iceberg's tip—a shock of icy, insurmountable pain, and still she could not, did not, comprehend the dark depths to which the rest of the iceberg plunged beneath the surface. She had never let herself accept it. She was not sure she could, even if she'd wanted to.

Hearing her mother speak of Fressa and ridding themselves of her belongings felt just as looming and unfathomable. Lena squared her shoulders, letting the cold settle into her bones. She would have to act fast now—faster than before.

The daylight was gone, but the village forged onward still. There was some rebellion against the darkness, after all. Lena rushed through the repairs her mother needed her to do, but stayed clear of her sister's belongings. The silence of the empty home suffocated her; she could not recall the last time a smile or laugh had occurred within these walls.

Lena's lips trembled, and she set down her hammer on the table. She clapped both her hands across her mouth, quiet tears cutting down her face. Lena had been the first to make Fressa laugh, as a baby. She'd been barely two years old, and doing nothing special. But Val loved to tell the tale—how Fressa, not even strong enough to hold up her head by herself—suddenly dissolved into laughter as she stared at her sister.

"Probably because I saw her for the ridiculous girl she is," Fressa had retorted with a grin, much later, when their mother recounted it.

Val had shaken her head, smiling. "No. You always smiled when you saw her."

Lena let her hands fall, and felt her tears drip down her clothes.

Lena's mother reappeared some hours later, wrapping her ash-blonde hair into a tight braid. At least, Lena guessed it had been a few hours—without the sun, and with her mind still panicked and racing for the solution to save her sister, the passage of time never seemed as linear or predictable as it'd once been.

"Lena?" she asked, her hands still behind her head, weaving together her hair. "You are ready, yes?"

"For . . .?" Lena blinked slow, leaning the broom she held against the wall.

Val sighed, quick and frustrated. "It's Odinsday.'"

"You want me to go with you?"

The village held weekly meetings on the evenings of Odinsdays, but it was typically a time for the married adults to go over any harvest or trading logistics. Since

Jannik's death, they certainly had a lot to review, in order to ensure they were not viewed as responsible for the trader's demise—which everyone seemed to agree had been a random, seizing attack of the heart. Lena's core ached and dropped like a bottomless pit.

"Yes," Val said slowly. "I told you yesterday."

Lena hesitated, biting back a rebuttal. Her mother rarely misspoke or forgot her words—they were her weapon of choice, and the only reason why she could maintain her control over the village without her husband around. Lena must have forgotten. She was losing focus, losing comprehension—and she could not afford to do so. Especially not now, not with the gods watching her.

"Oh," Lena murmured, rushing to the comb at her bedside table. She dragged it through her hair, her stomach doing a small flip at all the strands it pulled away from her scalp. "Ready."

Her mother gave her a dismayed once-over, but beckoned to the doorway, and they both walked into the night. They walked in silence toward the central hearth, the pressing cold too heavy to talk through. Lena cast a sideways glance at her mother—she had a strong jawline, something more present in Fressa than Lena. But her gaze looked vacant, her pace slower than it usually was.

Lena bit her lip, looking away. A faint misting of rain began to fall. She squinted into the dark, using her mother's movements in her periphery and the glowing fire of the hearth ahead as her guides. There were more attendees than she expected, even some she did not recognize. One look at her mother, and she knew that this was unusual.

Val's pace quickened, frost flying up behind her ankles. Lena jogged to keep pace. She caught Amal's familiar silhouette cutting against the tall flames of the bonfire. He was here too? Her first instinct was comfort—to have someone her age, someone she knew and trusted in an environment she knew little of. But the implications were obvious, and clear, even if Lena's mother thought she was being discrete.

Lena's chest tightened, and she had to look away from her mother. The bloom of anger that she was well acquainted with opened inside of her. It scared her, but it was the only thing that kept her from an abyss.

She glanced back at Amal now. He was already looking at her, his eyes weighted with a heavy sort of sorrow. The sort that was resigned, accepted. She shook her head slightly at him; she was not sure of what was about to happen, but he needed to be ready to fight for them—for Fressa—if there was a confrontation. The firelight dancing across them made his dark gaze look too light, too ethereal. She shivered, and stared at her boots instead.

Make no mistake. You are betrothed.

She kicked at the frost hard, until she could finally

see the earth beneath it. It was dark and almost frozen solid, but it was there beneath the frost—it was still there. Her mother cleared her throat subtly enough that Lena knew it was for her alone, and not the gathered men. A handful of wives were in attendance too, which pleased Lena to see—it was a more familiar sight, at least, with most of the men gone so often with her father.

"Welcome," Val said. Lena frowned slightly—this was her mother's *Freding voice*, reserved only for occasions such as this. It rang out like a falcon's cry but dropped like a stone; she sounded piercing and final at once. Lena and Fressa had always exchanged suppressed smiles. It was difficult to take their mother so seriously, when they never heard this voice within their own walls. "Please, be seated."

They sat upon the wooden logs that encircled the bonfire. Lena's mother stood tall and unflinching, but kept her face relaxed enough to make everyone at ease in her presence. Everyone but Lena, maybe. Her stomach dropped further and further, cold dread stopping up the blood in her veins.

"Magdalena came with me this evening."

Lena felt her shoulders roll back instinctively, and her chin rise. She was to be *Magdalena* tonight, apparently. A good chief's daughter would have certainly met the gaze of her people directly, appreciating and addressing as many as possible. But her eyes latched onto the flame in their midst, the only light aside from the roaring stars above. She fought the urge to walk closer, and wondered how close she could get to the fire before it hurt. Lena was cold enough that she was willing to burn, if it meant she could just feel warm, even if only for an instant.

"I know several of you have concerns," Val said, forging onward. A smattering of mumbled voices rang through the gathered crowd, but no one came forward. "But before I hear your issues, regarding the *weather* or otherwise, I would like to announce that in my husband's absence, things are still moving ahead."

Lena stared hard at her mother as she droned on for a few minutes about some alternate sea routes that could be taken if the mountain passes got snow, and went over the remaining stock of lumber and grain, and how it would be rationed should the weather not relent. She did not give voice to the suggestion that Lena imagined most of the village was thinking—they could leave. They could try to stake out and find a new home, like Bejla had done last autumn. But Bejla was one girl, and Lena knew the logistics of relocating over seventy people together would be overwhelming—destined to spiral into conflict and chaos. They were fragmented enough already, a web of icy cracks that spread further as the darkness around them fell deeper.

It will never relent, Lena realized miserably. *Not unless I can fix this.*

She felt dizzy, suddenly, for a reason bigger than her betrothal to Amal. She surveyed all the people gathered before her, all their tired and wane faces, feeling the weight of the children left behind in their homes, shivering through another impossible night. Her throat grew thick with rising panic. These were *her* people, and she had failed them already by not meeting Hela's bargain. She sat down hard onto a log a few feet back, ignoring the pointed glare her mother tossed her way.

"Finally," Val said, clasping her hands together and offering up a generous half-smile. She turned to Lena with that smile, but as her gaze switched from her audience to her daughter, her mother's eyes cut a quick and vicious blow. *Get up, now.* Lena rose to her feet fast, biting her tongue in the process. "As some of you may know, Magdalena's future has been on my and her father's minds for some time. Her marriage, of course, must be one fortified with strength and strategy, which will poise our clan for boundless success in our days to come, when Fredrik and I can no longer lead."

Did Lena imagine the doubtful glances exchanged between the clansmen? She crossed her hands behind her back, keeping her back straight as a rod. At the edge of her vision, she saw Amal sit forward. She realized Nana was not with him.

"We came to the decision years ago that Magdalena is well suited for Amal, son of Nana."

Lena switched her gaze quickly to her feet and tried to focus on the faint crackle of the fire finally burning through the damp wood, the sizzle of sparks lifting into the darkness. No one spoke. Why would they? If the match had been so obvious to Estrid, Lena feared what else her selective blindness hid from her. She shut her eyes tight. She could not afford to cry here—not now, not in front of everybody. Lena should have acted faster, should have been decisive and unrelenting and unforgiving. How had one simple exchange become an entire knot to untangle?

"Amal was not born here," one man muttered. Lena blinked hard, her mind clearing just enough to feel her surprise morph into anger. The man spoke in an ugly tone, loud enough with the intention to be heard, but quiet enough to make it appear like an honest, instinctive reaction. "Should not our chief's daughter be wed to one of our own?"

Without hesitation, Lena opened her mouth to argue—something usually only Fressa had ever been bold enough to do in public. But, in an act that almost redeemed Val to Lena, her mother spoke first.

"Henderson," she snapped. "You know well enough that clans are not of blood, but of chosen and championed bonds. Many of us come from lands far from this valley, found from trade or family or travel. The sole thread weaving us is the choice we made, and continue to make each day, to each other. If you feel otherwise, we will certainly be glad to discontinue your rations."

Henderson glowed red, even through the dark. Lena felt a sliver of affection for her mother arc through her, and caught Amal's gaze.

Val continued, her voice growing frost. "*I* decide whom my daughter marries. I decide what is best for us. You will respect it."

No other retorts followed.

I decide whom my daughter marries.

Lena dropped Amal's gaze, and the ice returned to cover up the fondness completely.

"The fact is that Amal and his mother have maintained crucial trade and diplomatic relations with several key allies," Val said, trying to meet as many of her clansmen in the eye as she could. "Amal understands, more than most men in this clan, how to maintain a level head and how to keep our trading routes flourishing. He understands the economics required to keep us on top, and he does so with ease and confidence. It is certainly an asset that he is also versatile in healing arts, weaponry, and casting runes. And through it all, he is easy to like."

Val smiled at Amal then, the sort of smile she reserved for only her children, and Lena remembered that her mother had always loved Amal. Truly, and like a son.

She had always wanted him for her daughters. Lena's heart ached.

"And that makes him nearly impossible to beat."

It was a convincing speech, and if Lena hadn't been so intimately involved in the fallout, she would have been wholly persuaded. Her mother was right—Amal was easy to admire, which made him a formidable enemy and a treasured ally. He would be excellent for the chief's daughter. But not *her*. Not *this* daughter. Could her mother not see that Amal was her brother? He was going to be, he was supposed to be—

Lena heaved a haggard breath, and some of the audience stared uncomfortably at her. She wanted to seep into the earth. Lena used to relish their focus and attention. She liked to be looked to for guidance, but she had never dealt with the brunt of their expectations alone. The emptiness at Lena's side where Fressa always stood roared louder than ever. The continued absence of her father pulsed through the air; Lena saw doubt and fatigue written across her people's faces. Her family's hold on this village weakened with every day he stayed away, with every second the sun stayed out of the sky in the middle of summer.

Who did they want Lena to be? Who was she capable of being for them? She had thought she would someday step up to be the formidable force required to keep a village of people thriving in an unforgiving valley of

Scandinavia—she believed it was her destiny, the reason underlying everything she pursued. But now the weight of their eyes whittled her away. Lena found she did not want to play a part, or indulge strangers with scripted words or forced strength. She wanted to curl into herself, to tear across the valley and into the river, and carve a path through Yggdrasil until she could claw her way into Valhalla herself and find her sister.

She just wanted her sister.

"I think he makes a fine choice." Lena followed the voice until she saw Olaf, grinning just at her. Her heart twisted—his face was so open and earnest, and she could tell that he was trying to be a comfort. Gunnar stood at his shoulder, smiling too, but Bejla must have stayed behind. But they couldn't know or understand why Amal and Lena would be disastrous together. Olaf's brow wrinkled the longer Lena stared at him, and she could not muster even a dismissive smile. *Help me,* she wanted to cry. *Please.*

"If I may," Henderson said. Val's back straightened, and she did a very poor job at concealing her irritation. His voice was no longer accusatory, but even Lena felt like she was suddenly on the defensive. "The boy's mother is not here. Neither is your daughter's father."

"My mother is not well today," Amal said. He stood, and Lena realized these were the first words he had spoken at the whole meeting. "Her health has suffered over the past few weeks, but I am sure you will join me in prayers for her swift recovery." Lena cut her gaze away. Nobody *recovered* from age, though she could not blame Amal for hoping otherwise. "As for the matter of Le—of Magdalena's father, Chief Fredrik—"

Lena cleared her throat. They shared a brief glance, packed full of their last hope.

"I want him present for the ceremony, of course," Lena said. Her voice was too soft and delicate, like the flimsy outer petals of a rose. "I want him here."

Murmurs of assent rippled through the crowd, thankfully. Maybe the gods had some pity for her, or perhaps they saw her as the lonely, sisterless daughter of a missing chief. Val stepped forward, taking away the attention from Lena, blissfully.

"My husband will return shortly, we are sure," she said. It might have been Lena's imagination, but as her mother spoke, the wind grew into icy gusts that seemed to whisper *we will not relent. This is just the beginning.*

The unspoken question dropped upon the crowd. How could Fredrik return through this weather, even if it didn't get worse? Lena assumed that somewhere, buried within her, she hoped her father was okay. But the thought of him never returning, or at least staying away until she could get Fressa back, was a deep, sturdy source of relief.

"Still," Val continued. "Preparations will certainly

begin in the meantime. We can discuss this further in the days to come."

The subtext rang clear. *In case my husband never returns. In case Nana's health worsens.*

Lena's heart warred, beating slow for a few moments before racing again. She was safe from this marriage—at least, for the time being. There was no time left to waste. For her sister's sake, and for her own.

"Now, if there were other concerns to be addr—"

"This darkness."

To Lena's surprise, it was Amal who spoke. He looked different at this meeting; she knew he could not have grown in the past day, but Lena thought he seemed much taller. His posture mimicked the older men of the village, and he spoke every syllable deliberately. Lena's stomach rolled. Was he trying to make them respect him, if he was to marry Lena? Why was he playing along with this game? The firelight painted him in flickering red.

"Yes," Val said. She paused for a long time, and no one else spoke. What was there to say? Val stared at the flames, then seemed to wake up from a trance. She shook her head quickly, throwing back her shoulders. "Well. We do have rations stored, and we can make it a few months more if we are careful. If it gets worse, we could try to venture elsewhere . . ."

She trailed off. Nobody wanted to finish that thought.

Amal nodded, and pivoted so he faced as many of the

clansmen as he could. "We are safe, for a while at least. But I just cannot understand *why* this is happening. By any calculation, summer should have continued for at least three more weeks. It makes no sense."

Nervous chatter rose up through the air like the diminishing sparks from the fire. Lena grabbed her hair and twirled it hard against her fingers. She thought she heard someone whisper *Fimbulwinter* but she did not recognize the voice. Her spine shivered, and she rolled her shoulders back. With a sharp inhale, she tilted her chin up and spoke, mustering the best chief's-daughter voice she could manage.

"Perhaps the gods are angry," she said. Immediately, she hated how she sounded—like a petulant young girl, speculating on the whims of a pantheon that she imagined half the people here did not even believe in. As she feared, a few bursts of surprised laughter escaped from the crowd. But others stayed quiet, glancing around themselves and up at the sky above. These were extreme circumstances—beyond the accumulating cold, it could no longer be denied that nature was acting out of stride, defying all the knowledge that had been passed down and experienced by them. The possibility of the divine rang clearer in times like these, Lena imagined.

Bolstered, she couldn't stop the next words from escaping her.

"It started when Fressa died."

Amal's face crumbled, his perfect posture collapsing. Val turned sharply to Lena with a ferocious glare. She mouthed harsh words that Lena could not decipher. Lena shrank into herself, raising a hand to cover her mouth. Everyone fell into total silence—the most uncomfortable breed of it.

"I'm sorry, I—" Lena caught herself. Villagers stared at their feet, or shuffled awkwardly in their seats.

Thank the gods they felt too afraid to speak, because Lena had no idea how she would have answered the questions that could have followed. *What do you mean by that? Are you suggesting this weather is connected to your sister's death?*

Why would Fressa have anything to do with this?

Lena wanted those answers too, and she had come far too close to the edge of hinting at her plans. The quiet was splintered by the sound of running feet. Lena glanced up to see Amal sprinting from the fire, his footfalls pounding into the earth. She whispered a curse. Val stared upward, obvious humiliation and frustration wrinkling her forehead.

"I'm sorry," Lena whispered again, and she took off after Amal.

CHAPTER
THIRTEEN

He'd run back to the doors of his home, which surprised Lena. She thought he might have run for the woods, or the river, or anywhere he didn't have to keep his shoulders back and chin up and forget about his lost betrothed forever. But he'd sprinted straight for his mother, with tears gathered at the ends of his eyes.

"Amal," Lena heaved, skidding to a stop behind him. He paced outside, his steps erratic.

"Now they definitely will not want me as chief," he muttered.

"They will understand," Lena murmured, her chest still heaving from the strain of running so far so fast. "They knew what she meant to you."

Amal shrugged with one shoulder. He kept his face downturned, so Lena could not see. "Exactly. And now they all know about us . . . this marriage . . ."

He trailed off. Lena's chest tightened, and she dared a step closer to him. "Not until my father returns. With this weather, and knowing him, it might be a decade."

"He will still come," Amal said, still staring down. His voice, usually full of the glowing richness of dripping honey, scraped like a blade across ice. "Or if he does not, they will bend the rules. In case you have not noticed, Lena, you are not getting younger."

Lena blinked. Her eyes stung from the cold and from the grated edge in his words. "Do you *want* us to marry? I'm trying to help us, Amal!"

"I know."

"I can fix this," she insisted. "We just need to wait—"

"Wait for what?" Now, Amal looked up to her. The tears in his eyes had disappeared, replaced by an angry sort of caution. He looked upon her as if she were a stranger. She clamped her jaw shut, forcing herself to maintain eye contact.

"Lena."

She shook her head.

"You worry me sometimes," he whispered. At that moment, part of Lena wished he would grab her by the shoulders and demand he tell her everything. She imagined the weightlessness of it—the words and secrets tumbling from her lips. They would crash around her, but she would be featherlight, if only for a moment.

Lena shut her eyes, letting out a deep breath. She

had instructions. A quest, of sorts. All she had to do was follow the steps, and this would all go away—the darkness, this marriage, everything. Lena could do it.

She had to do it.

"Go inside, Amal," Lena said. "I am fine. The others will leave the meeting soon, and unless you want an uncomfortable reunion, I suggest you go inside to your mother."

He stared at her for a long, aching moment, and she nearly buckled under his heavy gaze. It was awful to have such a secret from her best friend. She had made a stranger of herself to him, and the few yards between them stretched and rolled for miles.

Lena sat down hard in front of her fire, the events of the meeting repeating themselves again and again—an onslaught of anxiety washing her away with every cycle. She steepled her hands and tapped her feet erratically. The empty chairs surrounding the hearth seemed to stare at her. Lena wondered when her mother would return—and what verbal tirades she might be fighting right at this moment.

Lena tried to distract herself with needlework, but it lay untouched on her lap. Guilt swamped her for attempting something so trivial. Her eyes lingered again on the empty chairs beside her. She'd been sitting at this chair, on her mother's lap, so many years ago. On one of those rare nights where all four of them had been together, her parents had decided to tell them.

No child could forget the first time they heard the legend of Ragnarok. Some parents taught it with the utmost seriousness, making their children recite the warning signs and accept that its beginning could happen any day, at any time. Others told it as a story or myth, accentuating the drama of the twilight yet to come—how the gods would perish, who would slay whom, and how the sun would be consumed by the giant wolf Fenrir.

Fredrik and Val's explanation ended up both solemn and ridiculous at once, which spurred all kinds of questions, especially from their youngest.

"Will it be our rooster who cries?" Fressa had asked. "Will all the worlds hear Heimdall's signal?"

They'd answered these in flippant, general terms, but Fredrik's smile grew wide at Lena's one, sole question: "Why do the giants and Loki and everyone care so much about burning this world and making another?"

"Excellent question, Lena." He'd stared at her, and it became one of Lena's first memories of her father: lips upturned, a hand in his copper-colored beard, his eyes seeming to flicker from hazel to green and back again in the firelight. "Perhaps the gods get too comfortable in their reign. Remember what I always tell you of power, Lena?"

Lena had nodded, reciting the knowledge ingrained in her. "Good men do not want it. But whoever takes it and keeps it can decide who they want to be and how they want the world to be, and that is good. Right?"

"Something like that," he'd murmured. Fredrik's eyes drifted over to Fressa, who listened, rapt. "Those giants and Loki probably want to decide who they are and what type of world they live in."

"But why do they have to kill everything?" Fressa had asked.

Fredrik had just shrugged. "Power requires a strong, untouched foundation. Besides, I hear they will not kill all the gods or all the giants. It is impossible to guess, my love, even if we know it will happen."

When her mother returned later that night, Lena was still awake by their dwindling fire. She tried to appear busy with needlework, but she had made only nine stitches since she had left Amal. Val entered in silence, but Lena's back tensed on instinct. There was no father or sister here to bridge them.

"Is Amal all right?" her mother asked. Lena paused,

her fingers jumping. That had not been the first thing she expected Val to say.

"Of course not," Lena muttered. Val walked in front of her, standing between Lena's chair and the flames. "How could we be?"

Her mother crossed her arms, but only let out a tired sigh. "I need to rest."

Lena glanced up from her stitching as her mother made her way to her corner of the room, undoing her braid and shuffling her feet. Part of her wanted to know how the rest of the meeting had gone. Were they angry or sympathetic toward Amal? Had they discussed her father's raids more? Or had they fixated on the weather?

Her heart skittered, and she imagined Fressa's bright and insistent voice ringing through her mind, unearthing a buried fear. *This winter is not ending, Lena. Even you must know what that means.* She remembered the faces and the cacophony of the worried voices of her villagers.

"Mother—" Lena said, her voice rising in a panic. She needed help, or assurance, or anything.

Val turned to her daughter, eyebrows raised. Lena swallowed. Her mother was right—she did need rest. The firelight made her ash-blonde hair more silver than gold, and her face was webbed with wrinkles.

But Lena made herself keep speaking anyway. "Is this Fimbulwinter?"

Her mother's face went pale, which was a feat given

her complexion and the past weeks and of dwindling sunlight. But Fimbulwinter was a grave topic, to be certain—Lena regretted her question as soon as she spoke it, though something about the proclamation settled in her bones. Fimbulwinter heralded Ragnarok, the twilight of the gods, when Loki and his forces would begin their final destruction. It was not a prediction, but an accepted fact. It would come someday, though most tended to believe that if it were to happen, it would be to their great-great-great grandchildren.

"Magdalena." Val's voice cut sharper than blades, and Lena bit her lip hard. "Why would you say such a thing? What stories are your friends telling you?"

Friends? Lena wanted to ask. Besides Amal, she had hardly spoken to anybody since Fressa's death—she barely saw Estrid and Bejla now. She wanted to, but there was too much to do. There was too much they would never understand. Death happened, and it had happened to every family in the village. But not like this. Not death without a wound or a cause or a reason. She remembered Fressa's hands still outstretched on the forest floor, curling toward her blade but not quite touching it.

Lena felt glad that she was sitting down, for faintness and fatigue settled upon her like a smothering blanket. "Nothing, Mother." Her voice sounded so normal that it scared Lena. "This just isn't normal."

"Well, that does not mean we go around tempting any forces that may be," Val muttered harshly. She was not a particularly devout woman, though she found ways to weave their gods into village rituals. To Val, it was more about honoring a heritage than worshipping present forces. Lena had felt that way once. "It is just a shift in the weather—a short summer. Don't go spreading that nonsense. We cannot afford rumors like that now, without your father."

Lena nodded, sorry she had asked. Her mother shook her head again for emphasis, then turned to blow out the candle beside her bed. Lena turned around, setting down her needlework. Her mother's rejection of Fimbulwinter had not been a comfort. Lena had learned too much, done too much, and seen worlds beyond this one. There were already forces at play, and her sister was wrapped up in them. She stood quietly and lay on her pelts, but did not remove her clothes. Lena stared at the roof and turned over the bits of knowledge in her mind, glinting and precious and hard as diamonds.

Fressa had always been special, of course. She fought extraordinarily well, and when she had touched the blade her father had given her, it glowed. Lena felt furious with herself for not demanding an answer of Fredrik before he'd left. Though it was Fressa's capability, perhaps he knew the origin of the weapon.

And then there was Amal's translation of the runes

that appeared under her touch. His guess was *master of the wolf.* Lena's body sank into her bed, exhaustion making her limbs heavy, but her heart raced with sickening anxiety, and the knowledge that she was so close to the cusp of some discovery or revelation that could change everything. Whether that change was positive or destructive . . .

Lena frowned, focusing in again. *Master of the wolf.* What wolf? Was the knife the master, or the wielder? There was the massive wolf Fenrir, of course, but he was bound and chained by impenetrable rope. If he were even real. But if Hela and Helheim were real, then maybe she would have to assume Fenrir was too. She still had no notion of how that modest-sized blade was supposed to *master* anything. Lena had a momentary wave of panic when she realized it was not strapped to her belt, as it had been every day since Fressa died. No weapons were allowed at the Odinsday meetings, however, so she had removed it and placed it underneath her pelts. She reached her hands beneath it, tracing the familiar slope of its blade and the grasp of its hilt.

It was nothing special without Fressa.

Fressa.

She shut her eyes, tight, releasing the blade. Lena could do an excellent job of sorting and hiding information for herself, only allowing herself to consider what was necessary when it was called for. It had served her well growing up as a chief's daughter, and undergoing the stresses of apothecary training—but it served her best now, in the aftermath of her sister's elusive death. Lena did what she had to do to make it to the next dawn, however dim and far-off it was.

Now, alone for another night, Lena listened to her mother's breathing. She allowed herself to turn over the thought she had kept locked inside her all week; she opened it as she would a heavy chest, throwing all her strength into lifting away the cover and peering deep inside the dark.

I never said I had her soul.

Hela's words rang through Lena's mind as clear and brutal as if she were still there, standing in front of the goddess with her legs trembling beneath her. Lena clutched at her blankets, the rush of confusion and fear sweeping her out into an endless sea. She made herself recall the exact lines and curves of her sister's face. It was hard to do, and not just because it dredged up the sinking chasm of grief. Horror chased the blood through her veins, because for an instant, she forgot if Fressa's hair had reached past her shoulders or her elbows. She had to think to remember whether Fressa had freckles on her nose, or if they were just scattered across her high cheekbones.

A soft whine escaped Lena.

But she kept her eyes shut, and relaxed as Fressa's

image slowly, mostly, returned to her. This was the core of everything—it did not matter to Lena who had Fressa or why, or what interest Odin had taken in her. It bothered her, of course, and pulled her mind in endless, aimless directions. And if she were to succeed in retrieving her sister, she had to find her way through this hellish maze.

Lena examined all the information before her—Amal's translation, Hela's cryptic revelations, and her strange, almost enthusiastic willingness to work with Lena on returning Fressa's soul. The information was something to work with, but not enough to draw connections between. She was left with too many questions, and one impossible task—to kill someone as good as her sister had been.

It made sense, in a way. Valhalla's warriors were all handpicked by Odin and his Valkyries, because he needed only the very strongest and bravest to fight for him during the foretold final battle in the plains of Vigrid. How did they make these judgments? Did the gods watch them during their lives, or could they sense by retrieving souls who was worthy of which fate?

None of the fates seemed particularly enjoyable, Lena thought. You could die a second, final death while fighting if you ended up in Valhalla, or you could sink into the nothingness of the fog surrounding Hela's throne in Helheim. There were other fates too, but none that

Lena knew much about. Rán supposedly kept the souls of those who died at sea, and in her realm at Folkvangr, the goddess Freya also kept the souls of some who died fighting.

Was it all about *how* someone died? What about the life lived?

Lena was sick of the gods' whims and sorting and scales, not that she could afford to voice that aloud. She had one job and one task, however impossible it seemed. If Valhalla was as large as the legends claimed, perhaps Hela's switch could be pulled off. It had to be pulled off, but first, she needed to secure an equal soul. There was no other option. There was nothing else.

She stared at the ceiling, her eyes unblinking, until it seemed to morph into the clearing where she had found Fressa. Trees pushed through the earth around her, a canopy of leaves twisting to life above her. Lena blinked hard, wondering if she would find Fressa's body beside her—sprawled lifeless and woundless in the haven that had once been theirs. Instead, the scene was just as it had been the last time she'd set foot in the clearing. Zhao and Bejla stood whispering to each other in words Lena strained to hear. Bejla began to turn toward Lena, her pale eyes blazing.

Lena gasped a breath, and the scene faded away. She hadn't realized she had drifted to sleep until her eyes opened again, and faint light seeped through the boards of the wall. Lena was still dressed in her clothes from yesterday, and eased herself up to her elbows. She was in her home, alone. Her mother was already gone. It was unlike her to allow Lena to sleep in, but maybe she felt guilty after the announcements at last night's meeting.

Lena pushed herself up into a sitting position, her head pounding. What dream had she just had? It'd felt more lucid than any she'd had before—what was it that some believed? That dreams were messages, sent from gods and giants, like stolen glimpses between worlds.

Or maybe it had just been a dream.

In either case, Lena's heart staggered to keep up with a new realization. She had taken too long to connect the distant points, but a mountain of inexplicable occurrences culminated as she laid out all her information. There was someone else threaded throughout all of this—a recent arrival who likely knew where Lena had been the night Jannik died, but had said nothing. Someone who had been whispering in the woods where her sister died—someone whose familiar eyes had grown frightened and caged.

Lena's hands flew to her mouth as her stomach sank, because how had it taken her so long to realize? A sickening certainty crushed into her bones, but she made herself stand as the world swirled around her.

She needed to find Bejla.

CHAPTER
FOURTEEN

The trek to Bejla's home was one Lena could walk blindfolded. Her feet moved without her body really registering anything, but her mind reeled with every knotted tree and bend in the road that she passed. What was she supposed to say? To ask?

Determination prevailed over the anxiety, but barely.

Lena arrived at the door of Gunnar and Olaf's modest home too soon, but she did not hesitate before raising her knuckles to the oak door and knocking thrice.

It took too long for an answer, and it was not the person she wanted to see.

"Lena," Olaf said, with forced pleasantry. "Bejla—she . . . is not feeling well today."

Lena stood still, then stared at the earth beneath her feet. Olaf was a terrible liar. She did not want to disrespect him by pushing, but she was here to fix this; and if she did this right, it could all be over. Or at the very least, she would not be alone in all of this. The thought endowed her with a rigid will—a capability to do what needed to be done—that dulled her grief and sharpened her resolve. She looked up.

"I do not think that is the truth," she whispered.

Olaf's gray eyes widened, and he exhaled, glancing behind himself. Lena crossed her arms as Bejla slowly stepped out from behind him, her pale skin gaunt beneath her blue eyes.

"It is all right, Olaf," Bejla said. Lena winced at the sound of her friend's voice. "This will not take long."

He stepped aside and Bejla exited the home in a thin, woolen dress. Lena cleared her throat, and jerked her head toward the river. In silent agreement, they set their paths there.

"I hear you're to marry Amal," Bejla started. Yesterday, the words would have made Lena livid; they still stung, but she saw a way around them now. And it seemed trivial somehow, compared to the subject both the girls tiptoed around.

"Bejla." Lena kept her voice steady. The wind around them blew strong, and she resisted the urge to move the golden strands plastering themselves across Bejla's face. Above them, just beneath the gray cover of clouds, two ravens began to draw a lazy circle above her. It could have been a coincidence, but Lena's heart rushed with affirmation—ravens were Odin's birds. Yes, this was a sign. This would work. The other worlds knew of her, and they would comply. She would make sure of that.

"Bejla," Lena tried again, after another strained minute of silence. "I . . . have questions, but I know you do too. I mean you no harm."

Lena kept her gaze calm, but firm. She had not come this way for nothing. She would not let Bejla leave without direction. She would not marry her sister's fiancé, or lead this village without her sister by her side.

"Lena?" Bejla asked, her hands intertwining an anxious pattern. "I know that was you in Jannik's tent. I know what you did."

Was this a tactic to disarm her? Lena led them to a quieter spot, in between two trees whose roots dipped into the river.

"What do you think I did to him?" Lena asked. "With him?" Did Bejla believe she had killed him? Slept with him? Both?

But now Bejla mirrored Lena's stoic expression. "I will not play that game with you, Lena." Her expression dissolved slightly, almost like an innocence crumbled away—Bejla's eyes were pale, but brutally piercing. She took a step closer, and despite herself, Lena tensed. Did she know her friend at all? She thought of all the days they'd spent together—sometimes with Estrid, Amal, and Fressa—or just by themselves, wandering this very riverbank or market or forests. Now, she stood before a stranger. Bejla tilted her head, straggly golden hair moving across one shoulder. "Why would I care what you did *with* him?"

Lena swallowed hard as Bejla raised a brow, and they held each other at sword-point with nothing but their eyes, waiting to see who would crack first. The energy between her and Bejla had always felt murkier—more charged—than it did with her other friends. She wondered why it did, and might have sought an answer someday had Fressa not . . .

Lena rolled her eyes as her cheeks flared. Bejla's tactic had worked already. "Stop it. Who was that girl you spoke to in the woods? Where my sister—"

"What do you want me to say?" Bejla's cool veneer began to seep away, and Lena recognized real panic crowd out the haughtiness she had seen in her friend's eyes just moments before. Was this a tactic too? Bejla's voice dwindled to a whisper. "Do you have any concept of what is going on here?"

"Enlighten me," Lena muttered, trying not to faint—she was right. Bejla did not belong here, and Lena liked how her voice came out—haughty and confident. It sounded like how she wanted to seem, and so she raised her eyebrows.

"Odin is more powerful than any of us. Any of the gods. You spoke with Hela, and I cannot know what she told you or suggested you could accomplish, but I promise you that Odin is always one step ahead. Don't be a pawn in this war, Lena. You *will* lose. Odin may be the All-Father—the most powerful among them all—but there is no god trickier than . . ."

She trailed off, but anyone in the village could have supplied the answer. *Loki*. Lena's whole body vibrated. Bejla had spoken the god's name. She had been right— she was not alone on this bigger stage she had stepped onto. Tainted euphoria washed over her. To hear someone else speak about the same realms and gods that Lena had become entrenched with took away a fraction of her burden, though it added to the weight of confusion.

"So Loki *is* connected to this?" she asked, regretting her question even as the words slipped from her tongue. Lena cursed herself. She was starved for information and help, and hunger made any living being do unspeakable things without a second thought.

Bejla's eyes widened with a fear so tangible that Lena's spine tingled. Was her answer so bad?

"How do you know all of this? Where are you from?" Lena asked, panic growing. "Really?"

"Oh, by the gods." Bejla stared at Lena for a fleeting moment, but her gaze gripped the edges of the valley's river. "He is returned. I cannot say more now—" Bejla shook her head desperately, her mouth hanging open with a thousand unsaid words, but she only closed it miserably as her eyes darted manically across the clearing. "I am sorry, Lena. But we both have to go. *Now.*"

Lena blinked, and the space before her was empty. *As if she had never existed,* Lena thought. She swallowed hard. Lena swiveled, but there was no one visible. She tried to whisper Bejla's name, but fear stopped up her throat.

She walked closer to the water, and as soon as she took the first step, a horn tore through the valley. Lena's knees swayed. It seemed everyone in the village was out of their homes, moving as one in the same direction.

Toward the water.

She reached out a steadying hand to the nearest oak tree, sagging against it. Lena watched the tapestry begin to unfold before her, and almost sprinted back into the trees. Lena could see the gruesome dragon's masthead in the distance, splitting its way through the fog suspended above the gray river.

Her father was back.

CHAPTER
FIFTEEN

Lena stayed away from the main docks, staring down at the village as her world collapsed further in on itself.

This is my fault.

Her father had returned, impossibly, somehow, from somewhere. Through the thick fog, and in the changing weather—how had he managed? He was her one excuse, her once-impenetrable shield against an impossible fate. Some spear wedged itself into that shield, and her defense splintered away from the inside out. She braced both hands against the trunk of the tree she leaned upon.

This was not how a daughter was supposed to react when their father returned from far-off shores—especially not a chief's daughter. She sifted through her mind to try and remember the last words he had said before he left after Fressa's death.

I will not be scared away from my destiny, he had said,

with a quiet fury so intense that even the memory sent chills coursing through her body.

Regret fell upon her, swift and complete. She had not acted quickly enough; now her father was back too soon, and nothing had changed. Lena had obsessed over the details and logistics and the daunting burden of causing death, and she thought that those fears had made her wise and cautious and noble.

No.

They had made her weak, and now she paid the price.

If Lena squinted, she could see that the boat had already been shoved and pulled half-ashore. The silhouettes of Fredrik and a smattering of men disembarked. Lena accepted the cold dread that settled in her stomach. She needed to remember what this felt like, so she would never hesitate again.

Oh, Fressa. I have failed you—but I will make it up. I swear.

Inevitably, a clansman saw her perched by the tree line and hollered over to her, assuming she could not see the scene unfolding.

"Lena! Your father is returned!"

She raised her arm to let him know she heard, but she did not move to join the others. She would have to, she understood, but for now she stayed exactly as she was. Lena would never be able to pull off a public reunion right now, and she knew her mother would rather people whisper about Lena's absence than about her flimsiness or disdain.

Once she decided that enough people had made their way to the river, Lena slunk as fast and discreetly as she could away from the forest and back into the village. The pathways seemed empty enough now that the racing of her heart slowed a fraction. She had almost made it to her house when a figure darted out from behind it. Lena yelped despite herself, and she sighed in half-frustration, half-relief when she realized it was Amal.

"I thought I would find you here," Amal said. His face was torn; Amal's dark eyes looked almost black, and met her gaze with resigned steadiness. But his jaw quivered, and his hair stuck out at odd angles, like he had forgotten to brush it after a rough night's sleep.

A surge of defiance rose in her, and she rushed her words. "Amal, we can still fight th—"

At the same instant, he began to shake his head. Slow, deliberate, damning. "Lena. We have tried everything. Our only protection is gone. When they come back here—any minute—you know what will begin to happen."

"But—"

"They will not care how we feel," Amal said. She hated how calm he sounded, though the sadness in his eyes assured her that at least he was still heartbroken too.

"This is not a contract of love. It was never supposed to be. It is for property, for law, for a functioning society."

Lena rolled her eyes, not bothering to hide the hiccupping buildup of sobs growing within her. She knew he was right. What type of chief's daughter would she be to not understand that? If it were anyone but Amal . . .

"How am I supposed to do this?" she whispered.

For the briefest moment, anger glinted like a turned blade in Amal's eyes. "How are *you*? I was the one who was engaged, Lena."

She froze, the truth of his pain rubbing into her coarsely, like salt on an open wound. "So this will not be out of love."

Amal nodded once. "This is not for love. It never can or will be." He paused, the creases around his eyes relaxing slightly. "We can do this though, can't we? You are still my best and dearest friend. We will make it work, somehow."

She took some comfort in his words. They did know each other well, and she was not worried about romantic love developing between them. She nodded to appease him, but her mind already tangled itself in other logistics. They would have to live together, permanently. They would have to share a bed. Or, at least, make the clan believe they were. In more than one sense.

"I should go," Amal whispered. "I will tell them you are at home?"

Lena nodded again, and he turned away from her to jog down to the river. She watched him leave, and wondered if she could ever convince the clan of the legitimacy of their marriage. They would have to go through an entire ceremony of nearly two days, and that held no comparison to the fear that crept like ice into her veins when she considered what had to come *after*. All those rituals right before the wedding night. The expectations, the consummation. She knew Amal would not do anything she did not want, but how long could their charade last? What if they asked questions? What if Lena could not fix this before they began pressuring for children?

Lena quickly walked inside the house, slamming the door shut behind her. Her vision swam, and dizziness overtook her. *No.* She would make certain this was fixed and healed before anyone expected anything of *that* nature from them. Lena would not fail Fressa twice. She would understand, Lena thought, when she came back. Fressa would know that Lena did what she had to do.

So they could see another dawn, however dim and far-off it was.

She waited inside the house for a few hours, sitting on her bed and staring into nothing. Perhaps the reunions down by the river were taking longer than expected. Lena wondered if her father had brought back more jewels and gold and weapons this time, and if he believed these would be enough to justify his continual absence. A flash of rage brought her to her feet, and she paced the length of the room. He had not been gone all that long, Lena knew, which bothered her even more— how come he had to return so quickly? Even though Lena knew there was no way he could have known about her and Amal's impending marriage, the timing of Fredrik's arrival felt twisted and vicious and left her suspicious of something she could not name.

He had abandoned his wife and Lena when they needed him most. When the village was weaker and more uneasy than ever before. And for what? What did he need to prove? Their village was supposed to be rooted, trading people; not those violent, disgraced men from further north that raged against the southern lands and took to the seas, leaving smoke streaking into the skies and villages burned to the ground. She could not even focus on Bejla's strange revelations.

Lena stopped in her tracks when she heard footsteps approach. She clenched her fists as the door swung open, gray light pouring into the dark room. Her parents did not speak as they entered, and Lena wondered if they even noticed her in the corner of the room. The light rushed out of the room again as Val closed the door behind them. Fredrik stomped the snow off of his boots, and Lena wished he would do that outside instead.

Without looking up, her father spoke. "Hello, Magdalena."

Lena paused. Crossed her arms tight across her chest. "Father."

Val crossed the space between them to get to the fire, and shot her daughter a warning glance. Her pale hair hung loose across her shoulders, thin and stringy. "You should have gone down to greet your father, Lena. People wondered where you were."

"I was busy," Lena said.

Her mother shook her head, but there was no real bite in her words or gaze. Lena knew, deep down, her mother shared Lena's resentment toward Fredrik. Still, Lena's fate and marriage pivoted around her father's presence, even though he was hardly around to begin with. Somehow, he was deemed significant enough to stop or initiate the most sacred rituals and happenings of his clan, based on the merit of his attendance alone.

"I see," Fredrik said. No anger shook or deepened his voice. In fact, Lena wondered if she sensed an amusement in his words. A fascination. "Well, I was busy too."

Val stoked the fire, jamming in an iron rod so the wood could burn brighter, scattering a hundred tiny sparks into the air. The afterimage of them flashed around the room when Lena glanced away. Her father sat down to untie his boots. His beard was longer than it had been, of course, rust-colored and still speckled with bits of ice.

Silence settled, and Lena felt the tension of it wrapping around her. She wanted to run from the room, or break something, or scream at her parents until they could hear her—actually hear her. She could tell her mother felt the same way, given the fact that she was still stabbing the burning logs in the hearth, even though the flames shot up so high that it made even Lena nervous.

Fredrik seemed unaffected as he pulled off his boots. A subtle smile pulled at his lips, and Lena wanted to know what could possibly make him feel happy. The firelight danced across his eyes, and for a moment, the light that reflected looked like it burned from within. As if he felt his gaze on her, Fredrik turned to Lena.

"I hear your marriage will be soon." His voice was too casual for the words, and he stared hard at her, maybe angling for a reaction. "To Amal."

Lena gave a one-shouldered shrug. To hear the words aloud made her want to shrivel into herself, but she would not cry in front of her father. She did not trust herself to speak.

"Do not pretend to be surprised, Fredrik." Val said. She finally let the fire alone, and turned to face her husband. "She knows that it was what had always been planned."

"Ah," Fredrik said, inclining his head. "Yes."

His guise hardened, and he worked his hand across his mouth, looking down. Lena tilted her head, wondering if the death of his youngest daughter affected him more than he let on. She felt no pity, but at least she could understand grief. Lena had long pretended not to notice that her father preferred Fressa. He was not obvious about it, at least. It was not something she had detected until she was a teenager. Fredrik was neither cold nor disinterested toward Lena, but he always asked more questions of Fressa. His eyes lit up when she spoke to him.

It might have bothered Lena, but he was so rarely home. She could make herself forget.

But now, of course, he had chosen today to return. Lena clenched her fists hard, suppressing a scream.

"No use in putting it off longer, then," Val said, brushing her hands across her skirt. Dark smudges of ash streaked across the fabric. "Odin knows we need some semblance of order around here, and Lena wanted to wait until you returned for the ceremony."

"Did she?"

Lena did not dignify him with a response.

"I see," Fredrik continued, and Lena thought her father was perfectly aware of why she had wanted to wait for him to return. Because, in truth, she had not believed he ever would. At least, not so soon. "I will help however I can."

"Preparations have been in place for a week or so now," Val said. Her parents spoke over her, literally, and Lena slunk away to her corner of the room and let them discuss. "If we act quickly, I believe we can plan it for Freyasday."

Lena hugged herself, willing the nausea away. This morning had held so much direction and clarity. She had gotten one of her closest friends to confess harrowing knowledge. Now, her father had somehow returned from some faraway shore, and her mother claimed that—if they were only so *quick*—Lena would be Amal's wife by next week.

Her vision blurred, and her parents' conversation continued without her.

Lena refused to attend any sessions with Nana the next day. It was not a verbal refusal, for nobody asked Lena, but she still took some joy from her quiet rebellion. Nana did not seek her out; she wondered if it was because Nana understood Lena's anger, or if she was not well enough to do so.

Amal did not try to see her either. Lena almost wished he would, a thought that surprised her. It was still hard to wrap her head around the fact that they would be forced to marry soon, but in any case, he was still her best friend. And she needed someone who knew her, or most of her.

She paced by the river and through the village as soon as the sun rose, half-hoping she might run into him. Lena stopped by Olaf and Gunner's house a couple times, but Bejla always seemed to be away, and Lena feared to press them further. Panic and frustration chased through her veins as her deadline drew nearer. Some of the other girls in the village stopped to talk with her, and she was grateful for their companionship—but she knew they only spoke to her because she was about to be married, and their poorly concealed stares of envy made her want to laugh. She'd let any of them switch places with her in a heartbeat.

The darkest moment after her father's return came during one of these conversations, when Estrid called over to Lena when she walked by the fire in the village center.

"Hi, Lena!" she chirped.

Lena glanced over, her practiced smile appearing on instinct. Estrid's littlest sister, Kiali, was in her arms, and Lena fought back the swell of angry jealousy that slammed into her. She kept her smile plastered, and remembered that Estrid had tried to visit in the days after Fressa's death, but Lena had not wanted to see sad smiles or hear assurances that things would get better.

Estrid asked how Lena was feeling about the upcoming wedding and other pleasantries about the return of Fredrik, and how strange the darkness and cold were in the summer, and how excited she was for the marriage ceremony to come. Kiali wriggled in Estrid's grasp, and finally she let her sister go. Lena watched the small girl run into her house without a backward glance, and her heart surged with a hurt so terrible that her eyes prickled.

"But I'm not as excited as you are, I'm sure," Estrid continued, with a suggestive wink. Lena went red, and managed a choked laugh. Anger erupted within her— Estrid *knew* what Fressa and Amal had meant to each other.

It was in that instant that the thought slammed into her, as if someone else had shoved it in her arms. Estrid was still a kind person, and genuine, and hard-working. If Lena just slipped something into her food, or . . .

She blinked hard, and Lena's body ached with revulsion. She was not capable of that. Was she? She would have to be. There was no time. Realizations and logistics piled up inside her at once, and Lena stepped back, cutting off Estrid mid-sentence.

"I am so, so sorry," she rushed, her gaze flashing to the sky, the ground, anywhere but Estrid's concerned face. She needed to . . . to what? Escape? Act? "I just remembered, uh, I need to go help my mother with the nets now."

"Oh!" Estrid said. She laughed a little, but it sounded forced—Lena could not blame her. She did not want to imagine how she must look and seem. "I actually have some clothes to wash there—would it be all right if I came along?"

Lena sucked in a breath. What kind of a sign was this? Then again, she had believed Jannik was a *sign* too.

But if not her, then who? Lena thought. She had to remember what this was for. It was for her sister, and for something far greater—she had a divine audience, apparently, and she would not let them down. "Sure," Lena whispered, feeling along her belt to ensure Fressa's blade was still strapped to it. Her knees buckled, but she caught herself.

"Lena?" Estrid suppressed a laugh. "Someone must be nervous for Freya's Circle tonight. Let me just grab the baskets."

"Right."

Lena stumbled after Estrid as she walked behind her home. Estrid's family was large, but their thatched roof hung lower and smaller than Lena's. Clanging metal resounded from their nearby blacksmithing shop, and the air hung heavy with smoke.

Her hands trembled, but Lena grasped the hilt of Fressa's blade and tried to pretend she *was* Fressa—if only to keep her hands from shaking. But the thought of her wrung Lena's chest out like wet laundry, leaving her gasping for breath.

She shut her eyes tight, mouthing her sister's name to herself. When she opened them, she held Fressa's blade in front of her—and Estrid had turned around, her mouth hanging open and her eyes locked on the glinting metal.

Neither of them moved. Neither of them breathed.

"Lena . . ." Estrid's eyes did not leave the blade, but they were wide with fear. "What is this about?"

Lena couldn't make her lips move.

"I don't—" Estrid heaved a stuttering breath, then lifted her gaze. The confusion and terror pulsing through her gray eyes smothered Lena, whose hands trembled wildly. "I'll scream, Lena. Put that away before I call for help."

A part of Lena marveled at her friend's level-headedness. But most of Lena felt like she was hidden far away, behind the deepest corner of her consciousness, carved out of the darkest parts of her heart.

"But I'm the daughter of the chief," Lena whispered. The implication was clear—*whom will they believe?* Lena almost felt worse for saying these words than for raising her blade.

Estrid lurched back like she'd been slapped, her mouth falling open. Shame blossomed within

Lena—shame for what she was doing, and shame that she couldn't see it through for her own sister.

"I'm so sorry, Es—"

Her friend had never been a gifted fighter, but Estrid's arms slammed into Lena and the blade dropped into the grass. Lena's body went limp, the fury-tinted fear in Estrid's eyes banishing Lena further into herself. She fell to her knees, and watched Estrid run fast and far. *Would she tell?* Lena tried to muster the panic that was probably necessary, but felt nothing but shame. She dissolved into tears—she hugged herself, trying to keep the hiccups and wracking sobs contained, but it was of no use.

Plummeting perpetually, the shame carved crevices and chasms that emptied Lena from the inside out.

That night, Lena stared into the flames of their house's hearth until her eyes teared up again. Her mother sat behind her, yanking Lena's dark locks into a braid. Fredrik was meeting with some traders from the neighboring village that had arrived earlier in the morning, so it was just the two of them in their house.

The silence between them was oppressive, and Lena actually thought the one benefit of marrying Amal would be that she would no longer live with her parents. This, right now, would be the final evening she had to endure in this suffocating home. Nostalgia-tinted relief gave her a head rush, and she let her eyes wander the beams and corners of the place she had grown up in as her mother wrestled with her hair.

Lena's eyes lingered in the corner she and Fressa shared. They still had not removed her pelts, thankfully, but it was a reminder that Fressa was still out there, waiting, even if in another world. What if she could see her now? Could she? Lena bit her lips hard. She would have explaining to do, certainly. Lena had been so close to Estrid. Something had stopped her—made her limbs weak and aimless, her mind flimsy and breakable. The events of the afternoon flashed painfully through her mind, and Lena clenched her trembling jaw. She had tried. Why was she not strong enough?

But Fressa would understand. She *knew* Lena, and that was what Lena missed more than anything. If she wanted anyone else to understand her, she would have to try and articulate intimate, immense detail—but Fressa could just look at her.

Lena blinked hard. She just needed to make a more careful plan. The incident with Estrid had surprised her, was all.

Her throat grew raw with the effort of containing her tears.

"This will be good for you," her mother said, tying

the end of her braid. Lena had nearly forgotten she was here. "It will help you feel ready for tomorrow and what lies ahead."

Lena started to nod before remembering her hair was being done, and winced. "All right."

Val sighed a little, and Lena felt her mother rest her chin atop Lena's head for a moment, breathing her in. Lena suspected this was not how either of them had wanted or expected Lena's wedding to go.

"It is time." Val stood, offering a hand for Lena to stand. She adjusted her daughter's skirts. Lena wasn't wearing anything particularly fancy, but her mother told her to wear one of her nicer dresses. It was a dense, gray wool to ward out most of the cold, and long enough that it brushed across the ground as she walked. Val gripped Lena's hand. "Let's go."

Val led Lena all the way to the north side of the village. There was a low, wide building here with smoke billowing from the roof. This was where the religious ceremonies took place. It was where she would have to see Amal tomorrow, but it was also where she was supposed to go tonight—along with most of the other women in the settlement. Val paused before they entered, examining Lena for any imperfections. She pinched

Lena's cheeks to bring color into them, and heaved an aggravated sigh at the dampness on the bottom hem of her skirts from walking through the frost.

"You were supposed to hold them higher," she muttered. Val straightened, pulling Lena's braid across her right shoulder. "No matter now. This is it." Her eyes drank in Lena. "Are you ready?"

Lena raised her eyebrows, and Val pretended not to notice. She opened the doorway, and warm firelight poured out in golden streams across the frost-choked grass. It was nighttime, but the moon was full and the clouds were gone. Silver light doused the village. Lena did not want to think about what was supposed to be happening at this time tomorrow night.

She fixed her gaze on what laid beyond the doorway. Her mother entered before her, taking on the bulk of the greetings and pleasantries. Lena stood behind Val, her mouth dry at the sight of so many women surrounding her. She remembered attending a few of these circles when other maidens got married, but the last one had been years ago. Fressa had been beside Lena the whole night, and they survived by stolen, exasperated glances and whispered ridicules of the ceremony happening around them.

Lena fidgeted with her braid, and then her skirts, keeping her smile pasted to her face. The small, polite one that conveyed kindness without really acting on it.

It was easy enough to fake, and easy enough to maintain. She sighed inwardly. This was going to be a long night.

She murmured greetings as the women all stood to offer congratulations and well-wishes. Lena recognized the majority of them, relieved to see Estrid was absent, but glad to see a few other acquaintances among the crowd. That meant word of this afternoon hadn't spread, hopefully. Bejla was there too, twirling a golden strand of hair tightly around her index finger. Lena's heart pounded; she had not expected her to attend. Most of the attendees were older women, closer to Val's age. *They will share their wisdom,* her mother had said. Lena resisted the urge to roll her eyes.

The oldest in attendance was Nana, even though she was unmarried. Lena had expected she would be here as the groom's mother, but it still stung, and she kept her eyes averted from her as the bustle of her arrival dwindled.

Lena knew the next step. She walked to the dead center of the room once her mother motioned for her to go. The gazes upon her were not malicious, but so intent that Lena's hands shook. She buried them in her skirts, and knelt down to the ground. A soft rug of a wolf's hide cushioned her.

Val beamed at her, so Lena assumed she was doing all right so far. She didn't care for any of this ceremony, but it was hard not to feel a little nice at her mother's obvious pride. Her mother had smiled at her. Her mother loved her, and it was such a sweet, surprising relief after the look in Estrid's eyes that she nearly sobbed. She still felt like a stranger inside her own limbs, but Val's smile brought her back just a little.

Lena tilted her head up, taking in the rest of the room from her new vantage point. Torches lined every wall at exact intervals, and Lena had never before seen so much firelight in one contained space. She wondered if this was what Folkvangr was like, with its endless summer and eternally green hills. That was Freya's realm.

And this was supposed to be Freya's Circle.

She exhaled, letting her eyes adjust to all the light. Lena shifted herself on the rug, and her mother accepted a bowl from Nana as she strode over to stand before her. Lena didn't want to look and see what expression Nana wore—pride, worry, guilt, excitement? There was no answer that would satisfy Lena.

"Magdalena." Her mother's voice rang through the room, but it was not the voice she used in Odinsday meetings. It was her usual tone, clear as springtime sun, and she looked only at Lena. If she tried hard enough, Lena could ignore the gaping women encircling them and pretend it was just her and her mother. "This remedy is an herbal mixture used by Clan Freding for generations to assure our healthy, continued survival."

The implication was clear. *So you can have children.*

Lena flushed, and for a moment, feared that her mother might make her eat the mixture. Thankfully, the tradition unfolded as it always had, and Val dipped her fingers into the bowl and marked Lena's cheeks with the light-brown concoction. Two stripes beneath her eyes, and one down the bridge of her nose. It did not smell pleasant, but Lena kept her guise calm.

"May the goddess Freya be in step with you now and always. May you fortify our people with your strength and beauty," Val intoned. When she finished, the rest of the women echoed her prayer, wishing their words between the worlds, and Lena wondered if Freya—goddess of fertility and love and exquisiteness—could hear them, or if she even cared. Lena felt the words roll off of her like water off a duck's wings; she was not capable of absorbing them. If they understood who they were praying for, and if they knew that Freya very well might know all these things that she had done . . .

Lena smiled at her audience. She was getting better at that, at least. Her mother stood while Lena fell back into a sitting position like she was instructed to. It was not a graceful maneuver with the thick dress.

She racked her mind to remember what came next. Was it the advice or the wreath? Lena looked around the room, at all those faces staring back at her. Lena was sure to avoid Bejla's gaze—it would be too much to handle.

Val took a few steps back and cleared her throat.

"When I married your father, we had you right away. I do believe it was that very wedding night that you came to us."

Lena fought the urge to vomit. Apparently, it was time for the *advice* portion of the ceremony. All she could remember was Fressa doing a rubbish job at concealing her laughter as the women went down the line sharing the rather explicit successes and failures of their first nights with their husbands. Lena definitely did not want to hear any of this, but she sat back, the heels of her palms digging into the rug's fur.

"We Freding women have good luck, I think." Val pronounced the words quietly. Lena was unsure if she heard correctly, but the silence that followed turned decidedly charged through the room. Good luck? Lena could not imagine how her mother had gotten such a notion. "We prevail. And you are my firstborn, my—my . . ."

Nobody needed her to finish that sentence. In their minds, Lena was no longer just Val's firstborn, but her only child. Lena thought how dreadful that must be to believe. If she was all that her mother had left, then Lena felt truly sorry for her.

"All I mean is, daughter, I have no doubt that this is only the beginning for you." She paused, staring at her like she was the only one in the room. "This will be good. For us all, and especially for you."

Val's eyes sparkled with the start of tears, and Lena

had to look away. She twisted her skirts with her hands, blinking back an unexpected wave of sentiment. Before long, Val motioned to the woman at her left side, and thus began a cycle of monologues among the married women. Some poignant, some funny, some sad. Some of them seemed to be designed more for the other married women among them, who threw in their own interjections and jokes. All of them made Lena squirm and grit her teeth. Bejla and the other maidens offered no specifics, obviously, but wished her well in her marriage. She appreciated their presence, even though she wished desperately any one of them could switch places with her.

When it came time for Nana to speak, Lena hardened her jaw. Special weight was given to her, of course, as the mother of the husband. Nana had to lean her arm against the shoulder of the woman sitting beside her as she stood, but her voice still had its commanding, intelligent tone.

"Lena," she said. "My son is the single greatest thing that has happened to me in this life. You have the responsibility now to keep him safe and joyful and kind. If my time training you has taught me anything, it is that you know how the body and mind work. I have every confidence you will treat him well and be treated well in return, and this will be good for our people. I am glad he will be with you."

She sat down, and the others murmured their

agreements. Lena did not react, even though Nana was the last to speak. Not one of them had mentioned Fressa. Lena knew it was on the forefront of everybody's minds. It had to be. A sister marrying their dead sister's lover? It was a sick joke that nobody would acknowledge in front of her, but Lena felt certain her sister's name had fallen from all their lips in whispers when she wasn't there. Lena hated to see Fressa ignored, but knew it was for the best. If anyone here had spoken Fressa's name to her, Lena would have broken down.

In her distraction, Lena forgot what part of the ceremony came next, until her mother approached her with something in her hands. Once the light hit Val, Lena inhaled sharply. The circlet.

She had loved watching this part as a younger girl. The other clanswomen gathered together days before a wedding to weave together a circlet of bright cornflowers. Lena could not remember the last time she had seen a blue so bright and bold—they must be from Nana's special stock, since there was no way they could have grown in this cold summer.

Val knelt down and placed the flower wreath firmly atop Lena's head. It fit perfectly—tight enough to stay in place, but loose enough that she felt no pressure. Despite its significance, Lena wanted to ask for a glass to see her reflection in.

"Thank you," she breathed, for the whole audience

to hear. They had made this for her. Lena risked a touch, and traced her fingers across the interwoven stems and blooms with care.

"Remember," Val said. "You keep this on through tomorrow. Amal will take it off for you once the marriage is complete."

Lena nodded, removing her hand. The circlet made her feel a bit like a princess, though reigning this clan was not elegant and regal like it was in some stories.

"Beautiful." Val said the word with a touch of finality, making it more of a dismissal than a compliment. She swiveled to address the whole congregation. "Now—shall we?"

Lena frowned until she saw her mother signal to a group of the younger girls. Their faces split with grins, and in wavering harmony, they began to warble songs of Freya. The lyrics harkened to some faraway meadow overflowing with bright poppies and roses, where mead and honey flowed from rocks like waterfalls. For a moment, Lena lost herself in the music, despite everything.

Some of the women began to dance, urging Lena to stand with them. She fought them off for a couple songs, but finally relented and pushed her way up to her feet. Lena got more attention when she excluded herself from something than from when she actually participated. She had never been particularly well-versed in the songs and dances reserved for Freya's Circle and other ceremonies, but they were easy enough to imitate. The next hour was spent in a strange space—Lena felt like her life was ending, somehow, with the dawn.

But now, with the bright, warm light and the simple beauty of the repeated songs ringing through the room, Lena imagined she was someone else, somewhere else, and managed to enjoy herself a little.

The older women began to trickle out of the room with waved farewells. Lena did her best to say goodbye to them, but pretended not to notice when Nana made her exit. The music died down too soon, and Val grasped Lena's shoulders.

"I think it is time for me to leave you," she murmured, tucking back a stray strand of Lena's braid. "But I will see you soon, in the morning. Whom did you select as your maiden-companion?"

Lena cursed silently. She had forgotten she needed to select her best unmarried female friend to keep her company on the eve of her wedding—allegedly to act as a supervisor to ensure the marriage was *legitimate,* as if the night prior was the only possible night for Lena to engage in any uncouth behavior.

She quickly surveyed the room, panic rising. Lena had made Fressa promise years ago that they would be each other's companions when the time came. Lena had never considered choosing an alternative. Her eyes wandered around the girls' faces, a lonesome ship desperately seeking harbor. Several of them smiled and nodded vigorously, obvious invitations. Lena mouthed her thanks, but when she turned to her mother, she knew whom she had to say.

"Bejla."

Val raised one eyebrow. "All right. Well, I will leave you both and see you soon. Good night, Magdalena. Try to get some rest."

Lena nodded, and Val pulled her in for a tight embrace. "It will be so strange to sleep in that house without you. Without either of you."

Tears sprang to Lena's eyes. It had been too long since Val spoke of Fressa, and she was glad she did so when they spoke in private. "I know," Lena said.

Val gave her one last smile, tinged in sadness. When she left the room, the rest of the maidens did too, save Bejla, who sat on the floor with her legs tucked delicately beneath her. She avoided Lena's gaze relentlessly, her jaw taut.

Lena stood for a while at the door her mother had left through, almost wanting to call her back. She finally heard Bejla stand and walk around the room, extinguishing most of the flames. She kept a few burning, but the room still felt oppressively dim and hollow.

"You must be exhausted," Bejla said, making a terrible attempt at small talk.

"I am." Lena turned around, and gently removed

her cornflower crown, traditions damned. She hung it across one of the poles that made up the pair of cots in the corner.

Bejla nodded, walking over to sit on her cot.

Lena gave her a small, mock-polite smile. "That was an interesting exit you made last week by the river," Lena said as she undid her braid, sifting her fingers through her hair. Bejla leaned down to untie her boots, offering no response. Her mother would come first thing in the morning with the dress.

Tomorrow.

She exhaled shakily, a panicked cry stopping up in her throat. Lena choked on the hatred for what she had done and failed to do, and the fear for what was yet to come; a suffocating desperation clawed its way up her throat.

Bejla glanced up at her, worry widening her blue eyes. "Lena. Are you scared?"

It was not the question she had anticipated. *Are you okay? What's wrong?* But no—was she scared? Lena stared down at her, letting the tears primed behind her eyes fall.

"Please tell me what you are." She wished her voice could reflect the anger that simmered within her, the furious desperation clawing down her ribcage. Everything filtered through an exhaustion denser than Lena could penetrate.

Bejla ran a hand through her hair, eyeing the door.

Lena half-expected her to vanish again. "I want to, Lena. I swear."

Lena wiped at her eyes, and knelt before Bejla. "I won't tell a soul."

Bejla laughed, and Lena saw that her eyes shone too. "You are the one soul I should not tell." She shook her head. "Cannot tell. I am so, so much like you, Lena. More than you know."

Lena's heart pounded. In what way did she mean? She moved to sit beside Bejla on her cot, and wished her friend would look at her.

"Odin has my sister, doesn't he? In Valhalla?"

Bejla looked over at her, and Lena swallowed. Their proximity was too much, suddenly. "Odin is a terrible god to be indebted to, Lena."

Lena blinked. "He has my sister. Why did he take her soul? How?"

Bejla bit her lip, her jaw clenched shut. Lena reached down and grabbed Bejla's hand, surprising herself. "I know about debts and deals, Bejla. Let me help you." She shook her head, but clutched at Lena's hands harder.

"Your sister is safer with Odin, Lena. I'm not just saying that," she whispered. Lena's body shook. "If he knows—if he ever learns I even *spoke* to you, Odin will kill me."

Lena shut her eyes. "Odin does not own my sister,"

she said through gritted teeth. "Whatever else is going on—"

"You know not what you say," Bejla urged, her voice rising. She leaned closer into Lena. "I know you do not know what you say, for your sister is more than you knew. Stop this before it's too late for you. You have to."

"I just want my sister back," Lena whispered.

"I have a sister too," Bejla said tentatively. "She lives in the land I came from. Something awful happened to her, Lena. I saved her, but it came at a cost—Odin owns me now. I am his to serve."

"What did you do?"

Bejla shook her head again, her eyes brimming with tears. She removed her hands from Lena's, and held Lena's face with a surprising tenderness. Despite her frustration, Lena found she did not hate the sensation. "It doesn't matter. My sister is safe."

"But mine isn't!" Lena shouted, her voice cracking, exploding her caution. She shoved Bejla's hands off of her. "And something is wrong in Midgard! This darkness—this cold—it happened after Fressa was taken. Why can you not understand?'

"I do understand," Bejla said, her voice steely. "Believe me. I am still doing you a service when I say you need to leave this alone. Your sister *is* safer in Valhalla. She will not be anywhere else." Lena opened her mouth, but Bejla cut her off. "Do not ask more of me. I have said more than I ever have or should. If you love me at all, you will let this alone."

Lena sagged. She did not want to endanger Bejla, but the questions had only piled on.

"This is the eve of your wedding," Bejla continued, with a sharp laugh. "Focus on anything else, or tomorrow will be even more miserable."

Lena's heart urged her to ignore Bejla's words, but her mind knew to relent. She had pushed Bejla hard—too hard—and would get no more information out of her. Bejla would be of more use later if Lena did not stretch her too thin.

"Marriage," Lena muttered. "I guess I knew it would come someday. Amal is a good man, but—I am not the one who loves him in that way."

"In that way," Bejla murmured. "I understand."

They stared at each other for a long moment, and she wondered what exactly Bejla meant. Lena's heart twisted in a strange way, and she wished that many things were different. Too soon, Bejla cleared her throat. "Get some rest," she instructed, standing up. "You will certainly need it."

Lena laughed bitterly. "I'm afraid so."

She walked over to her cot and laid herself down, folding her hands across her stomach and listening to the soft sounds of Bejla preparing herself for bed. Lena expected she would stay up the whole night, staring at the ceiling, cold with dread and fear. But she already felt her eyelids collapsing, the burden of tomorrow pulling her under. Lena fell hard into sleep, and dreamed of a blizzard. A huge swathe of snow and ice burying her village, smothering the fires and inhaling their houses.

The snow stopped, but the village was gone. Buried. It was impossible to tell that anyone had ever set foot in the valley before.

CHAPTER
SIXTEEN

The knock came later than she expected. Lena woke up an hour before her mother arrived, nauseous and starving at once. She tried to focus on Bejla's steady breaths coming from the cot beside her, but it was little comfort. Once the knock came, Lena swung her legs down to the floor, shaking off the cold as best she could.

The sooner she began this day, the sooner it would be over, and the sooner she would be erasing it all.

"Good," her mother said, as Lena swung the door open. The sun had barely risen. "You are awake."

Before Lena could comment on her mother's acute observational skills, she had pushed past her and into the room. Bejla startled awake, blinking rapidly and pushing herself up onto her elbows. When she squinted through the dark and saw Val, she was out of bed faster than Lena could really register. Her mother had quite an effect when she wanted to, and today Val's face held no trace of the nostalgia that had softened her gaze last night.

Today she had to be Fredrik's wife, and Lena would have to be *Magdalena*, heiress to Clan Freding and the picturesque bride—brimming with youth, fertility, and promise. Lena massaged her cheeks, suppressing a groan.

"Let me help you with that," Bejla rushed, jogging over to Val and helping her hang up a dress. Lena's breath caught for a moment—never before had she seen such white, pristine fabric. The hemlines were expertly crafted, with ivory-threaded designs arcing and twisting across the bodice.

"Where did you—" Lena started. Val smoothed the skirts with a tender hand, holding the cloth like she might a newborn. "Oh. Was this yours?"

Val nodded, some of the softness of last night returning as she glanced back at Lena. "Believe it or not, but your father was different back then. He courted me for months, as if I would ever have dreamed of saying no to him. Chiefs' sons are highly sought after, you know."

Lena shrugged, keeping her lips pursed. It made her sad to hear her mother speak of her father as a different man from the one she knew. She wondered if it was her own entry to the world that had caused such a divergence to occur.

"I would have said yes to him even if he'd been a

farmer's son," Val said, her voice dwindling in volume and speed. "Back then, I would have."

Val stared at the dress, her fingers still buried in its folds. Bejla hovered in the corner, looking trapped. Lena bit her lip, trying to think of anything to say to that, but her mother got a hold of herself. She turned around with a quick shake of her head, and the tresses of her hair shifted across her back—golden waves cutting against the dark sage color of the dress she wore.

"Let's get you dressed."

And with that, the day descended into the chaos that every village wedding fell victim to. Val helped Lena step out of her clothes and into the dress she had worn years ago, cooing in delight to see the fabric fall across Lena's frame, the bodice just tight enough to highlight her waist without feeling constraining.

The fabric was soft, but held the musty scent of an untouched, forgotten relic. Lena shared the same tall frame as her mother, even if her curves weren't quite as pronounced as Val's or Fressa's. As her mother worked on adjusting the fit, Bejla hovered around, trying to hand a cup of milk and piece of bread to Lena, who accepted them readily.

Then, Val marched Lena back to her cot and sat her down. From her satchel, she pulled out the comb Fredrik had given Lena last month. Val stared at it, flipping it over in her hand and letting out a tiny sigh. Lena tried to smooth out her hair while her mother gathered sections at a time, pulling it through her tresses with surprising care. Usually, she yanked and dragged her daughters' hair until it met her expectations, dismissing their cries or poorly concealed tears.

But there was a lot different about today.

The sun had already risen by the time Val deemed Lena's hair acceptable. The light from outside was staggeringly bright—the first cloudless day Lena could remember since before Fressa's death. She longed to be out of this room with a surprising ferocity and shock of energy, but her mother was just getting started. Val smeared rouge across Lena's cheeks, then stared at her for a while, grimaced, and tried to remove most of it. Bejla ducked outside at one point, and Lena resisted the urge to bolt after her. But she returned minutes later, probably from Nana's—she had oils to streak through Lena's hair and pansies to rub across Lena's wrists and neck.

Lena breathed in the scent, sweeter than any other herb or flower she'd come across in her training. She wondered what Nana was doing right now. How she felt on the morning of her son's wedding. Would Amal be getting ready too? She wished she could speak to him before the ceremony, to gauge what he was thinking now that he was about to marry the wrong Freding sister.

Lena hurriedly placed the cornflower circlet atop

her head, and Val said nothing, but adjusted it at least twelve times before approving its fit. The bold, solid blue of the petals was still mesmerizing, and based on Bejla's delighted clapping, it must have complemented Lena's hairstyle well.

"Oh," Val sighed, her eyes misty. Lena could muster apathy at best, which was only slightly preferable to the baseline sensation of drowning. She wondered if her mother would say anything today like, *I wish your sister were here,* or, *she would be so proud of you.* Lena hated to hear Fressa's name spoken in the past tense—it was just a devastating reminder of what she had yet failed to do, and a harsh warning against the dwindling time she had left to see her plans through. Even so, it felt equally as strange to *ignore* Fressa so consistently. This was supposed to be *her* circlet and dress and day.

Lena blinked, feeling out of her own body. If the sun was up already, she knew there were only a few hours before it would be gone again. Which meant that Amal and the rest of the clan would be entering this room soon—in less than an hour, at the latest.

"Are you ready?" Val asked, her voice returning to its regular commanding timbre. "We need to start setting up."

Lena nodded, splaying a hand across her chest as if that would slow her heartbeat. She stood, and Bejla moved behind her to hastily fold and remove the two cots from the room. Lena watched the main door open and close, light flashing into the room in tantalizing bursts before disappearing again.

Other women began to file in when Bejla reentered with a chair in her arms. Val held open the door as more clanswomen brought in chairs, until most of the room was covered in the dark, carved oak. The walls looked barren without the traditional chains of flowers that were supposed to line the ceiling. They had already splurged enough, Lena imagined, on the cornflowers needed for her circlet and the blossoms to perfume her.

Lena stood in the center of the room as preparations were made, aimless and adrift. Some gave her tight, hurried smiles, but most rushed around her like a swarm of bees, transforming the room. There was a hearth on the far wall, opposite the entrance door. A small fire flickered quietly, left from last night, but the room still froze. Lena felt the cold, but only on her skin—beneath, she burned and raged and flamed.

The door heaved open again, and this time two women had to hold the chair that was being brought in. It was massive—engraved with runes and knots and branches of Yggdrasil. Lena knew it was where her father was to sit. Another pair of women entered holding a similarly large chair for Lena. The two chairs were set down gently, but with relief, directly in front of the hearth. Lena knew it would be rude for her to go sit in it now, but it was hard to restrain herself.

She stared at the pair of chairs. The one for her was dwarfed by her father's—simpler, smaller, and unassuming. Long, narrow tables somehow maneuvered their way inside with lots of groans and shouted instructions from their handlers. This was another weather provision. The wedding feast should have been outside, by torchlight; but even though the clear sky was beautiful during the day, it meant that tonight would be colder.

Lena examined the sleeves of her dress, which came to a hem perfectly at her wrist bones. The fabric at her chest was slightly loose, but it still felt suffocating. Her ankles ached already and no spectators had yet arrived.

The door swung open again, and this time, heaps of brisket and loaves of bread were carried inside. Lena was unsure of how anyone—including herself—was supposed to get through the first part of this ceremony with the warm, savory scent of the food wafting through the enclosed space. That was something of a comfort—the vows could not last forever, if they were the only thing holding back the guests from the wedding feast.

Lena tried to walk casually by the food tables, making sure nobody was looking in her direction before snatching a slice of bread. She shoved it into her mouth just as she heard her father pronounce her name.

She whirled around to find him in the doorframe.

The first man to enter the room today. The other women nodded to him, while Val motioned for them to finish up the last decorations. They filed out soon after, and Val walked briskly to Lena, giving her one final nod of approval after smoothing down her hair a final time.

"I will see you soon," she whispered.

Lena nodded, her mouth still too full of bread to respond verbally. Val followed the rest of the women outside so they could get dressed and ready for the ceremony. Fredrik watched Val leave, then closed the door behind him and strode over to Lena, also grabbing a hunk of bread. He gave her a wink, like they were in on some exciting secret.

"How are you feeling?" he asked, his mouth full of food.

Lena shrugged, keeping her face passive. She did not have to dignify him with a response. He waited for her to speak more, but once enough silence passed, he shrugged back at her and sauntered over to his chair: the bulking, massive one that nearly blotted out the hearth behind it.

"This should be interesting," he muttered. "My first time officiating the same wedding in which I'm giving away the bride."

He was right. The chief always did the marriage ceremonies for members of the village when he was present, but it was also customary for fathers to give away their daughters—hence the enormous chair that was designated for the father, where he sat until he was replaced by the husband after the rites were completed.

Lena swallowed down the last of her bread. "I will be glad when this is over with."

He tilted his head at her, relaxing into the armrests. "Will you? I thought you did not want this wedding. That you felt it would be an insult to your sister."

Her mouth hung open. "Wh—"

Fredrik cut her off with a grim smile. "You could have stopped this, Magdalena. If you'd only tried a little harder, a little faster."

She froze. Did he know something? Or did he merely mean she could have convinced the clan not to move forward with this marriage? Her skin itched, and blood roared in her ears. Fredrik motioned to the empty chair beside his, and she sat down automatically.

"Time to begin," he said. His voice sounded light and airy, like clouds in springtime—had she imagined his words before? She gaped at him as he stared at the doorway, the voices from outside growing louder and persistent. "This will be fun."

CHAPTER
SEVENTEEN

Lena knew this village was smaller than most she had heard of, with a settlement of about seventy people. It still seemed as if the stream entering the ceremony house might never end. Already, the sun began its descent, crashing down to the horizon after a blissful three hours of daylight. The door stayed open as the guests arrived, and Lena caught glimpses of blood red and singed orange cut between the shadows of the entering figures. Each of them held a small torch, which Lena half-feared might burn the whole place down. At least that might postpone the wedding.

With so much fire in the room, she could almost forget the growing winter asserting its claim on the village. It hurt to stare out at the gathering crowd taking their seats, with so many blazing dots of pure light. Her father looked over the guests with ease, greeting them by name and shouting pleasantries over the dull roar.

Lena twirled the same strand of her hair over and over again until her fingers turned white under its grasp. She knew they were waiting for the final guest—the important one. When Amal arrived, it would be the worst blessing imaginable. It would be a point of no return, but she also longed to glimpse the familiarity of his kind eyes.

Bejla stayed close, sitting at the far end of the front row, in case Lena needed anything during the ceremony. The youngest children sat on the floor as the chairs quickly filled up. They stared up at her in wonder, at the flower wreath and pretty dress. She tried to smile at them but found it easier to look elsewhere. Children could see through all sorts of lies and disguises, and Lena knew that if they stared too long at her, they would see all she had to hide.

At the edge of her vision, she saw her mother enter. Her golden hair was wrapped in a braid that twisted its way atop her head. Val beamed as she entered, looking to her daughter and husband only briefly before turning her focus to the gathered crowd. Her people. Lena sighed, tapping her feet. She wanted this over with. She never wanted it to happen. She glanced at her father, and heard his words clearly in her mind.

You could have prevented this, Magdalena.

She breathed through her nose, her eyes dancing across the tables of food. Where was Amal? Val made her way to the front, taking the seat beside Bejla. Her role in the ceremony had taken place last night in Freya's Circle and this morning as she prepared her daughter's appearance. Now, she stepped aside to let her husband finish the job. Lena watched her mother lean over to Bejla and whisper something. Bejla glanced up at Lena and laughed, nodding in agreement. Lena drummed her fingers across her armrest. She hated knowing she was the subject of words and conversations she could not hear.

The din of voices grew louder as the waiting continued. Lena watched as a discrete smile played across her father's lips, and then the door creaked open one last time. The noise in the room rushed out, as did the air from Lena's lungs.

Every head turned to the entrance. No light came in with Nana and Amal, for the sky was the deepest blue before black behind them, and they held no torches. Nana hobbled in first, looking far worse than the last time Lena had seen her only a few days ago. As she preceded her son, she used a steady oak branch to lean upon as she walked down a haphazard aisle carved between the chairs. Normally, the father of the husband would lead her to the front row, where they would sit in the designated seat beside the mother of the bride.

But it had only ever been just Nana, and she made her way by herself—albeit slowly—to her chair. Val reached over to clasp her hands, and they shared a solemn smile. Lena dared to look to the back of the room. Amal wore a sage-colored tunic she had never seen before, with threads of gold stitched into the front. His thick, dark hair was combed and oiled back, his beard trimmed and even. He did not look at her as he approached the hearth, nor did he smile.

Lena grasped her armrests tight, for they were the only things keeping her upright. Her chest seized. She should be sitting by her mother, not at this chair where Fressa would have sat—she could see her sister, her hazel eyes alight with adoration, Amal's meeting hers with equal fire across a room full of smiling people. It all played out for her, as if it were superimposed on the scene before her, in sickening, vivid color. Amal walked fast and sure-footed to Fressa, and held her hands like they were carved out of precious gold.

But here, and now, all Lena and Amal could do was try not to cry or run from this place. She blinked, and he was before her, standing in front of her and her father, in the empty space between their chairs. Fredrik smiled, though it did not reach his eyes. Lena was hit by the memory of Fredrik's arrival all those weeks ago—at how nervous Amal had been to see Fredrik, who had not yet known or approved of his engagement to his youngest daughter.

Amal did not look nervous now. His eyes were vacant, merely reflecting the firelight from the room, but desolate within. Fredrik stood, and it was strange to see that he was not all that much taller than Amal now. He used to tower over them all, a daunting hulk of a figure that said "chief" as well as any word could. But Amal was seventeen, and developed enough that their frames were comparable.

"Amal of Nana Freding," Fredrik said, voice booming through the room. Lena stared at Amal's feet, at the polished-leather shoes that accompanied his wedding outfit. "You are here to accept and commit to Freya's domain by taking Magdalena of Val Freding as your wife. Yes?"

Amal must have remembered that he too might be chief one day, because his voice sounded far richer and louder than his downcast face suggested. "Yes."

Fredrik looked down to his daughter, and as she rose, he turned back to the crowd. "This part is a bit odd, is it not? I do two jobs this evening."

The crowd laughed at his aside, appreciating any levity that came with such a ridiculous ceremony. Still, she wondered how many of them harbored resentment for his prolonged absences and for stealing away some of their husbands and sons on far-off raids.

A fresh wave of resentment rippled off of Lena as

she stood. Her father gently guided her arm so she stood directly in front of Amal, only a couple feet away from him. She stared at the ground, at how their shoes pointed right at each other.

"Magdalena," Fredrik said, mostly under his breath. She inhaled. Looked up into Amal's eyes. Exhaled. He nodded slightly at her, as if to say *we will survive this.* "You are here to accept and commit to Freya's domain by taking Amal of Nana Freding as your husband. Yes?"

Lena was certain she had never seen Amal's eyes so dark. She stared at his forehead instead as she forced herself to say, "Yes."

"Excellent," her father said. A few of the children shuffled from the ground, readjusting. It must be cold and uncomfortable, Lena thought. And there was plenty of food waiting to be eaten—her mother had insisted there be a *proper* wedding feast, despite the fears of rations to come with the weather as it was. Fredrik cast a silencing glare their way before continuing. "Join hands."

Lena reached out, but Amal did not reach out far enough, and she had to gently guide him closer to her. His fingertips were freezing, and his nails held a bluish tint. She gripped them tightly, hoping she could convey all the commiseration and regret she felt through her touch alone. He squeezed back, once, and she offered a small, grateful smile.

"Repeat after me." Fredrik looked between the two

of them. "What is mine is yours. What is yours is mine. From here until the twilight of our worlds, my soul shall not be undone from yours."

In stilting, awkward fragments, Amal and Lena did their best to repeat the words in unison. They avoided eye contact relentlessly until the last few words. For a moment, Lena's heart swelled. Not out of romantic love, but of the thought of her and Amal's souls bonded together through something that transcended time and circumstance.

She gave him a half-smile until she realized the room was still oppressively silent. Even the youngest child was completely quiet, and only the soft rushing of torch flame resounded. Amal stared back at her, his lips growing thinner. Fredrik cleared his throat. Lena looked to him, confused. He subtly jerked his head back to Amal, and her heart tumbled down and out of herself.

Of course.

She had to kiss him.

Lena swallowed, aggressively evading Amal's eyes. She would have to pretend this was someone—anyone— else. She would just pretend she was not Lena. Or she could try both. Lena slowly reached out her hands to grasp at Amal's vest for balance. This was too slow. Too miserable. Better to burn fast.

She pulled him closer and tilted her head up in one motion. Lena had certainly seen her sister do this to him enough times. Even if Lena had never kissed anyone before, she hoped she could do this right. Her lips collided with his—mostly. She had definitely missed half of his mouth, but it was too late. He did not move against her, and she yanked back as fast as she could.

Lena's stomach roiled. She resisted the urge to wipe at her mouth with everyone staring at them, and with one apologetic glance to Amal, she could tell he was grappling with the same sensation. He was completely frozen, his back ramrod straight.

"Well," Fredrik said. "The vows are fulfilled."

Lena's mouth went dry. She felt no different. Was she supposed to? The ceremony still had more components left, and she would not be officially considered *married* to him until tomorrow morning, after . . .

She clutched at her neck as subtly as she could. The bitter, acidic taste of vomit touched her throat but she swallowed it roughly down. Amal and Lena were turned to face the crowd—their first introduction as a couple. The clan erupted into applause. Her mother looked proud, her eyes glowing with fierce love. Nana sat beside her, clapping in slow, measured beats. She seemed satisfied, if not happy. Her lips were not upturned in a smile, but she stared at her son and Lena with a relaxed expression, her property and family's standing preserved. Lena jutted out her chin, her lips still burning and poisonous to herself.

The wedding was not yet over.

Blissfully, the crowd was quite ready to turn their attention from the wedding to the food. Lena exhaled as most of the eyes moved away from her and Amal. Still, they were to eat before the others, and Fredrik led them over to the food, walking between them and holding their hands. Lena tried to catch Amal's glance over her father's shoulder, but his gaze was fixed straight ahead on nothing in particular.

Her stomach sank. Did he hate her? The bond between their souls was so irreversibly altered, marred, changed. But he had always known—or at least, suspected—that he was meant to marry Lena, and he had never told her. Frustration simmered and she fought off angry tears, though she knew intrinsically that he had only withheld the information to protect her.

The torches the guests held were either hung along the walls or extinguished. The temperature had already dropped.

A woman in front of Lena already had a plate outstretched to her. She took it with a crumbling smile, offering her thanks. Her voice cracked, even though it was a whisper. The plate shook wildly in her hands, and she set it down with a clatter at her spot at the head of the other empty table reserved for the family and couple. Amal touched her wrist gently, a subtle reminder that she was not alone in her sadness. But it was also a dismissal—an assurance that it would be dealt with later.

Always later.

She sat down hard in her chair at the head of the table, and Amal took the seat beside her. On Lena's side, her parents sat next to each other, with Nana opposite them. They seemed lighthearted and casual, and not at all like the world had shifted beneath their feet. Lena tried to taste the word out on her tongue—*wife*. She cut a sidelong glance to Amal, who poked at his brisket with little interest.

Lena had been so hungry before the ceremony, but now she only ate when her mother urged her to. A few other close family friends took up the seats at the far end of the table, while the rest of the guests conglomerated around the chairs in the rest of the room. Hardly anyone spoke to Amal and Lena, too preoccupied with their own conversations and laughter. Amal and Lena certainly did not speak to each other.

Time stretched through the meal, and Lena readjusted her cornflower circlet several times out of a wretched combination of anxiety and boredom. Then, all too soon, her father was standing up and motioning to Gunnar across the room. He stood with a smile, and some part of Lena took comfort in his presence. Gunnar pulled out his pan flute and played a lively jaunt that Lena recognized from weddings past. The older couples began to clap in their seats, urging the children and younger couples to dance. Now, expectant faces turned to Amal and Lena.

Amal cleared his throat, pushing back his chair. He offered a hand to Lena. She looked up to him for a long moment, but his eyes were grim and resigned. Lena used to enjoy dancing—but now it seemed too frivolous, attention-seeking, and monotonous at the same time. Especially if everyone would be staring right at her.

But it would be far worse attention if she stayed sitting, and so she grabbed Amal's hand. She rose, and Amal led her to where the others had already formed a large circle after moving chairs to the sides of the room. Lena and Amal held out their hands, expecting to join the chain—but the others laughed and beckoned for them to stand in the center.

The effect was disorienting. All those familiar faces flew around Amal and Lena, fabrics soaring, shrill voices raised in song. They moved fast and faster still. Bejla broke off from the dancers, grabbing Lena's hands and pulling her in a tight circle. She probably only meant to include Lena and make her smile, but Lena could barely suppress the growing nausea and confusion she felt as she stared into her eyes. Lena backed away with a polite grin, feigning a desire to be closer to Amal. Her circlet lay askance across her head, and he reached out absently to correct it.

After a couple songs, Amal and Lena were able to communicate with one look. They edged their way out of the circle and returned to the pair of seats by the hearth. Since the male one was so much bigger, the height difference between Amal and Lena felt daunting and unfamiliar. Before them, the dancing continued. The flute and voices clashed in a cacophony, and Lena rested her chin on one of her hands.

The music changed. It shifted like the breeze, from abrasive boldness into slow, sweet notes ringing out in a minor key. The effect consumed the entire room—even beneath the heavy fabric of her long sleeves, Lena felt the hair on her arms raise. She could see Amal tense, and see the short breaths heaving out of his chest. This was the song that played when the ceremony left this room.

She clenched her jaw hard as the attention returned to the two of them. Amal's arm leapt over to Lena's hand like a viper, but Lena welcomed the assurance. They would get through this together. Val strode toward them, her expression unreadable. She came to a stop before them, the somber music still piercing through the stuffy room. Lena stood, meeting her mother's eyes. Behind Val, the maidens of the village each took hold of one of the torches along the walls. They held them up, barely avoiding each other's elaborate, loose hairstyles.

Lena saw Amal rise to his feet beside her, still holding her hand.

"It is time for Amal to take you to your new home," Val announced. Even though she said *you,* it was still her chief's wife voice—the one catered to the audience, and not a person. "He will carry you, and we will follow you."

Lena glanced over to Amal. This was always a part of weddings Lena had loved watching—the bride fitting perfectly within her new husband's arms, the two of them laughing and drinking in the sight of each other as they entered their home as a married couple for the first time.

Awkwardly, she looped her arms across his neck. Amal's hands slid down to her waist, she gave a graceless jump up, and he caught her. Despite it all, her lips quirked in a suppressed laugh. He shifted his arms, one beneath her knees and one around her back. She held tight to his neck, terrified of falling, but he seemed steady enough. His arms did not shake or tremble. Amal had always been stronger than Lena gave him credit for.

"Shall we?" he murmured under his breath.

She raised her eyebrows. What choice was there? He walked forward carefully, Lena bouncing slightly against his chest. She stared over his shoulder as the maidens began to follow them with their fire. It was definitely ominous. She wondered if Amal could walk a lot faster, or just run.

When they stepped outside, the air burned her

lungs—but it was such a relief to be out of that room that she felt liberated for a few steps until the cold lashed into her dress. Her body convulsed despite her best efforts to stay steady, and she curled into Amal instinctively.

"Almost there," he whispered. "Almost done."

Tonight would not be as unusual for Amal as it would for Lena, for they were moving into his home—Nana had said days prior that she would move into one of the rooms of the apothecary hut. *All the closer to my herbs,* she'd joked. *To keep me alive.*

If or when her father passed away before them, Lena and Amal would replace Val and Fredrik in their home, the one Lena and Fressa had grown up in. For the foreseeable future, she would be just next door.

Maybe things would not be so different, Lena thought, as the fires followed them home. Maybe she could pretend she and Amal were just . . . spending a lot of extra time with each other. She could survive until she could fix this. Lena's eyes roamed across the faces of the smiling girls. Any one of them might be the answer she was looking for. It would be hard, yes, and sad—but Fressa was the one who could stop this winter. Lena was certain of it. What chief's daughter would not act in that interest?

Amal stopped moving. They had arrived at his house, and the procession following them came to a halt, fanning out around them. Val walked toward them, parting through the girls. She wore a strange expression—pride muddied with caution. Her hair and face glowed gold in the firelight.

"Carry her across your threshold, Amal," she instructed. "And bring out the wreath when it is done."

Lena bit her tongue. She and Amal had never discussed this in words, though she knew nothing would actually happen. Now, with every pair of eyes staring at her, thinking they knew exactly what was about to happen, she felt faint. Amal's arms shuddered, though he kept his jaw clenched. A brief wash of panic hit her. Maybe they should have talked about this before, explicitly. What if—

No.

He would never.

Still, when he raised one leg to kick the door open and carried her across the threshold, her heart rate only accelerated. Lena thought she would be happy to see the door shut behind them, away from their eyes for the first time all week. But even without their gazes on them, the fact that they were *thinking* of her and Amal . . .

She leapt away from him as soon as he set her down.

He sighed, dragging a hand through his hair. "Lena—"

"Listen," she whispered, her voice hysterical even to her own ears. "I don't want—we cannot—"

"I'm not going to touch you," he said, voice low and angry. "Why would you even think I could?"

She grabbed at the sides of her face, shaking her head. "I am sorry."

They both stood far from each other, despite his home's modest size. Someone must have visited the bed to prepare it for tonight—rose and thyme lay scattered across the blankets. She hastily shoved them to the floor, sitting down hard on the bed. It was more comfortable than her pelts back home, at least.

After a few moments, he sat down too, their backs facing each other. "How long do you think we should wait before I go back out there?"

Lena flushed, even though he wasn't looking at her. "Did—didn't you and Fressa ever?

Amal was silent for a few moments more. "Too risky."

She hummed her agreement, trying to see what her new home—her *very temporary* home, she reminded herself—looked like. It was familiar enough, for she had visited Amal a number of times growing up. But she had not been back in a few months, and it looked very different in the dark.

"Besides, we thought it would not be too long," he said, with a bitter laugh.

"I know," Lena said. The silence between them, at least, felt not as charged or tense anymore. She reached up to her head and pulled off the wreath. The cornflowers sagged, dull and wilted. "I think you should go out now."

He stood, taking the wreath from her. "I cannot say they'll think I am the epitome of manliness, but all right."

She smirked, watching him approach the doorway. Amal swung it open and flung the wreath into the crowd of onlooking girls. He did not pause to watch who caught it. Closing the door one last time, he leaned his forehead against it for a long moment. His chest shuddered enough that Lena could see it through the dark.

"You can cry if you want to," she murmured. "It's just me."

There had been a time—a long time—growing up, before Fressa folded into their friendship, where it had just been Lena and Amal, after all. He nodded, wiping at his eyes, but made no sound. She stood up and moved to the door, as if he were a wounded animal. Tentatively, she reached her arms around him, resting the side of her face against his back.

"I'm so sorry," she whispered, her voice thick. "I can fix this."

His body went taut beneath her. "What do you mean?"

She sighed, releasing him. Her explanations would be lost on him. "I just mean—I'm sorry, okay? But we can make this work."

He turned around, facing her with doubt clouding his eyes. "Oh?"

"Nobody has to know!" she said, her voice taking on fervor. "Right? Nothing has to change between us. We just have more responsibilities around the village, and more expectations, but—"

"It's those expectations, Lena." Amal moved past her, falling back on the bed and lying down. He stretched his legs across the bed's length, folding his arms across his stomach. It was a relaxed gesture, but his voice held the tension of a primed arrow. "We cannot repeat tonight for forever."

This will not be forever, Lena thought. *Believe me.*

"What? You mean have a whole wedding ceremony every night?" she asked, trying to keep her tone light and airy. She moved over to the other side of the bed, sitting primly on the edge.

Amal sighed. "Lena. You must know what I mean."

She pulled her arms around herself, shutting her eyes. He couldn't be suggesting what she thought he was. "What—I don't—"

"Lena." His voice, soft and pleading and brutal, wrought tears from her closed eyes. "We will have to eventually. They will wonder, they will pry, if you do not . . ."

"Oh, gods," she managed. All this time, she'd leaned heavily upon the unspoken agreement that everything between them would be an act. A show that they could pull off because they knew and loved each other, but not a show that would ever exist behind closed doors. "Even you? What will Fressa say?"

"Do *not*." Amal sat up then, the tension roiling within him finally escaping. "Do not speak to me of what she would say."

Lena covered her mouth, trying to conceal the cries wracking at her core. He had not balked at her use of *will* instead of *would,* and she wished badly then that he would ask her what she meant. That he would ask her where she went that night—that night that felt so long ago now, where her greatest, only hope melded so completely to her darkest fears.

She swallowed back the tears with anger. Fury at Amal, for buckling under the pressure of their clan's expectations. Rage at Hela, with all her talk of balance and maintenance, as if finding her sister were a simple act of keeping a scale even. In a vehemence that scared even her, she blamed her parents and Nana for arranging all of this to begin with, and dredging it up from the ground so soon after her own sister was taken.

How could they do this to Fressa? To her?

Lena leaned back onto this new bed that she and Amal were to share. Everyone in the clan believed she had given herself to Amal within these walls tonight. He had already shifted to lie on his side, his back facing her. She mirrored his image, staring into the dark wall beside her bed. Her limbs shook slightly, from the cold and the anger.

There was much she could not understand or comprehend, but she knew this anger. It was the fire that burned her alive, but kept her alive. And she would let it consume her if she had to. She and Amal had gone too far already, and Lena's inaction was the root of it all. Lena wondered again of her father's cryptic words before the wedding, and she knew this would have to be the last night of her cowardice and weakness.

Fire burned bright within Lena, but she still felt cold. The endless winter settled around her, burying her under mountains and mountains of snow.

When sleep came, it brought a dream so seemingly ordinary that Lena slipped into it like a pair of well-worn boots.

She was five years old again, and Lena watched from the shadows as Nana knelt over a coughing man. The man was old and nameless through Lena's young eyes, and he would not stop coughing. Lena even saw small bits of blood fly from his mouth. She wanted to tell Nana that some was on her face, but Nana was very busy.

Lena stayed put, under strict instructions not to interfere.

She glanced at the tables of herbs and remedies, wishing one of them could help.

"The good ones are on the tops of the tables," Nana had explained to her solemnly, weeks before. "You must only use those. Do not touch the bad ones, even if some look pretty. I keep them hanging here, way up high, so only I can use them. Understand?"

Lena had nodded, though she did not understand. She was always told their job was to heal and restore. What would they need bad remedies for?

But Lena trusted Nana and stayed put, waiting for any instructions that might come. She stayed there all afternoon, watching as Nana walked fast between the man and the tables until the light outside turned shades of pink and orange. The man had stopped coughing, Lena realized, and she looked back. Nana stood above him, her face paler and more tired than Lena had ever seen. She did not know what was wrong, or why her instructor had gone so very still.

"Nana?" she asked, her small voice quavering. It was the first word she had spoken in hours.

"Go, Lena." Nana's voice sounded stronger than she looked. Lena's eyes stung. She felt like she was being scolded, even though she'd done nothing wrong. "You need to go. Get your parents."

And so Lena had left, running the short distance back to her home. She knew something had happened. Something bad and big. She couldn't understand what, but the ill feeling took all night to leave her. Fressa wanted to play—it was summer, and the sun was still making colors outside. But Lena stayed in, hugging her knees to her chest as her parents walked briskly next door.

They had said that Nana's job was an important one. Lena thought "important" meant something big and exciting, but now she wondered what else the title held.

CHAPTER
EIGHTEEN

Lena was surprised she had slept at all, but she rose to the sound of a distant rooster crowing. Her eyes slammed open, her chest aching. She relaxed slightly. It was just one of her neighbor's roosters. But she couldn't help remembering the fireside stories from her childhood.

The loudest rooster cry. The permanent winter. Ragnarok.

She exhaled, taking a steadying breath. The dream she'd had of Nana and the coughing man already seeped through her fingers like sand, but the shape of the scene stayed firm in her mind. She felt incredibly lucid and disoriented at the same time. Amal slept beside her, a familiar figure in the oddest of places. It was strange, certainly, to wake up beside him—but not as strange as she'd feared. But the blinding anger she'd felt after their conversation last night had not faded.

Lena grasped at the side of the bed, her fingers white with strain. Her feet touched the cold ground before she realized she was standing up, and she braced herself against the bedframe for a moment, making sure Amal still slept. She was still wearing her wedding dress, but her other clothes were back with her parents. So was Fressa's blade, but it was still dark and black outside.

That did not stop—or rather, could no longer stop—the village from stirring to life. She opened the door slowly, peering outside to make sure there were no lingering or persistent spectators. But most of those awake seemed to cling to the snow-clad outskirts of the village, pulling along horses or bags of grain.

Lena slid outside, closing the door as quietly as she could. Maybe it was just because she'd woken up so recently, but her mind felt choked and distant. She was hel-bent on eliminating the reality around her—her new role as Amal's wife, the ice crunching beneath her boots. Fressa's absence.

Lena blinked, realizing she had already crossed the distance between the house and the apothecary hut. Her heart slowed, but she raised her hand in a fist. She knocked on the door of the room in which she had spent half her childhood. Nana's home, now. Lena kept her fist clenched at her side as the door cracked open a few moments later. Nana had to lean outside to see through the dark with her clouding vision.

"Lena?" she asked. Her voice held the fragile, unsteady weakness of the first layer of ice across a lake in winter. It would take nothing more than a light touch to shatter. "Is that you?"

"Yes," Lena replied evenly.

Nana took another long moment to reply. Lena could not see well through the dark, but the thick wrinkles lining Nana's face creased enough for her to register. "I . . . I did not think we had training today."

"We do." Lena kept her words short and succinct. Somewhere deep within her own mind, Lena felt like screaming at herself to run far from here.

"Oh, I—I must have forgotten," Nana murmured, turning around to walk back inside. She left the door open, so Lena assumed the invitation. She entered, her heart calm and steady, her core numb. Lena knew Nana's mind was slower in the morning, but it was still surprising to so easily convince her of a lie.

Nana's gait was uneven and painfully slow to watch. "How are you, my dear?"

Lena braced her hands along the edge of the table—the table of *good* remedies and herbs and plants. "Considering the events of yesterday, I would say . . . not well." Lena meant the words, but they came out too nonchalant.

She turned and saw Nana's face in the dim firelight. Nana frowned before nodding in recognition. "Of course. Yes. You looked beautiful."

Lena stared down at the ivory fabric flowing down to the ground. "I do not feel beautiful."

Nana's head tilted in confusion, and Lena swallowed back choice words. Did Nana not remember the horror Lena had voiced when she first heard of the arrangement? She smashed her hands across the table's surface, relishing the brief flash of surprise that rippled across Nana's face. Lena would make her understand.

"This was your plan all along," Lena said. "Was it not? What about when my father brought Amal back with him from Baghdad? When you saw him, what was it you felt? Did you see, even then, your chance at security without a husband? Your chance of securing him for a guaranteed future as a chief's daughter's husband? For comfort in the last months of your old, withered life?"

Nana backed away from her, and Lena gasped a breath. The onslaught of questions had rushed out of her, pent up too long. She tried to inhale again, but she could not catch her breath. Lena drowned, standing upright and speaking the words she had buried too deep. Here they were, unearthed, but morphed by the too-long darkness.

"You—you must have known how I would feel. How your son would feel. And now," Lena sucked in air again, her chest still tight and aching. "You took Amal away from Fressa. What am I supposed to say to her? What am I supposed to—?"

Lena cut herself off. She had to breathe. She felt her own face, tracing her hands down her cheeks, but she found no tears. Nothing at all. Nana stood far from her now. Her mentor did not look at her with fear, but with pity.

"Oh, Lena." Nana stared at her with clouded eyes. "You speak of your sister as if she is still here with us."

Lena barked a short laugh, blood rushing to her head. "Not in this world."

Nana's brow creased again, the lines around her mouth drawing in. Lena thought it was regret playing across her face, but now she saw it was confusion.

"What are you doing here, Lena? I did not think we were training today."

Lena's mouth fell open. Was Nana that far gone? A ray of pity cut through the dark redness of her anger. But it did not kill the rage—the fury that scared even her. "Do you not remember?" Lena asked, her voice so quiet that Nana leaned in. "I told you last week. I tried to make that remedy you told me of. The one for headaches in the front of the mind."

Lena walked over to the table. And she looked up. Hanging and hovering above all the good was the bad. She reached up and grabbed a handful of white flowers, but her fingers began to shake. Her breath caught, nausea swelling up inside her. Lena had done this before, she reminded herself. It was Nana or her sister. There was no in between. This was never going to be an easy decision, and Lena reeled. She focused on the words Hela had instructed her with. Over and over again, Lena thought *Nana or Fressa*.

It was difficult—unspeakably so. But there was no contest when she looked at it that way. And if the mind was gone, what was really left? Bile rose in her throat as she smashed the tiny blossoms with Nana's stone pestle. She gathered some herbs from the table and mixed it in a small bowl.

"Oh, yes," Nana murmured, her gaze elsewhere. "I'd forgotten about that."

"It's all right," Lena said, making her voice soft. Her vocal cords ached from her outburst. "I have it here with me. How about you test it for me? To make sure I did it right?" Lena set down the pestle, and held out the bowl. She thought her arm would shake. It did not. "Go on."

Nana accepted the bowl, not quite looking at Lena. She was definitely not lucid if she had noticed nothing amiss as Lena mixed lethal hemlock into the root right in front of her. This, then, was a kindness, was it not? Her son's future was secure, with or without her. And what was an apothecary who could not see the small petals of hemlock in a paste gathered in her own fingers?

Nana reached into the bowl, dragging out the pale paste and putting it to her lips. Lena seized, then, her mind settling upon the rosy memory of some childhood summer afternoon, fingers tracing flowers and roots, Nana's gentle, lilting tone reminding her of their names and functions.

"Don't—" she gasped.

But the bowl already clattered to the floor, shattering across the stony floor. Bile rose further and further until Lena could not hold it back. She turned to her side, her stomach emptying itself violently, staining the front of her white dress. And at the same time, Nana crashed to the floor in a series of falls. First, she doubled over to the table, holding it with what little strength reigned in her arms. Then to her knees on the freezing floor, before falling all the way down, one arm splayed away from her, the other trapped beneath her own body.

Lena's hands flew to her mouth, and she retched again and again, though nothing was left to come up. The warm salt of tears bled into her mouth, and she could not rip her gaze from the floor.

Fressa.

For the first time, her sister's name did not bring comfort. Or purpose. Or assurance.

Lena sobbed, the sound cracking through her, any innocence left in her flying out from the gaping hole. Nana's last breaths came slow and soft through the room where Lena had spent over half her life. Lena had fallen to the ground at some point, but saw nothing through her tears—she could think of nothing, really, save for the hysteria exploding through all her veins. When had it all come to this?

The room fell silent. Her mentor was dead.

Most of Lena was too.

She stayed on the ground for what could have been hours, tears and numbness chasing each other in a vicious cycle. Lena wanted to be outside of her body. She wanted to claw her way into Valhalla and take her sister back, to find some proof for why she had done this. How she had become this.

This time, the thought of her sister—trapped and alone—brought with it a thread of practicality. She pulled herself over the floor to the shards of the bowl—it had split into four pieces, which Lena retrieved and tossed into the hearth. Lena rose on shaking legs and grabbed a ragged cloth from the table, making herself lean down and turn over Nana's body, which already felt limp and lifeless beneath her. Lena said her sister's name over and over, out loud, as she wiped away the traces of hemlock from Nana's mouth and face. Then she threw that cloth into the fire as well, and sat back on her haunches, waiting until the flames dissolved it.

Finally, she rose, on legs not quite strong enough to stand. Lena leaned her weight on the table, gasping until she nearly made herself sick again. Tears still flowed from her, and she wiped at them furiously before realizing they might be the only thing standing between her and execution. She took a few staggering steps backward, letting the tears slip down and off her chin.

Lena walked back and back again, feeling behind her for the door. She flung it open and entered the pale blue of a late dawn. More people milled around the village streets, which would help. Lena pointed to the apothecary house, letting screams tear through her, and she shouted like she had on the morning that she had found no pulse, no beating life beneath her sister's skin.

"What—what happened, exactly?"

Her mother sat across from her. Lena was wrapped in a blanket, sitting at the table back in her parents' home. How strange to be back so soon after her marriage. How strange to have ever left at all. Lena wrapped her fingers tight in the wool, and shook her head again—a gesture so practiced and repeated over the past couple hours that it came as automatically as blinking.

"I just walked over. I thought we had training in the morning," Lena whispered. "Nana . . . was just on the ground. She was not breathing."

Lena did not have to try to give her words their

scratchy, mournful remorse. She felt the weight of what she had done. It crushed her into the ground, and the only thing keeping her from falling through the earth was the hope that this would be enough. This would be the deed that saved them.

If only she could escape from her village's watchful, piteous gaze.

She knew they must be wondering and whispering amongst themselves about just how terrible and unlucky and mysterious it was that Lena had stumbled across her sister *and* her mother-in-law's dead body.

Lena had not stayed to see Amal's reaction. It would have shattered her. The thought of it—the endless imagination of it—broke her enough. Lena had lost a sister and then lost her mentor to get her back. But Amal had lost his fiancée and now his mother. Lena had never considered anyone to be more brokenhearted than her, but Amal was a serious contender.

She knew there was no coming back from this. Not really. Lena could be his wife no longer—his rightful one would return. Had to return. And if not, Lena had no reason or right to stay, after everything. She half-expected Fressa to walk into the house at any moment—because if this had not been enough, what would be? Her mother still stared at her, hazel eyes narrowed in what Lena hoped was concern. Lena looked down at the floor, wondering if she was not doing a convincing enough job. Could her mother tell what had happened?

Val grasped the side of Lena's face, pulling her in to kiss her forehead. "I am sorry, my love. So sorry. We knew it would come soon, but to happen *today* . . ." She shook her head. "It is so strange."

Lena wiped at her nose. "I know."

Val sighed, dropping her hand from Lena's face. "I should go to your father. He is telling the village now. You can stay here if you want."

Lena nodded, sniffling. "Wh—where is he?"

"In the ceremony house," she answered, bundling herself up with a wolf-fur pelt.

"All right," Lena said. "Maybe I will stop by later."

"That might be nice," Val said, cautiously. "If you are up to it." She paused a moment to study Lena again. Her gaze was meant to be comforting, or sorrowful, Lena knew. But she felt like she was being studied and seen through. When the door closed behind her mother, Lena sagged in relief.

She waited a few minutes. Lena tried to stand, but her legs would not stop shaking. She lowered herself back to the edge of her cot, putting her head between her knees and trying hard to breathe. *This is how it ends,* she told herself. *One way or another.*

With that, she managed to rise to her feet. She made her way to the door, then walked to the back of her house and took the long way to the river, evading visibility from the village. It seemed empty and quiet, anyway, the inhabitants either with her father and Nana's body in the ceremony house, or too tired to rise from last night's late, mead-filled festivities.

Lena walked unsteadily at first, but the closer she got to the river, the more her feet tore at the ground beneath her. When she caught a flash of the bright white hide of the hel-horse she had seen so often in her dreams and mind, the heaviness cloaking her heart started to fade. If Hela had sent her horse for Lena, something must have gone right.

But then again, the hel-horse had come for that trader Jannik's death. Was it Lena or Hela who had summoned it?

There was no time to ponder that, so she quickly swiveled around to see if Bejla was watching with whatever directions Odin had given her. Lena gave herself a running start, then slung herself across the hel-horse's flank and squeezed her thighs, urging him onward.

The tilting, erratic gait did not faze her anymore. She stared down the river, no longer marveling at how the horse made no sound walking across the frozen river. Or how he had walked across all those weeks ago, when there was hardly any ice at all. Lena kept her eyes peeled ahead of her, trying to detect the moment when Midgard faded away into the shrouded darkness of Helheim.

She did not blink, but still discerned no transition or change that her mind could process. The bleak light of Midgard was replaced—in a movement not meant for mortal eyes—by the unsettling darkness of Helheim, which was total and complete, but somehow still penetrable. Lena gripped the reins hard, keeping her gaze averted from the writhing coils of souls surrounding her. Was Nana among them? Lena swallowed back tears. This was the worst part of traveling through Helheim—the knowledge of breathing in the realm that you would enter one day forever.

In a movement as strange and sudden as switching from Midgard to Helheim, the throne of Hela appeared in front of Lena. The goddess seemed almost happy to see her, though it was hard to tell with half of her face decayed.

"Magdalena," she breathed. "I can see the soul of Nana now—such a beautiful one. Heavy with love and intelligence and dedication."

The words were promising, and Lena's heart surged with hope—though the reminder of Nana's goodness was not lost on her. Lena dismounted, walking as close to the goddess as she dared. Hela stayed silent for too long, her eyebrow furrowing in confusion.

"But she is old, Lena," Hela whispered. "So old."

Lena swallowed, the sadness in Hela's voice pulling her under. "So? I thought bodies did not matter—"

Hela sighed, her fingers tracing the human bridge of her nose, as if she were suppressing an outburst. "From the start, Lena, I have explained that this is about an *exchange*."

"Right," Lena rushed. "Like evening out a scale. But Nana is—was—kind like Fressa, and brave, and smart."

"They are far too different, Lena. In age, skills, everything." Hela pinched the bridge of her nose again, releasing a controlled breath. Her voice rang out in brittle tones. "You think Odin would not notice that?"

Lena opened her mouth, but had too many questions to choose from. Most, she could barely articulate or wrap her head around. "What does that even mean? Valhalla is enormous, isn't it?"

"How many warriors do you imagine are still fighting in their seventies? She would be obviously out of place, no matter how large Odin's hall is," Hela said. "Valhalla is Odin's attempt to create some semblance of a defense against what is yet to come. Soon to come, if we can get your sister free. We are so close, Lena, but only you can do this part of the job. You need to find someone as similar to Fressa as possible, and we can make this work. We have to. We're so close that I can almost see our sister."

Lena's mind went silent. She tilted her head. "Our?"

"*Your*," Hela rushed, flipping her hand dismissively. "Your sister."

Lena nodded once, but her stomach was leaden. She needed to get out of here. The gods were keeping something from her—something big.

"I should go," Lena whispered, backing away to the hel-horse.

"You should," Hela said. Lena felt the goddess staring at her, but she needed to get out. "Do not give up now, Lena."

Lena did not reply, and did not look to Hela. She mounted the hel-horse and quickly flicked the reins, even though she knew by now that the horse would take her back to the valley. She flicked the reins again and again, urging him to run faster, and did not stop until her valley emerged once more.

It was dark again when she returned. Had she been gone so long? She did not understand how time passed between the worlds, but then again, the light lasted shorter and shorter. After dismounting the hel-horse, Lena did not even look behind her to see him leave Midgard. She ran from the freezing riverbanks, the slippery ice slowing her pace.

Once she returned to the village, lit by a few smoke-trailed fires, she ran harder and faster until she arrived in front of the apothecary house. Lena did not last long, tearing her gaze away so she wouldn't throw up. She hesitated, wondering if she should enter Amal's house or her parents'. Maybe she should try to find Bejla again, trapped as they both were by the gods, and try to figure out what was happening.

Tears of frustration welled up. There was no place she belonged in. Not anymore. Amal did not deserve her, her parents barely knew her, and she despised who she had become. She wanted to break through her own body. She clapped a hand across her mouth to muffle the sound of her crying, but it was too much.

"Lena?" Amal spoke not from his home, but from behind her. His eyes were red, and his skin blotchy and pale. He ran to her, throwing his arms around her. She sobbed against him, clinging to him and hating herself for doing so. "I just came from the ceremony house." His voice held the strange, simultaneous thickness and fragility that she had not heard since Fressa died. "Your father said it was you who found—" He stopped himself, and took another gulping breath. "I looked for you all day."

She nodded into his shoulder. "I'm sorry. I'm sorry, I'm sorry—"

He shushed her, but she couldn't stop muttering the words. His chest shook, and she knew he was crying. How often had they held each other in their lives? So many celebrations and weddings and funerals over their lives, and none of them holding any sort of weight anymore. There was familiarity in his arms, but it was only glimpsed. The Amal and Lena they had been with Fressa were worlds away now. She held the shadow of him, and no longer quite knew who reigned beneath this skin of hers. Lena gasped, unable to catch her breath through her tears.

"What are we supposed to do?" Amal whispered. She shook her head, still more tears spilling over. "What do we do now?"

It was a terrible scale to balance.

Amal believed Lena had found his mother's dead body, but Amal was the one who had lost his mother. Who had suffered the worst trauma in the village's eyes? Lena tried to comfort Amal, to hold him close to her in private while playing the role of his supportive, attentive wife in public. But Amal asked too many questions and inquiries into her state of mind, fearing that her withdrawnness had shifted from concerning to deeply troubling, and that finding another cold corpse had sent her over an edge. Or a waterfall—somewhere there could be no backtracking or retracing.

She barely made it through the next day, confining herself to her and Amal's home, while the others milled in and out. Sometimes, she heard Amal speak of funeral arrangements, but she tried to stay hidden when visitors came inside. Lena's mind rang a deafening, splitting tone—she spoke barely a few sentences, ate only enough to keep herself breathing, thinking of nothing but her sister and Bejla's words and Hela's misspeak—*our sister*.

Then spiraling, she would grow furious at herself for not thinking of Nana.

And the cycle began anew, rotating viciously through what was left of her, taking more and more out of Lena with each passage. She stayed in bed, incapacitated with indecision and confusion. Amal took the opposite route, eventually, wiping away the tear tracks from his face often and braving the world outside and ahead.

When he allowed himself to lie down, he had to do so beside her. There was nowhere else for either of them, though Lena had already asked her mother if it would be okay for her to return. She'd been met with strict refusal.

Their bed was small, barely long enough to contain his long limbs and both of their broad shoulders. Lena thought he would lie with his back to her, as he'd done on their wedding night, but he faced her, and she reached out her hand instinctively, tracing the side of his jaw. He grabbed her hand and she expected him to shove her off, but he pulled her closer.

Nothing stirred between them but a need for warmth. To stave off the winter still settled around them, and to remind them that there was someone out there whose heart pulsed with life and love for them. She lay against his side, a hand stretched across his torso. He held the back of her head with his free hand, stroking her hair until he fell asleep.

Lena could not sleep. She knew with certainty that she had never before felt this breed of exhaustion buried in her bones—rooted deep into her core, embedded into her very sense of self, however dwindling that was.

A harsh knock on the door woke Amal with a jolt, and Lena's eyes blinked open, though she had not been asleep. She untangled herself from him, giving him the space to remove himself from the bed. He winced against the cold, but rushed to the door and pulled it open. Fast, frantic tones rushed into the house in whispered tongues. Lena's eyes drifted open and shut, pulled along by a tide of unrelenting fatigue that would never fully take her under. She wished it would.

Then, Amal stood above her, his jaw set but his eyes leaking. "We need to go," he said. He had never commanded her to do anything before, and couldn't really, but Lena felt herself start to sit up without thinking. "My—my mother's body is missing."

His voice cracked and shattered as he spoke the words. Lena's panic surged, washing away some of the tiredness. Why would Nana's body be gone? She had not touched it. Had Hela done something? She slung her feet over the edge of the bed, and laced up her boots with fragile fingers.

"Amal," she whispered, as he touched the door. He swung back to look at her, his eyes frantic and crestfallen at once. "Wait for me."

She would not let him walk alone this time.

CHAPTER
NINETEEN

The teary exhaustion and grief melted from Amal's face the moment he entered the ceremony house. He charged inside, Lena right beside him, and his gaze cut sharper than she had ever seen.

"Where is she?" he demanded.

Lena came to a stop, examining the room's inhabitants. There was only her father and a few of his closer, dwindling number of supporters. They sat among a messy conglomeration of chairs, a wooden pitcher of mead standing full and untouched at a nearby table. Dim torchlight painted gruesome, pointed shadows across their faces.

Her father sighed, standing up. "Amal—"

"She was under your watch, you promised!" Amal's voice exploded and careened off the walls, but despite its depth and volume, it made him sound like a small child. Like he was five years old again, wondering where in the worlds his mother had vanished to.

"Amal," Fredrik said again, his voice firmer. Lena tensed. It was the voice he'd used when she or Fressa misbehaved as children. It seemed too trivial, too condescending for the gravity of the situation. "We do not know. We will find her."

"Who was watching her?" Amal forged ahead, and Lena made a feeble step toward him, wondering if she should say something. "Who would do this?"

Fredrik heaved a short sigh, glancing at the men sitting by him. Lena knew he hated when his leadership was questioned publicly. "Perhaps it was an animal. A wolf."

Lena frowned. "But how—"

"They might be confused by all this . . . weather," Fredrik said, with a flippant gesture.

"Oh, do you think?" Lena muttered.

Amal glanced back at her, his expression guarded.

"I will look into this tomorrow, Amal," said the chief. "Do not worry."

Amal shifted his weight between his feet, looking like he wanted to run far from this room, but also like he wanted to stay and make sure Fredrik really would look into it. Lena sighed, raising a hand to Amal's shoulder. "You should rest, Amal."

He melted slightly under her touch, but he did not move. "No. This will not wait until *tomorrow*."

Fredrik shot Lena an annoyed look, as if Amal's stubbornness were somehow her fault or responsibility. Lena let her hand drop from Amal, still staring at her father. It was strange. In the firelight, his hazel eyes looked much greener than usual.

"You really want to push this?" Fredrik asked, standing. Lena stared at her boots, wishing Amal would back down. "Right now?"

"When else?"

Lena watched Amal and Fredrik stare at each other for a long moment. Amal had always been a strong man, but never before had she seen him act so abrasively. Her heart pounded—if he did not back down, they might start asking for answers that she could not afford to have revealed. Besides, Lena had no idea where Nana's body could have gone.

To Lena's surprise, her father broke first. "Fine." He turned to the men still sitting behind him, and jerked his head to the door. "Go call a meeting at the bonfire." They nodded, and looked relieved to get the chance to leave the tense room. As soon as the door shut behind them, Fredrik looked back at Amal and Lena. "You may have married my daughter, but I am still chief, Amal."

"I know," Amal said. "But with respect, this is about my mother, and nothing and no one else."

Fredrik studied him for another moment before walking past him and out the door, bound for the hearth.

Amal moved to follow, but Lena caught his arm and shot him a silent look—*give him space.*

Amal pursed his lips, collapsing into a chair now that the men were gone. He dragged his fingers through his hair, and she watched as he tried to take calming breaths. Lena stood in front of him.

"We will need to go soon, though," she whispered. He nodded, staring into nothing. "Amal."

He blinked, focusing on her. His face crumbled, and he took her hands. "Lena. I am sorry for taking so much of your energy and grief. I know it was you who found her. I know you loved her." Her tears came swifter than they ever had, and she pulled one of her hands free to wipe her eyes. "I know none of this has been easy for us, or you. I am sorry you had to marry me."

She shook her head, looking down at him. "We had no choice. It was not your fault."

Amal's eyes misted, but he did not cry. "We were friends first, Lena. Before I really knew Fressa. Do you remember that?"

"Of course I do."

"Then you must know that I love you," he said, his voice dropping to a whisper. "I love you entirely, Lena. Not as I loved your sister, but as I love you."

She smiled at him, her heart shattering with light and grief. He would not love her if he knew what she had done. What she would still do. She would treasure him as he was now, staring at her with open loyalty and unconditional love. Lena touched the side of his face.

"I love you too, Amal."

The village gathered around the fire, as they had on so many nights. But there had never been a night like this, and never would be again. Just days after a wedding, there was a funeral for a prominent woman in the clan—but now the body was missing. And they stood in a snowfall that should not have started for months.

Lena saw her mother standing just behind her father, her eyes tired and anxious with the unexpected news of the meeting. The rest of the attendees were bleary-eyed and shivering. Amal walked to stand with Fredrik. The absence of him from Lena's side, however brief, was brutal. He was the only thing holding back a mounting tide of oblivion. And he was the only one she knew she had hurt irretrievably, irrevocably, even if he did not know. Maybe he would never know. Maybe Lena could make this right before he ever found out.

She looked at Amal across the crowd and barely processed the words her father spoke. She wanted to grab him and run back through time, until they found Fressa, and some sunlight, and things were back to the way they should have always been.

Her heart leapt wildly as Lena saw Estrid standing with her family toward the back. Her arms were crossed tight against her chest, and though the distance between them was considerable, Lena was certain Estrid stared right at her. She swallowed back a wave of guilt and failure and shame, but she had gone so much further—her altercation with Estrid felt like child's play now. Lena wondered if she had just tried harder then, perhaps none of this would be happening now.

She wanted to cry, and almost let herself dissolve. But it was too cold out here. Her tolerance for the weather was typically fierce and strong, but now she felt like collapsing. Never before had she understood what people meant when they said the cold was in their bones. Now she felt it—she felt the aching frost inside of her, the freezing from within.

"I apologize if we woke any of you," Fredrik said. His voice dripped with self-preservation. "Amal insisted on a meeting."

"My mother's body is missing," Amal said, keeping his voice controlled and measured. Lena saw the attendees tense, looking among one another as if they might find Nana sitting with them. "We need to find her."

Val blinked in surprise. "Missing? How?"

"That, I still do not understand."

Amal's words were innocent enough, but Lena could detect the serpent beneath them, the subtle insult at her father. Fredrik must have felt it too, because he straightened and took a step forward, edging Amal backward.

"None of us harbor any malevolent feelings for Nana," he said. The crowd nodded solemnly, the shared grief hovering over them all. Lena tried very hard to keep her composure. "So there is no reason she would ever have been touched—much less *taken*—by anyone here."

"I understand," Amal conceded. "But that does not solve the issue. She is still gone."

His voice cracked just a little at the end.

How much more can this man take? Lena thought. And then—*this is because of you.*

"Then it must have been another clan," Fredrik said. "I keep telling you we are not strong enough. This is why we raid—we are not feared enough." His voice pierced the gathered men; some nodded readily, but most looked skeptical at best. Lena glared at her father for bringing this up again. There was no way or any feasible reason another clan would risk taking a body—and of Nana? Even if some invisible enemy harbored ill will, Lena still doubted they would have done anything with the dead body of an old woman.

"Father!" Lena said, because it was what Fressa would have done. And if she still was not back, then Lena would speak for her. "You know that's highly improbable. What are you hoping to achieve with this entirely unfounded accusation?"

Fredrik spread his hands. "It is your husband who demands an answer, Magdalena."

Amal gritted his teeth. "Stop this. Lena's right."

Her father raised his eyebrows, studying his congregation. "Either way, I do have a proposition. Regardless of Nana's whereabouts, we need to put an end to this."

Lena, somehow, grew colder. "An end to what, exactly?"

His words were for the crowd, but he spoke only to Lena. "As I am sure you have all noticed, winter is somehow here. It shows no signs of leaving soon."

Amal coughed. "So, what you're suggesting is—?"

Fredrik turned to Amal, and grasped his shoulder. "Surely you understand the economics that keep us alive, Amal. Soon we'll need to depend on rations, but it is growing too cold for any agriculture. We are losing valuable resources. It is a simple calculation—we need more."

Amal went pale. "Another raid?"

His voice held no inflection or emotion. Silence settled over the gathered crowd.

"It's them or us, son." He stared at the crowd. "This winter reigns. We have to make difficult decisions. Find our resources another way. Every man, at daybreak—we must go. This is not a mere request."

Lena and Amal gaped at him and at the crowd already rising with angry voices. She knew Amal was thinking the same thing—Fressa would have been livid. Furious beyond control. Amal pushed roughly past Fredrik and the mounting chaos, grasping Lena's arm and pulling her a few steps away from the congregation.

"I'm not going, okay? You understand? He cannot make any of us."

She nodded vaguely. Lena would help him however she could, because it was what Fressa would have wanted, and so it was what Amal wanted and what Lena needed to see through. Besides, she wanted him here in this village, next to her.

But Lena realized now that she would never get to lead this village. Her father did not have enough support. Was he purposefully *trying* to be overthrown? Something felt deeply wrong.

Amal went back to the people and tried to calm them down. Lena watched numbly as Val left Fredrik's side and moved to stand beside Amal. Clan Freding's grip loosened from the perilous cliffside it clung to—Lena felt the freefall.

"Lena? Can I have a word?"

She paused, blinking up at her father. How had he moved so fast? He had just been by the fire, and now he faced her, apart from the crowd. She stared over his shoulder, at her husband and mother and all the people—but not one of them noticed where she stood with her father.

Lena swallowed, and nodded once. He beckoned

toward the river—a pale serpent under a starless sky. She walked beside him, the air between them electric and shivering with something she could not name. Lena realized there was no noise from the gathered meeting behind her. She looked over her shoulder— there was no meeting at all. Lena knew the meeting hadn't been a mere illusion; still, time had assumed a strange, slippery sensation that made her afraid to blink. She stared at the spot that had been crowded a moment before. Only the central flame burned in isolation. Lena expected panic to well up within her and braced herself. But only dread seeped through her veins. She stopped in her tracks and looked up at her father.

"That raid suggestion was just a distraction, Father, and you know it," Lena said, forgoing any pleasantries.

"Well, they stopped asking about Nana, did they not?"

Lena glowered at him. He stood close to the water's edge, beckoning Lena to stand beside him. She did, but kept several feet between them. They stood in silence for a long while, staring into the dark distance.

"You asked to speak with me?" Lena finally asked, frustration building. "What is this?"

"Amal wants to know where his mother's body is," Fredrik said, evenly. "And I want to know what you know about that."

Lena's hand flew to the nearest tree trunk to steady herself. "I know as much as you do."

"I see," he said. "The issue, Magdalena, is that when hemlock is mixed in a paste like that, it leaves quite a distinct bile and foam a few hours later. Not to mention the odor. Now, I assume that would have been covered in all those years of training, but here we are. You can thank me for protecting you from anyone who understands how those poisons work, such as, say, your own husband. That's twice now I've had to clean up your mess."

Lena tried to move away. The world inside her head superimposed itself into this reality, and to hear someone speak of the secrets she had worked so hard to conceal nearly broke her. "Father—"

He moved just as fast and gripped her wrist hard. "I know why you did it, Lena, and you are so close to succeeding."

She fought his grip hard, but then froze at his words. They were so similar—almost exactly—to what Hela had said. "Oh my gods," she breathed. Her father met her eyes, and now she knew it was no trick of the light—his eyes were green.

Lena blinked too many times, expecting the scene before her to alter somehow.

Fredrik smiled, though the gesture held no warmth. The movement looked as slippery and unsteady as her own insides felt. He let her wrist go, and she watched him cross his arms behind his back.

"There's no need to be afraid, Lena." He walked closer to the river, staring into it without blinking. "We both want the same thing. Winter is here, and you know exactly why. It means we are closer than ever."

Lena flinched at his continued use of the word *we*. She wanted to sprint from here, but she knew it was too late to run from any of this.

"I went too far," she whispered. "Didn't I? I do not know—"

"You think you really had anything to do with this?" Her father laughed. "Lena. It has all happened exactly as I imagined."

She froze with her mouth still hanging open, tears of fear and confusion brimming at the corners of her eyes. Lena hadn't known until this instant what she had done—of course, she had made her decisions and actions deliberately and consciously, with a purpose so clear and forceful that nothing in the worlds would have stopped her.

But to hear someone here, in Midgard, in her own village—her own father—speak of the things she had done? It felt like a curtain had been ripped from her while she was in the middle of changing clothes. Because only *she* had trekked into Helheim. Only Lena had ever spoken with Bejla—in private. Perhaps, somewhere deep within her, it had all felt a little bit beyond her, or outside of her. As if she could pretend it was all a bad dream if she tried hard enough.

Now there was tangible, breathing proof that it was all real. Lena had killed a trader, and then killed her own mentor. She had married the man that should have been with her sister.

And Fressa was still gone.

Dead.

Lena stared hard at the man before her, letting her hands collapse at her sides. She knew, then, with absolute certainty who he was. Who else could know?

She exhaled. "Loki."

The man who claimed to be her father nodded twice, but did not let his expression shift or ripple. And as soon as Lena spoke the name aloud, despite everything, she laughed. Because her father could not be a *god*. Lena was . . . Lena. She would have known if she were more.

"Give me the blade, then," Fredrik said, unfazed. Lena swallowed her manic laughter, reaching down an absent hand to grasp the blade. She frowned, passing it to him. He made sure she was looking as he wrapped his fingers around it. Lena stared at his strange, green eyes, and watched them burn in the light that illuminated the flat of the blade.

Her stomach dropped. "You—but only Fressa could . . ."

He widened his eyes at her, as if waiting for her to understand something obvious. "And where do you believe she got that from?"

"But . . ." Lena paused, frowning at the runes—shifting purples and greens—and grabbed the blade from his hands. Instantly, they diminished. The light blinked away without a trace, the plain silver of the blade glinting in the firelight, showing Lena the gaunt, haggard reflection of a girl that must have been her, though she did not entirely recognize. "It does nothing for me."

"For you are not *of* me," he replied. "I merely wear the guise of your father, Lena, for I found a way to carve my fate through his body. Understand?"

Lena shook her head.

He sighed, short and annoyed. "Your father ruled this clan and married Val, but the first time he ever tried to raid, it went miserably, laughably wrong. He needed wealth, I suppose—you came along faster than your parents anticipated."

Lena grabbed her stomach, nausea and panic warring within her. She wanted to shout at her father—*no*—this man, this god? Lena needed him to slow his words, to speak clearly, or to vanish entirely.

"He died separated from his men," he said. "I saw everything as it unfolded, for there are few moments in these worlds and this existence where everything aligns just so. You must claim them with all the fight left in you. I managed to assume his form before anyone took notice. I returned here"—Loki tossed a hand toward the village—"and if anyone noticed a change, they wrote it off as a result of my travels. I bedded your mother as soon as I could."

Lena was definitely going to throw up now. She sank to her knees, the snow seeping through her clothes. The strings and yarns that made up this tapestry were easy to pull apart now. A demigoddess daughter, in Midgard, with abilities strange and spectacular. To do the bidding of a disguised god that could not attract attention to himself. But . . .

"Loki is imprisoned," Lena said. Her voice felt brittle and breakable in the air, like snowflakes already dissolving. "Is he not chained in the innards of his own son, with poison dripping into his eyes? The Aesir gods put him there for his mischief."

"Mischief," he said, through laughter. "They always boil it down to that, do they not?"

Lena stared hard at him, hoping the terror in her veins was not readily visible. She watched him sigh, pinching the bridge of his nose. "It is not easy, assuming this form. Why do you think Fredrik goes on all those raids? Why is he gone so constantly, with little reason or explanation, and unpredictably? I must conserve my energy and watch the gods, to know when to strike."

She backed away from him but made herself meet

the god's eyes. Could this be why there were discrepancies about where he went? Francia, England? If this was Loki, there were a thousand questions she wanted to ask, but only one she needed to: "Does Fressa know?"

Loki blinked. "Of course not. That was one of my first observations of people, Lena. They rarely work for you if they know they are doing so. It's better that they never know at all, or do not realize what they do. I needed my blood in this world—one strong enough to do my bidding, but hidden and mortal enough not to arouse suspicion."

"Then why did you let her get killed?"

Loki's eyes flashed black. "I cannot be everywhere at once. Odin must have figured her out—perhaps I gifted the blade too soon. He must have sensed it. He stole her from here, without her even understanding who she was. *That*," he said, with a flourish, "is where you came in. No god would have anticipated you, a human girl, would dare summon Hela or trek between worlds. It's preposterous. Utterly insane. Which is why I am so fond of you, and why you are my most treasured asset now."

"I thought you were—I thought I had a father," Lena said. "But now you say I barely had him for a year? I do not even remember him, though I've looked at you for seventeen years."

Loki tilted his head, his mouth lifting in a smirk. "I

thought you would be more bothered by the fact that Fressa is only half your sister."

"She is my sister," she said, without a second's hesitation. "Blood means nothing. I have always thought so, and now I know so."

He rolled his eyes. "Well. Glad to know that won't be holding us back from finishing what we started."

Lena frowned. In her core, a mounting dread spread in thin coils. After a few moments, she named it for what it was—doubt.

"I know what I want her for," she whispered. "To have her back. That is all. The village loved her, and Amal needs her, and I need her." She faltered at the apathy in his eyes. "And she can stop this winter, can't she?"

"She can," he said, but Lena did not like the way he said it. "Fressa can stop all of this and birth us anew. She is the straddler of worlds—the one with the power and inconspicuousness to use the blade I gave her, to release Fenrir and begin the chain of events that lead to our victory. Our new world."

Lena's heart pounded. Fressa would never agree to his plans—Fressa did not even know what or who she was. But if Loki was suggesting that bringing her back could somehow spur Ragnarok? She clenched her fists where Loki could not see them. *No.* She knew her sister better than anyone, and her parentage did not faze Lena. Of course it did not.

"You—" Lena stopped herself, held back the tide of anger and confusion surging at her skin. "You are beginning the chain. Or think you are. But—but we are all taught that you too will die in Ragnarok. Heimdall, watcher of the worlds, will kill you, as will you him. Your efforts are always for nothing."

"And who is teaching you that?" Loki asked, and staring at him directly, Lena felt relief that this man she had believed to be her largely absent, unpredictable father was not actually hers. "Your clan leaders all want you to believe there is some poetic *justice* in what is coming, and there is—but *for* me, and not because of me. Can you grasp what the gods have done to me? As I speak to you now, I am not fully here. I am bound in what is left of my son, with my wife at my side doing all she can to keep searing poison from scarring me further. And Magdalena, just look at what they have done to *you*."

He knelt in front of her. She leaned back, but could not shake her gaze away from his. "They took your sister without warning or reason, for the mere possibility that she might be used for my purposes." Lena wanted to add that this part was true, but she too felt the anger in Fressa's sudden and devastating absence from Midgard. "Then you were forced to marry her lover. And you have *killed*. They have made a murderer of you."

Lena swallowed hard, her jaw trembling. The gods had ruined her, but was the present company excluded?

She did not know or care about all the ridiculous hierarchies and separations that existed within her gods. All she paid attention to was who hurt her family. And the two gods who had were Odin and Loki, both on opposite ends of a terrifying spectrum, both with quite different problems of their own to solve.

Loki wanted his own world, a new world. Odin wanted to prevent that for as long as possible. But both, Lena thought bitterly, viewed her little sister as an item to serve their purposes.

What about Fressa's purposes? What about the gaping, eternal holes in Lena and Amal? Lena knew, then, what to do. She made herself maintain Loki's gaze. His eyes had been hazel all her life, a terrible god looking at her through the body of her dead father. But they were green now—poisonous and nauseating, perhaps the very hue of the liquid dripping into Loki's eyes on some other plane or realm of existence right now.

"Let us finish this, then." Her words held the steely resolve of the unilluminated blade in her hands. It was a staggering thought to know what this weapon was capable of, in the right grasp.

Loki grinned, impossibly and unnaturally wild. "If you do this, you will be spared, you know. From the carnage to come. In my new world, you will see that I am not a bad god—just a mistreated one." Lena nodded before her courage gave out. But Loki was not finished speaking. "I think you understand what the price will be, Lena. Do not lose your fire now. I can feel her, you know—inside of Valhalla."

Lena's knees went wobbly. She did not know what price Loki meant, and the knowledge that he could sense Fressa actively made her heart surge with wild, intertwined hope and panic.

"Go," he said, finally. "Go back to Amal. I will remain here for what is to come. I want to be the first to welcome Fressa back."

Lena wasn't sure how to exit, so she gave him a curt nod before walking fast from him. She had slept hardly at all over the past couple days, but now her mind tripped over itself with all the thoughts and revelations crashing in. Her body surged with untapped energy, but it felt too manic and sickening to invigorate her.

Nana. Lena kept forging ahead, trying to put as much distance between herself and the god as she could, but her eyes misted again. A dry sob coughed from her throat. *They have made you a murderer.*

He was right about that. The gods had done that to her, but she was the one with blood on her hands. She knew how she would be seen if anyone ever found out, and suddenly the thought of returning to Amal was too horrifying to take a single step forward. She came to a halt, as more snow began to fall across the village. Lena peered in the direction of Amal's home, with her mother's so close by. She could not go back to them—not yet.

Her mind felt stuck in an endless loop of imagining the look on their faces if they found out what she had done with that hemlock—to the trader, and then to Nana. The cold seeped further into her since she wasn't moving. She turned diagonally until the tree line came into view. Lena had done evil—did that mean she was evil? She feared so.

Lena stared up at the sky, indecision pulling her apart. She blinked away freezing tears and let her gaze settle again on the forest. There was maybe only one place left to go now—to Fressa. Or as close as she could get.

She broke into a run, which was difficult through the collecting snow. Her knees and feet and everything ached, but she did not relent. Lena inhaled, feeling the cold arc its way through her as she sprinted.

Sure that she had not been followed, she sank her knees into the snow and stared up at the haggard, bare branches of winter reaching above her, blotting out the stars. This was the place she had often wandered to with her sister, and Amal sometimes, far enough from the village to relax from the expectations, but close enough that there was still a sense of belonging.

Lena kept looking up, knowing this was the last sight her sister had seen. She must have been so angry at Lena for considering marriage to Amal. And now Lena was his wife, despite everything. She sobbed into her hands. Because she could not have gone all this way for nothing. Loki could claim Fressa as his all he wanted, but he did not know her like Lena did.

Lena grabbed for her blade as she heard a deliberate footstep crunch through the ice behind her—from the side facing the forest, not the village. Lena froze, cursing her distraction. For how could she not have seen Bejla right there, and on horseback?

And she was not alone.

CHAPTER
TWENTY

"Lena," Bejla hissed. "What are you doing here?"

On either side of her, a handful of girls with cruel expressions fanned out. All of them sat astride their horses, washed in the silver light of nighttime, staring down at Lena on the ground. She recognized one of them as Zhao, the woman Lena had seen Bejla speaking with in this same clearing earlier. Lena imagined herself sinking further until she disappeared beneath this world.

"*Lena*," Bejla urged again, cutting her a private glare that the others could not see.

"I don't know," Lena rushed, and it was the truth. She knew what she wanted, and maybe even what she would have to do—but the thought of carrying it through, the thought of all the forces at play in this small valley . . .

Bejla turned, flicking her horse's reins. Lena had never even seen Bejla ride a horse before. She watched her shoot the other girls an apologetic, dismissive smile. "I think having us all here might be disturbing the girl. I'm sure you can imagine the distress. Shall I speak with her alone, to help her understand?"

The girls did not object, but they did not visibly agree either. Still, they led their horses to the far end of the clearing, giving Bejla and Lena a small sort of privacy. They shared one frantic look as soon as their audience vanished.

"They're Valkyries," Bejla whispered. "Odin sent them to accompany me, he sensed *him* here."

"I know about Loki," Lena rushed. "Who he is. What he wanted to do with Fressa."

Bejla nodded once, and bit her lip. Her eyes flitted to the ground and back to the sky, where the bright beginnings of the northern lights shimmered. Lena had always loved them, but tonight's were green—a shade so similar to Loki's that she did not let her gaze linger.

"And now do you understand why I did it?" Bejla asked, softly. "Why I took your sister?" Lena stared at her. There was too much between them—too many un-answered questions and feelings, but Lena felt them all drop away as the implication hit her.

"*You* were the one who took her?"

Bejla winced as if Lena had slapped her. Lena wanted to. She wanted to grab her by the neck and wring her until she brought her sister back. Lena supposed she could have inferred this once she learned that Bejla served Odin, but—but it was *Bejla*. How could she do this to Lena?

"There was no pain. All I had to do was *touch* her—Odin did the rest, and Odin understands more than you and Loki know," Bejla whispered, her eyes pleading. "He is here, through us, watching and waiting."

"Waiting?" Lena's mouth went dry. "For what?"

Bejla shook her head. "I don't know. But I feel it—don't you? Something is coming."

Lena's gut wrenched. Her mind was still fixed on the fact that it had been Bejla who had stolen Fressa's soul, but she forced herself to consider Bejla's words—their small valley was used to accepting visiting merchants and scholars. To have gods converged over it felt completely claustrophobic—and she knew it meant that something truly devastating was at stake.

She met Bejla's eyes, the line drawn between them pronounced. "Whatever it is that you had to prove to Odin," Lena whispered bitterly. "I hope it was worth it."

Bejla's lips parted, her eyes widening in small surprise. "Lena—"

"I need to return now," Lena said, standing up.

"Lena, *wait*—whatever bravery and fire brought you this far, do not underestimate what is at stake. I cannot turn a blind eye, or Odin will know. If you get any closer . . ."

Lena nodded, her jaw firm. "I understand."

They held each other's gazes for a long moment before Bejla moved back to the Valkyries. Lena exhaled. Bejla did not feel like her real enemy, but it was hard to shake the knowledge of her role in all of this. Lena would have to work against her now. She backed away from the clearing, and the Valkyries made no move to follow her. She tried not to think about why that might be, soaking in the view of the space that had been so dear and secret to her throughout her life, full with the dark shadows of strangers from another world.

She left with all the bravery and fire she could muster—the very stuff that Bejla had warned her to leave behind. What Bejla did not understand was that it was all Lena had left, and the only thing that could save her.

Lena heard the din of blades and screams echo through the forested valley as she approached. She had torn herself away from this village not even an hour ago, sprinting fast enough to outrun the wind, but now she walked slow, pushing through an invisible fog.

It was inevitable, this return. There was nowhere else for her to go. Nothing else for her to do. She felt unnervingly calm as she broke through the tree line, though she was still too far to be noticed in the dark.

The chaos unfolding edged away at whatever pride she'd scraped together. It seemed the clan had divided itself now, in her brief absence—those who stood with Fredrik and those who did not. Lena was smart enough to know which side was bigger. Loki might be manipulating this situation for his own sake, but he still could not force the village to forgive Fredrik for his behavior. Now, it would be dangerous for her to go back as Fredrik's daughter. But they did not know who he really was. For a moment, she imagined telling them that he was Loki, had been Loki for seventeen years—she almost laughed, but her eyelids fluttered. Exhaustion weighted her feet, but she pushed onward despite the danger. When she heard the sharp sound of her name ring across the distance, she was almost relieved.

She recognized it an instant later as Amal's. Her heart slowed, and her feet stopped completely. He ran to her, moving faster than she had ever seen him. Amal skidded to a stop before her, practically tackling her, angling her body away from the village.

"I tried to stop them, Lena." His voice was frantic, verging on hysteria. "They're saying they want a new chief—my gods, people are dead." He shook his head, grabbing her roughly and moving them back toward the tree line. "You cannot be here. They'll hurt you."

Lena turned over his shoulder, staring back at the fiery chaos unfolding. She saw her father—no, not her father at all, but a god—standing on the fringes of building chaos, unmoving, even as his own people tried to take him down.

And through it all, though he was impossibly far away, she saw Loki turn to her and wink. Lena's stomach flipped. Had he known? He had known. She shut her eyes tight, a sob wracking her. He had known the village would revolt. Loki had planted the idea in their minds by ordering another raid. He had known that would make Lena a target—ruin her reputation and standing forever, and giving her plenty of reasons to spur herself into action. All so he could have Fressa back.

Nothing in this village would be left for her, so what would she have to lose? She opened her eyes again, knowing that Loki still stared at her across the way. Amal's arms wrapped around her sides, trying to urge her farther away from the village so she would not be seen. He still trusted her, still protected her, even after everything.

Though he did not know everything.

She ripped his arms from her, stalking back to the village. Loki stood still as the men loyal to Fredrik clashed with the rebels, and watched her approach with Amal at her heels. And then he jerked his head ever so slightly to her left, where Amal was catching up. He gave her a hardly imperceptible nod—of what? Encouragement?

Lena fell still again, letting Amal crash into her.

The world dimmed, turning silent and dark around her. Loki had beckoned the dark, definitive answer to Lena's quest from the deepest parts of her. It was the answer, perhaps, that Lena had guessed all along—but every bit of who she was and every tiny memory of her life had suppressed it, buried it so deep that she had never consciously considered . . .

Her hands flew to her mouth. Loki was right. If he was urging it, he must know that it would work, that this would match the scales.

But tears blurred her eyes, burning in the cold. There was no satisfaction in finding the solution. She let her hands fall to her side. Suddenly, the volume surrounding her rushed in again. The cacophony of blades and men's voices crashed through her, and Amal's voice just beside her, begging her to leave.

She turned to face him slowly. He faltered at the look on her face. "Lena?"

"It's you," she whispered.

Amal blinked. "Le—"

"You loved her as much as I did," she said. "Just in a different way."

Who else understood Fressa like Amal? Who else was as brave, and kind, and fierce, and passionate? It was all, suddenly, painful but obvious. The simplest answers always were. She eyed him, and his lips pursed.

"We need to go," Amal said, his voice quiet but

terrified, glossing over the words Lena had said. "If they find you, they will *kill* you."

"For what?" Lena mused, in a daze. "For being heir? For killing that trader last month? Or for—"

She cut herself off in time, but Amal's expression had already crumpled. The manic energy behind his eyes and limbs faded, clouded away by something the two of them had never felt for the other—doubt.

"You did what?"

"Amal," Lena said, her voice breaking into jagged pieces. "You know I love you. You must know how sorry I am. But if you love Fressa—" Her voice broke away, dissolving into a sob. She caught her breath, trying to search over Amal's shoulders for Loki. She could no longer see the god.

Lena slowly pulled out Fressa's blade. Amal did not flinch, but he stared at the blade with shocked confusion. He switched his gaze quickly to Lena's eyes, and she wished he hadn't. She looked away from him, and the soft brown of his eyes, at the concerned furrow of his brows. How many memories were etched into the slopes of his face? She chased them all away with the image of her sister, with the sound of her laughter rolling through the village.

She gripped the hilt hard, and tried to remember how Fressa had described her lessons growing up—how to fight or kill a man. Lena inhaled a sob, and made one strike.

Her blade stopped. Amal's wrist grabbed hers so hard that she feared it might shatter. He wrestled Fressa's blade from her grip, and shoved her arm down. She fell with the momentum, and her sobs tore her apart. It had been a feeble strike, one that never would have killed or even hurt Amal. Maybe Lena had known that, even as she'd done it.

She would do anything for her sister—that was what she always said, always believed. But what if she could not do this?

No—she knew she could not do this.

Lena felt Amal grab at her clothes and force her back to her feet. She stumbled, her cries hurting her core. Amal dragged her over to the nearest building— some wooden tool shed at the fringes of the village, and slammed her into it.

These hands had held her so often; they had fed her in the days after Fressa's death, when the thought of eating never crossed her mind. They had wiped away tears from the training sessions gone awry in childhood. They had cradled her on a night not long ago, carrying her through the village with a tenderness reserved for only the closest of people.

Now they held Lena fast against the wall. His eyes flashed with an anger dark and complete, and Lena knew then that she had lost him forever. Tears fell thick and constant down her face.

"What have you done?" he hissed. Amal looked furious, but his voice betrayed him. He was broken, too. He had lost more than Lena had.

"I want Fressa back," she cried.

"Lena," he said, voice insistent but fragile. He risked a glance behind his shoulder, making sure nobody approached them. "What have you done?"

"I only meant to save her," Lena said. She would try to make him see. She would try to restore something in his eyes. "You summoned Hela for me, and she wanted Fressa back too."

Amal's hands slid away from her, but she stayed rooted in place by the ferocity in his gaze. Under different circumstances, he could have made a formidable chief. He shook his head.

"That wasn't real," he murmured. "The runes and those castings—they're just myths and tricks."

"I know you don't believe that, Amal. I went somewhere that night," Lena said. "You saw me. I know you did."

He kept shaking his head, refusing to believe what she said.

"Amal," she continued. "She said she could get Fressa back if I just found another soul to replace hers with."

"Do you hear yourself?" Amal snapped. "Do you?"

"I do, but—"

"So, what? You killed that trader? You were going to kill *me*? You—" He froze then, the realization hitting him. Lena sagged against the wall. "Did you kill my mother?"

Lena opened her mouth, considering a lie, but he knew her too well. One look, and he stepped away. He rubbed his hands across his jaw, a terrifying mixture of laughter and sobs escaping him. Now, the others took notice and started heading in their direction.

"You—*you*—killed my mother?" Amal was screaming now, his eyes wild with betrayal and rage. Lena eyed the approaching clansmen.

"You have to know, you have to understand—it was all for you, for Fressa—"

He whirled on her then, grabbing her wrists and slamming her against the wall again. His glare was fragmented, chaotic, and streaked with disbelief.

"Was it?" He shook his head angrily, tears cutting down his face. "This was for *you*, Lena."

She stared at him with an open mouth, but no response or rebuttal came. Because he was right. He was always right. Amal's hands worked through his hair again, and his gaze caught on the gathering men behind them. There was no telling how much they had heard. Amal faced her, though he looked disgusted to do so.

"They will kill me," Lena whispered, more as a

revelation to herself. Even if, by some miracle, they had not heard Amal's words about Nana, she was still the daughter of the man they wanted to overthrow. But something in Amal's eyes softened at her words. It was barely perceptible beneath the rage, but Lena clung to it. He eyed the blade laying in the snow between them. It was a boring and ugly blade without Fressa.

"Amal, they will kill me," Lena said again. It was true—they hated Fredrik, and considering the punishment for killing an elderly clan member, a quick death would be generous. Lena did not run, nor did she look for an escape route. Amal knelt down and picked up the blade.

She wondered if the same thought crossed his mind. "Please."

He glanced at her, his jaw quivering. "Lena," he said. "How could I—"

"After all that I have done?" she asked, bitterly. "You will make it quick. I would suffer far worse at the hands of anyone else." She drew a haggard breath. The sky lightened slightly.

Amal closed the distance between them, his hands shaking wildly, Fressa's blade shuddering with them. Lena wondered what it would look like from a distance, for the clansmen weaving their way toward them. She thought it must look like an embrace, Amal pulling Lena close to him, her back to his chest—aligned perfectly.

She felt the leaping thrum of his heartbeat through his chest. He reached his arms around her, and she clutched onto one of them. She wanted to apologize again, but the divide between them was pronounced and permanent now. Still, she had precious seconds left.

"Do you remember what your mother told you?" she whispered.

He held her tight. There was anger in him still, but she leaned against him and shut her eyes. "There is a way back to the light," he recited. "Crawl to it, if you have to."

Lena nodded, letting Nana's words settle between them. She felt the cold press of Fressa's blade against the corner of her neck, and fought every instinct within her. She stayed frozen. Eyes still shut, she heard the crunch of footsteps approach them. She squeezed Amal's arm, urging him onward. If he didn't act now—

The impact was staggering—more like a punch, instead of an entry. Fressa's blade raked across the front of her throat. A drowning sensation surged up in her, buried in shock. But as her blood poured down her body, for the first time since Fressa died, Lena felt warm.

CHAPTER
TWENTY-ONE

A s Lena's body fell, a part of her did not. From some-where else, she saw her own body collapse at Amal's feet, a growing puddle of blood unspooling from her. Lena raised a hand to her throat, but felt nothing. She glanced down and saw only a shadow of herself.

Around her, the colors leaked away. Everyone around her stood frozen. There was Amal, with tears falling suspended from his eyes, the blade discarded and red-stained at his feet. In the distance, she saw her mother mid-run toward her, mouth outstretched in a silent scream. Lena wondered what words were said. She wanted to tell her mother to run away from Lena's body—away from the village. They would hurt her. She was Fredrik's wife.

Lena swiveled around, but it did not feel like she was moving. Panic surged up from a muted, invisible source—this was not what any afterlife was supposed to look like. She should not be standing in a frozen Midgard, in this horrific tableau.

Faint hoofbeats shattered the silence. Lena whirled around, clutching at her throat, still expecting to find it ripped open. But that was the Lena on the ground, in the red snow. She stared at her crumpled figure. When had she gotten so frail? Seeing herself from above, with her spindly limbs and too-thin hair, disturbed her almost as much as the dark stains around her.

The hoofbeats got closer and louder. Lena peered through the shadowed world, until a familiar silhouette stood before her.

"Bejla?" Lena's voice cracked. "I don't understand—"

"This is a surprise," Bejla said. Lena had never seen her look so unsettled. Her eyes held a measured panic, taking in the carnage around her. She was alone, thankfully. She frowned, staring at the two Lenas—the one dead in the snow, and the shadow speaking. "Although, maybe it is not a surprise at all."

Lena watched her swing her legs over her horse, and stride forward to Lena's dead form. Bejla bent down, somehow retrieving Fressa's blade from the snow. In a swift movement, she grabbed one of dead-Lena's hands and shoved the hilt into her palm.

"There," Bejla pronounced unceremoniously. "You died with a weapon in your hand."

Lena frowned. "What?"

Bejla shot her a glare. "Understand?"

Lena nodded, turning the thought over in her mind. That was one of the alleged qualifications of entry to Valhalla, which meant . . .

She frowned, then stepped forward and knelt down— trying not to look at her dead body—and picked up Fressa's blade. Somehow, even in this in-between state, she could grasp it. The blade stayed in her hands, still as gray and dull as it had always been in Lena's grasp. Bejla grimaced, but said nothing.

She jerked her head back to her horse. "Let's go. Quickly, before the other Valkyries see."

Lena did as she was told, walking on weightless legs to the horse and mounting. Bejla followed, sitting behind Lena but holding the reins. Lena's mind still swam, but she was certain of one thing—Bejla had done something deeply profound and staggeringly kind for Lena, and if anyone found out, her punishment would be terrible.

A lump of gratitude stuck in her throat. She glanced one last time at the scene before her—at her body, at Amal and her mother, and the jagged pattern of the mountains that held the valley of the only home she had ever known. Bejla urged the horse on, and though Lena shouldn't have been surprised, she gasped as it took flight.

"Are we—" Lena turned her head backward, slightly,

so that Bejla could hear. She almost dared not ask the question, to speak aloud the gathering hope surging within her. "Are we . . . going to Valhalla?"

Bejla stayed quiet for a while. "Yes," she said, finally. "We need to hurry. And we need to be discrete."

"Won't Odin know who I am?" Lena asked. She stared over the horse at the dark nothingness dropping beneath them. Lena had not remembered when her valley disappeared, but now she guessed they flew over Ginnungagap—the endless void between her world and the worlds of the gods.

"Not if we do this right," Bejla muttered. "He still thinks I am with the other Valkyries."

Lena's heart jumped. "Bejla. Why are you doing this? What are you doing?"

"I told you of my sister," she rushed. Her voice sounded angry. "She nearly died after a devastating famine in my clan. We were in the mountains above you. Snowed in completely, last winter." Lena heard her exhale, controlled. "We did not realize how dire the situation was—I don't know what went wrong with the rationing."

Lena hesitated, keeping her head half-turned to hear Bejla.

"I could see my sister was close to death," she said, "My family's patron god was Odin, and so I begged and begged for him to come and save us. In the end,

I convinced him to save my sister—my whole clan, actually."

The story had more to it, Lena could tell. She waited for Bejla to speak.

Bejla flicked the reins again, and the horse shot forward faster. "But I paid the price. I pledged myself to him when I prayed. I did not realize quite how literally our gods interpret our words."

"I understand," Lena whispered. "He made you help him thwart Loki's plans," Lena realized. "And take my sister."

"Yes." Bejla said. "And if I said no—my whole family lives there, in the balance of Odin's favor. They think I died. Except now I'll never die, so long as I'm in Odin's service. He enjoys making his servants immortal," Bejla laughed. "I was sent here. The All-Father sensed Loki somewhere in your village, and the more time I spent there, the more I spoke to you, the more I saw myself in you. There are big and terrifying things in these worlds, but you ignored them all for the only thing that really mattered. Your family."

Lena felt uncomfortable. She spoke of Lena as if she were some sort of noble hero, and not the murderer she was.

"I followed you," Bejla continued. "And as soon as I saw what was happening, I knew you had found the way to answer Hela's terms."

"Amal?" Lena asked, her voice thick with shame and regret. She remembered her one, feeble strike toward him. That could never be forgiven.

Bejla stayed quiet for a long while. "No," she said, finally, but there was something wrong in her voice. "Is that what you thought?"

"Yes," Lena said slowly. She turned all the way back, as far as she could without falling, to see Bejla. Her face looked stricken, as if Lena had just slapped her.

"Oh gods," she whispered. "Lena, no. It was *you*."

Lena held Bejla's gaze. "What do you mean?"

"Look at how hard my horse flies," Bejla said. She shook her head. "Your soul is heavy, Lena. As heavy as your sister's."

Lena blinked, and turned her face quickly from Bejla so she couldn't see the tears pooling in her eyes. She stared into the cloud-filled mist ahead of her, waiting for Asgard to emerge. Her heart sank, knowing now that there would be no reunion waiting for her. At least there was the slight comfort of knowing that Bejla was immortal, and worked for the god whose hall Lena would now reside in. They could see each other, perhaps—a strangely comforting thought that fought its way through her mind.

"I'll make sure she knows what you did, Lena," Bejla whispered. "She will live because of you."

"But—Loki's blood is in her—"

"Once someone knows what they are capable of, it changes everything. I trust your sister will not be keen to help her father now that she knows who he really is."

Lena knew she should hold on to the horse, but she clutched one hand across her mouth and jaw, trying to hold down her cries. How had the answer been so simple and brutal? It had been her all along.

For who else knew or loved Fressa as Lena did?

Nobody. Not another soul.

And now she knew that Amal was right. Lena had done all this with the hope of reuniting with Fressa. She wanted her sister to live, but she'd done it so they could live together, as they always had and were always supposed to.

But it was not up to Lena how Fressa lived her life, or whom she chose to be. Lena would not be with her as she walked Midgard again, but she was still the one who could bring her there. She blinked away the tears, letting her vision clear. Her heart stilled. She stared beneath her for a moment, though Midgard was long gone by now, and said a silent farewell. With a stilted breath, she reached for Fressa's blade—the one Loki had power over. Without ceremony, she let it fall into Ginnungagap. Into nothing. She knew there was no permanent solution to Ragnarok, but at least this would delay Loki and his plans.

At least, long enough for her sister to live the life she deserved.

Lena turned her gaze upward, at whatever waited for her beyond the mist they hurtled through. She wrapped her hands around the horse's neck. Lena let the wind tear through her.

"Then we'd better hurry," she said.

EPILOGUE

Fressa understood one thing.

She could never let her village know she lived. The truths she had learned of herself in Valhalla already felt like a distant, hazy dream, but she held on to them—and she had returned to find her home in disarray. If anyone else found out who she was, and if they saw her breathing and walking again? Fressa's heart sank. She had loved her village, once. But there was too much they would never understand. Her mother, at least, had regained a fragile control of the village, but Fressa's father had disappeared without a trace. Without a husband or heirs, Fressa wondered if her mother would choose another family to lead their people. She hoped she would—Clan Freding had had more than their share of political chaos.

Fressa stayed by the riverbank, hidden behind the

thick pines, and waited. She had appeared here yester-day, with her sister's face in her mind and Amal's name on her lips. Fressa had found him—through tears and suspicion and elation, he had explained what he knew. And how he had killed her sister.

It felt strange to be in the cold, though it seemed as though winter was ending. The ground felt more damp than frozen, and the sky held a dim but encompassing light. Fressa risked a glance in the direction of the ruined village, wishing Amal would hurry.

Her heart twisted as she saw him approach, winding through the trees to the meeting place they had planned. The sight dredged up all the familiar feelings she had missed for so long—complete belonging, devotion, desire. But it would always be a bit marred now, with the knowledge of the last moments between her sister and him. Even if she understood what Lena had done, and what Lena had asked him to do.

Fressa stood from her crouch, and walked to the riverbank with her pelts wrapped around her face and hair. She boarded the small boat, cringing at the sound of the water and ice moving around her. Once Amal broke through the trees, she beckoned at him to hurry, but froze when she saw who was with him.

It was a young girl, maybe eight at most. Fressa vaguely recognized her as Kiali, the little sister of one of Lena's friends. She had thin wisps of ash-blonde hair, and eyes so blue that Fressa suddenly yearned for a cloudless summer sky. Amal shot her a placating look, like, *I'll explain later*. Fressa swallowed nervously, but she did not object when Kiali and Amal hastily boarded the boat. He slung over a worn satchel full of dried meat.

Amal's face was weighted with exhaustion. He was every bit as handsome as she remembered, with his strong jawline and deep brown eyes, but the skin beneath his eyes was a dark plum shade. Fressa knew they needed to move, but she still leaned forward and kissed him hard.

Happiness bloomed from her, despite everything. The sun was returning, and her father subdued for a long while. After all, there was a fierce breed of joy that accompanied the achievement of the impossible. Her sister had done so much so she could have Amal back—so she could roam this earth again—and she did not intend to waste a single breath.

Kiali pointed at the oars with a question in her eyes. Fressa nodded, and picked one up. They both rowed furiously, Amal eyeing the valley with his hands on his bow, until their home was gone in the mist and fog.

Finally, they let the oars down for a moment to breathe. Amal glanced between the girl and Fressa. "She's Estrid's sister."

"I know," Fressa said. "I remember."

"She said her family—" Amal stopped, and lowered

his voice. "I don't think they made it through the revolt. I didn't know what to do . . . I thought she should come with us."

Fressa's heart swelled, and she rested her hands on his knees. "Of course."

They shared a smile, small and tentative. Things would be different and difficult for a while, Fressa knew, but this was still her Amal. They would figure it out, even if they had to begin life anew far from their home. Where no one would search for them.

The blade her father had given her a lifetime ago was nowhere to be found. It seemed to have disappeared along with Lena's soul. Fressa swallowed back a staggering tide of grief, reminding herself that Lena wanted her to be happy. Lena wanted her to live. There was still a guilt imprinted within her, one that might never fade. But she would not waste this chance—that much she knew.

Fressa was not naïve enough to believe that all her father's plans hinged on the missing blade, but hopefully it would delay Loki, and force him to gather his strength from where his essence was imprisoned on a world far from here. That was all any of them could really do, anyway—try to delay him. He would win one day, but Fressa had a feeling that it would be a day far from today, when she and Amal had lived and loved enough for a thousand lifetimes.

Amal stared at her. She did not blame him for his curiosity and confusion—she had explained to him as much as she could yesterday, and there was still much she needed to tell him, but they had time now. The greatest luxury of all.

"I was afraid you might be cloaked in the darkness you returned from," Amal admitted. He studied her face—just as he had done a thousand times, and would do a thousand more. "But now I see it is not you I should fear, but your father. Loki has an uncanny ability to be many. To be anything. He lived among us, ruled us, for years before Lena learned who he was."

Fressa flinched slightly at the sound of her sister's name, and knew that they both felt the absence of her in this boat. She reached over and clutched Amal's hands tight, wishing she had an answer. A new world waited for them beyond their home, and they had no way of knowing what fortune or tragedy was in store. Because Amal was right—Loki could be anywhere. Anyone.

And as Fressa and Amal stared over the dark waters ahead, the girl's blue eyes flashed green, then back again.

Just for a moment.

AUTHOR'S NOTE

My great-grandfather emigrated to the United States from Sweden when he was only nineteen. Without knowing a word of English, he made his way from New York to Utah, which is no small feat—unfortunately, my grandmother tells me that the experience was so traumatic that he vowed to never speak Swedish again. Though my family immigrated relatively recently from Sweden and Finland (hence my last name, Tammi, which is the Finnish word for "oak"), we no longer have the language or intimate cultural knowledge of these places, beyond the occasional meal of Swedish meatballs.

As a mythology enthusiast, I knew I wanted to explore more about the Norse myths, which likely originated close to where a lot of my family comes from.

The Weight of a Soul allowed me the perfect framework to interact with Norse lore, while also focusing on the Freding family's dynamic, particularly between Lena and her sister Fressa.

Like I did with my debut novel, *Outrun the Wind*, I want to acknowledge that mythology has various interpretations and that my versions of Loki, Hela, the nine worlds, and the role of the Valkyries might be different from what you've previously learned. At mythology's very core is contradiction, and I think that's exactly why it's such an exciting realm to write about.

Historically, I tried to ground Lena's village and settlement in the context of the so-called "Viking Age" in Scandinavia. Most of my knowledge comes from a history course I took in early 2018 at Oxford's Trinity College, or external readings since then, some of which I've included below. However, at the end of the day, this is very much a fantasy novel—anachronisms are certainly present for the sake of me telling the story I felt I wanted and needed to in a mythological context.

For instance, Lena historically would've been married off *way* younger, and due to the almost nonexistent written sources from this time, there's no way to make any consistent or definitive consensus on how ceremonies like funerals and weddings would have gone, so those scenes in this book are total imagination and guesswork.

In this book, I also wanted to acknowledge and embrace the prominent relationships a lot of Vikings had with the Middle East and Asia—there is certainly historical grounding that Amal could have been raised in Scandinavia as a result of extensive trading routes and interaction. I think a lot of people (including myself, initially) have a misguided assumption that Vikings were all northern European white people. As I learned more about this age, I came to realize that's definitely false to an extent. Their trading routes and travel were absolutely massive, and it's undeniable that Vikings were far more culturally and ethnically diverse than we acknowledge.

If you're just getting started with Norse mythology and want to learn more, I'd definitely recommend *Norse Mythology* by Neil Gaiman—it's lyrical, hysterical, and evocative, and proved to be an instrumental source of inspiration while I was preparing to write this story. If you're looking for a fun, modern take on the Norse myths, I'd absolutely recommend Rick Riordan's *Magnus Chase and the Gods of Asgard* trilogy, which was my very first extended introduction to Norse mythology as a teenager.

REFERENCES

The Penguin Historical Atlas of the Vikings by J. Haywood (1995)

The Cambridge History of Scandinavia I by K. Helle (2003)

The Oxford Illustrated History of the Vikings by E. Roesdahl (1997)

Vikings: Raid, Culture, Legacy by M. Stein and R. Dale (2014)

The Poetic Edda, trans. B. Thorpe

ACKNOWLEDGMENTS

All of my author friends warned me of the dreaded "second book syndrome." They told me it would be particularly tough to write, and unsurprisingly, this came true. I drafted this story while I was enrolled in some of the most demanding classes I've ever taken and going through an amicable-but-devastating breakup, all while coming off the high of six months abroad. Obviously, these are extremely minor problems in the grand scheme of things, but difficult for me to work through nonetheless.

That being said, I can't emphasize enough what a powerful, fulfilling, and worthwhile journey this has been at every stage in the process. *The Weight of a Soul* allowed me to explore my deepest fears, questions, and passions—I've really had the time of my life getting to tell this story, and Lena gripped me from the first page.

It was clear from day one: she was never going to let me give up.

But I never would've been able to figure out what she was trying to say without the help of so many others.

This book is very much centered around the distant heritage of the paternal side of my family. I especially want to thank my grandmother Madeleine for her excitement about this story—I do hope this makes you and Axel proud.

All my grandparents have been instrumental in providing me with the resources and support that have led to so many opportunities. Thank you for your love and guidance. Growing up, I never doubted that I was cared for and unapologetically supported, and for that, I have unending gratitude.

My parents, of course, deserve countless thanks for the commitment and devotion they show my sister and me every day. I know for certain that I would never have been a reader, let alone an author, without your enthusiasm and encouragement.

Kelsy Thompson, my editor extraordinaire, has been a beacon of light and inspiration with both this story and my debut novel. I can't thank you enough for helping to shape the stories I want to tell, or for your critical insight and infectious passion for this craft. This story simply never would have happened without your thoughtful, guiding presence and our wonderful video calls. It's been an absolute pleasure to work alongside you, Mari Kesselring, and the whole team at Flux.

Amanda Harlowe and Lilia Shen are both talented, extraordinary writers that I feel beyond lucky to have as my critique partners. You both played vital roles in shaping this story from the ground up. My panicked emails and rubbish first drafts haven't driven you off yet, so I hope to keep writing alongside you for as long as possible.

I like to call this story the best souvenir I took home from my semester abroad, which might be an obnoxious thing to write. Still, it's true—a narrative poem I wrote while studying creative writing at Oxford in early 2018 became the basis for this novel's plot. I remember plotting this out at a very strange Costa/Odeon/church trifecta on Magdalen Street, and I can't quite believe that it's a real book now! Endless thanks to the fantastic friends I met while in England, who managed to simultaneously keep me humble *and* hyped me up—you were each truly one of the greatest parts of my entire Oxford experience. Thanks to Emily, Ellie, Autumn, Mary, Bethany, Abby, Haleigh, Hannah, and the whole Regent's Park crew.

As my graduation from Mercer University draws near, I'm reminded of how incredibly fortunate I've been to study at such a driven and creative institution. My professors are beyond supportive of all my ambitions, and I can't express how deeply I love the friends I've made here. When I look back on *The Weight of a Soul* and my first novel, I know I will always associate them with my time at Mercer.

My Mercer experience and studies abroad would not be possible without the generous support of the Stamps Family Charitable Foundation. Without them, I never would have seen Greece or Oxford, and I truly believe that those experiences are rooted with the publication of my two novels, respectively. Annie Stamps passed away while this novel was drafted, and I hope she knows how much gratitude and admiration I have and will always have for her—I will continue to write and explore as much as I can to honor the enormous impact she's had on my life.

As I referenced in this novel's dedication, so much of who I am and what I do is connected to my younger sister, Erin. Writing this story was difficult, but imagining and empathizing with Lena was easy because we both share one huge thing in common—an unconditional, omnipotent love for our sisters. I'm beyond proud to be your sister, and am so fortunate to have grown up alongside you. I hope our adventures are only just beginning. Thank you for everything.

ABOUT THE AUTHOR

Elizabeth Tammi has lived in California, Florida, and England, but currently resides in Georgia, where she studies creative writing and journalism at Mercer University. When she isn't writing, you can find her holed up at a coffeehouse, or at work for her college's newspaper and literary magazine. Her debut novel, *Outrun the Wind*, came out in November 2018. You can find Elizabeth online on Tumblr (@annabethisterrified), Twitter (@ElizabethTammi), Instagram (@elizabeth_tammi), and at elizabethtammi.com.

Read More By
ELIZABETH TAMMI

THE HUNTRESSES OF ARTEMIS MUST OBEY TWO RULES: NEVER DISOBEY THE GODDESS, AND NEVER FALL IN LOVE. BUT WHEN KAHINA ENCOUNTERS THE LEGENDARY WARRIOR ATALANTA ON A ROUTINE MISSION, A DANGEROUS LINE IS CROSSED AND BOTH GIRLS LEARN THAT THEIR ACTIONS HAVE CONSEQUENCES AND RULES WERE MADE TO BE BROKEN.

ELIZABETH TAMMI

OUTRUN THE WIND